A Reckless Heart

by

Jennifer Wilck

Scarred Hearts, Book 1

A Reckless Heart

Cover Art by *Jennifer Greeff*

The Wild Rose Press, Inc.
PO Box 708
Adams Basin, NY 14410-0708
Visit us at www.thewildrosepress.com

Publishing History
First Edition, 2021
Trade Paperback ISBN 978-1-5092-3517-9
Digital ISBN 978-1-5092-3518-6

Scarred Hearts, Book 1
Published in the United States of America

Dedication

To Laurie B.
I still remember our plotting sessions (and coffee!)
and the huge help you gave me
when I was coming up with this book and series.
I couldn't have done this without you.

Meg walked with Simon on the rocky beach, waves on her right, cliffs on her left, and seagulls overhead. This time, her lungs expanded, her respiration slowed, and she became hyper aware of him. He took longer strides than she did, but after they'd gone a few feet, he shortened his.

She appreciated the consideration. It only made her more aware of his muscular thighs. Their arms brushed as they walked, and tingles shot up her neck. It was an accident, wasn't it? He stepped away, but a few strides later the uneven ground pushed them together, and their bodies brushed against each other. She listened to his breath hitch at the contact, and he didn't move away.

Nervous laughter bubbled in her chest. They'd been close before and held hands. Granted, he'd covered hers on the ladder, but still. It wasn't the first time they touched. Why was this different? She remembered the sensations when he'd covered her hand on the roof—warmth and roughness and safety. And she wanted it. She bumped her hand against his, on purpose, to feel his skin. It wasn't smooth like hers. Its texture, unique to him, fascinated her. A moment later, he rubbed his arm against her.

Chapter One

Maybe this wasn't such a good idea.

Meg Thurgood exited her car and shook her head at the ramshackle gate in the stone wall. To her right and below was the ocean. She walked toward it, drawn to the salty smell and the pounding surf. Waves crashed against the sand, and a rocky cove sheltered a small beach. The wind whipped her hair across her face. She'd always loved the beach—especially now after her prison release—but this was wild, untamed, and deserted. Different from the California beach scene she frequented before.

Movement drew her gaze to blue-gray water. She caught her breath as a man arched out of the water. Light reflected off his wet skin, his dark hair was slicked away from his face—he was beautiful. What kind of person swam in the ocean at this time of year, Meg wondered as she walked along the cliff path? Before she could study him further, he disappeared below the water again.

The old Meg—the one who lived to socialize— would have gone and introduced herself, started a conversation, maybe splashed in the water with him. Then again, she couldn't picture the old Meg in a deserted place like Gull's Point, Maine. But in the three years since she'd left her former identity behind, she'd learned to value her privacy and embrace change.

Still, her chest ached at the solitary life she'd lived. Her friends deserted her years ago. Not that they were real ones. She repeated her mantra in her mind—repay the last of the money she owed, convince her dad it was time for her to take control of her life again, and announce her innocence.

She opened the gate, climbed into her car, and followed the dirt road. Far in the distance was a burned, tattered roofline of a large building. It reminded her of a setting in a horror movie, or maybe a ghost story. The realtor said her rental house was part of a compound— her gatehouse, a larger home where the landlord lived, and the burned shell of the former estate. She approached a small, weathered, blue-shingled house on her left with a hand-carved driftwood sign: The Gatehouse. There it was, her home for the next three months, with an option to continue afterward. She parked her car and walked up the fieldstone pathway. Tucked inside the front door was an envelope, with a key, and a poorly scrawled note on embossed stationery inside. Despite the bright sunshine, she squinted to read it. After several attempts, she managed to decipher the words:

Heat, electricity, and water are turned on. If you need anything, call the number and leave a message.

Neither warm nor sociable. The realtor said the owner kept to himself. From the equally spaced words, full sentences, and shaky handwriting, she surmised her landlord was an old man. Who was the man in the ocean? She pulled her suitcase from her car and entered her new home, saying a silent prayer this wasn't a mistake. The inside was dark but clean, and she opened the windows to let in the ocean breeze. The place was sparse and functional, with a sitting room with a fieldstone fireplace, a small kitchen with a breakfast nook, a bedroom, and a full bathroom. She'd have to add personal touches to make it her own.

Her phone rang. She sighed. "Hi, Dad. Yes, I've arrived. It's small and clean. No, I don't want your penthouse in DC. I don't like the confines of the city. No, I don't need your money. I'm fine." The quick conversation ended, and she hung up the phone, glad to be done with her familial check-in. Her mom died when she was a small child. Although it had been her and her dad for as long as she could remember, they were polar opposites.

After she unpacked her meager belongings—she'd left most of her old designer clothes and expensive jewelry with her old life—Meg drove the four miles into town to find a grocery store and research possible employment.

She wandered the aisles, chose enough food for the week, and congratulated herself on not worrying about being recognized. After three years out of the spotlight, far from the prying lenses of the paparazzi, the likelihood of recognition in this tiny town was doubtful.

At the cash register, she withdrew her credit card to pay for her groceries and asked about employment opportunities, when a photo in one of the gossip magazines distracted her. "High As A Kite." Meg recoiled. Her question, "are you hiring," died on her lips as she skimmed the cover. Flashes of her old life played in her mind—the clubs, the crowds, the carnage. She forced herself into the present. Different people, different situation.

The woman tipped her head toward the magazine.

"Such trash. Can you imagine someone wasting that much money on drugs and parties?" She shook her head. "Where are the parents?"

Meg swallowed, glad she didn't have to answer.

"You new in town?" the woman asked as she bagged.

"I'm renting for a few months."

"Oh, where?" She showed no sign of recognition, since Meg wasn't here with her former friends, the reality stars and socialites. Then again, out-of-the-way places were never their style. It suited her fine now.

"The Gatehouse, near the beach on the cliff."

Surprise flitted across her face as she tallied the bill. "Awfully isolated."

Meg shrugged, hesitant to talk too long to a stranger. "The beach is pretty." She picked up her bags of groceries.

"The house stood empty for years. I never thought he'd manage to get a renter. Good luck."

Once again unease snaked through her, as it did when she first arrived at the house. Meg squelched it and paid for her items. "I don't suppose you know of any employment opportunities in town?"

The woman examined her, and Meg resisted the urge to squirm. "Sorry, I don't. Maybe try the library."

She returned to her car and considered the woman's comments as she drove home. She'd look for employment the next time she came into town.

Once home, she inhaled the crisp fall air and pulled out ingredients to make zucchini bread. Humming, she baked for the next hour in her tiny kitchen. The yellow-painted room was cheery, the oak table and chairs comfortable, and the stainless appliances worked. It

A Reckless Heart

was far different from a professional kitchen with a home chef, but she could get used to it.

Sweet spices filled the house. Her mouth watered. When she removed the bread from the oven, she held the pan to her face and inhaled. She hadn't met the old man yet, but it might be nice to give him one of the loaves as a gracious gesture, regardless of the vibe she got about him from the townspeople. She put it on a plate, wrapped it in tinfoil and added a note.

Thanks for renting to me.

~Meg

Outside, she zipped her jacket as the light breeze ruffled her hair. She took the plate and walked along the dirt and gravel road. The exercise warmed her. She peeked behind her once in a while and shook her head over her nerves. There was no sign of the swimmer. No matter how aloof her landlord sounded, no one objected to baked goods. His two-story house was identified by a sign next to the front door "The Guesthouse" and sported a wraparound porch. She'd live on the porch if this place were hers. She knocked on the door. When there was no answer, she placed the plate on the rocker next to the door. It was time, once again, to start over.

****

After a swim in the same water as always, Simon McAlter returned to The Guesthouse, his home for the past seven years, removed a beer from the Sub-Zero fridge, grasped it with care in one hand, and walked onto his Brazilian walnut-floored balcony which overlooked the ocean. In the past, October was his favorite month. The days were warm but the evenings were cool, the grasses turned from deep green to a washed-out sage, and the water frothed. Soon it would

5

be too cold to swim. For most people, it already was. But he loved the chill of the water, and his scarred flesh prevented him from feeling it as much as others. There was an upside to his injuries.

He stared at the water and breathed in the salt air. The peacefulness didn't soothe him as usual. Isolated on an inlet, miles from town and farther from any other houses, the seclusion was a balm for his soul. Or it used to be.

Until his seclusion was shattered earlier today.

He had waded into the ocean. As expected, the cold water shocked his system, but he dove under once he was past the shallow shore. Beneath the surface, silence surrounded him. It was supposed to refresh and restore him. It didn't. He remained there until his lungs protested and he shot out of the water, droplets splashing. When he glanced up, a figure stood on the cliff far above. He'd frozen.

His heart pounded. He ducked under the water before he realized it wasn't possible for the person, a woman, to see anything from where she stood. The freedom made his curiosity bloom. He treaded water and stared at her on the cliff. From there, he couldn't make out more than her outline. Long hair billowed around her shoulders. A flowing top flapped around her body and some sort of pants clung to her legs. As if the wind chilled her, she hugged her arms around her waist, retreated a few steps, and disappeared.

Once again, the beach was his. Nothing to see but the harsh beauty of nature. Nothing to hear but the wind, the surf, and the seagulls overhead. Like every other day for the past seven years. Only today, it stifled him.

His beer finished, he changed into gardening clothes and strode toward the mansion. He planned to work on the gardens around the burned-down mansion a few hours today until his hands cramped. In his free time, he experimented with landscape designs and used the mansion's grounds as his laboratory. He had no plans to ever touch the mansion itself—it reminded him of what he'd lost—but the grounds were another story. Someday, he wanted to transform them into an all-season garden, with acres of walking paths through bushes, flowers, herbs, and trees. Someday would have already come and gone if he'd hired people to execute the work he designed. But hiring people meant daily interaction. So he worked on the gardens himself, in irritatingly slow steps. After digging, planting, and weeding for a couple of hours, his hands, as expected, stiffened.

Flexing his fingers as much as he was able from the scar tissue as a result of the burns, he walked to his house and stopped short. There was an object on his porch that wasn't there this morning. He jogged up the steps and frowned at the rocker. A foil-wrapped plate sat on it. He hadn't put it there, which meant someone else had. *Wow, you're a genius, Si.* Taped to the foil was a note. He ripped it off to read it. Meg. His renter's name was Meg, and she'd left him a gift. He unwrapped the foil and inhaled. Zucchini bread. The spicy smell made his stomach growl.

His mother had given baked goods to local people to show appreciation for something. Granted, the cook baked, but it was the thought that counted. He'd left specific instructions with his listing agent to rent the house to an older man or woman who wanted peace and quiet. Apparently this one baked. Striding into the kitchen, he grabbed a knife and cut off a piece of the bread. He took a bite and groaned. It tasted better than it smelled.

He cut a second piece. His hands pained him, and the thought of writing a thank-you note was more than he could deal with right now. Should he call her? He knew her number. But if he called her, he might encourage her to visit. It was bad enough she was his tenant for the next three months. When Larry called and begged him to rent the unused house, he should have said no. He'd have to explain his scars. He hated socializing. That was why he refused to rent to a single twenty-something. There weren't many of them in this area, but with the beach, the last thing he wanted was all night parties and bonfires and… He shook his head to banish the memories.

The money didn't matter. The insurance money from the fire, plus his multi-million dollar inheritance ensured he'd never have to work again and could focus on things he loved—like landscape design and online teaching at the local college. And then there was CAST Ltd., an investment group he and his three college friends formed after graduation. Each was an expert in their chosen career fields—he in landscape architecture, Caleb in media, Alexander in architecture, and Ted in computer security—and they'd grown their combined assets to over $200 million in the fifteen years since they'd graduated. While each of them possessed enough individual wealth to live well on their own, they all needed to do something worthwhile with their money. They used their investments for philanthropic projects—healthcare in underprivileged communities or funding the arts in schools. He spoke with them weekly to discuss current and future projects. He should have been fulfilled. Except what should have soothed him frustrated him of late. Whereas he once awoke content with the routine, for the past few weeks he'd faced the day with a sense of dread.

Maybe dread was the wrong word. He didn't dread his days, but he didn't look forward to them anymore. He needed a change, but he didn't know what kind.

You need to hire a crew, his inner voice whispered.

"Inner voice be damned," he responded.

Shaking off his thoughts, he turned on his computer and opened an email from Claire, one of his few remaining local friends from his childhood.

"Has your tenant arrived?"

He pecked at the keys. "Yup." He sorted through his mail until she replied.

"Met her yet?"

"Nope."

There were two requests for proposals from existing clients, a few assignments an eager student turned in early, bills to be paid, and invoices to mail.

"Probably a good thing, since you only give one word answers. She might think you're unfriendly."

He cracked a smile. "I am."

He looked at the designs he was in the middle of, and his mind went blank.

"You're impossible."

"Talk to you later."

He opened another file on his computer and looked at the garden renderings he'd created. His friend Ted, one of his CAST partners and a computer security genius, provided him with the latest technology.

Remote design via computer, garden experiments on his own property, and communication by phone or email—nothing required in-person interactions. The situation should have been perfect.

He scoffed at his persistent dissatisfaction. He didn't need people. He was fine on his own.

Besides, alone, he didn't have to share the zucchini bread.

Chapter Two

Meg squatted outside her home the next afternoon and examined the placement of her mums. Purple and orange alternated on each step. It looked homey and inviting. Already, the place was prettier than when she'd arrived.

Maybe she should become a gardener, or at least see if the local garden center needed extra help. Ever since her release from prison, she craved the outdoors. Gardening was perfect.

Her soft laugh was bitter. Former socialite turned gardener. What would her friends think of her drastic change in circumstances? She snorted. Her "friends" wouldn't care. They'd abandoned her when she'd needed them the most.

Despite the cool fall air, the sun beat on her neck and warmed her. She wiped her brow. The idea of running in the sand and dipping her toes in the ocean appealed to her. She ran into the house, changed into her bathing suit, grabbed a towel, and went in search of a walkway to the beach.

The path to the inlet led right past her landlord's house, and she glanced at the front porch. There was no sign of the zucchini bread. The beach called to her.

She walked with care along the rocky path and stopped when her feet hit the sand. With a cry of joy, she removed her flip-flops and dug her toes deep into the soft, cool sand. Dropping her towel, she spun around, arms out, before she raced to the water's edge. Like a sandpiper that approaches the water's edge and runs away from the water, she did the same and laughed. Finally she stopped and let the water lap over her toes. It was cold, but not unbearable. She waded in to her ankles. The tide rolled in, and the waves splashed as high as her knees.

She took a belated look around. No one was there. Her landlord's house was visible, but she doubted he watched her. Interest in her died a long time ago. At least, she hoped so.

No one watches me anymore. No one cares.

After ten minutes, she became chilled and walked toward her towel. She shook it, lay down, and closed her eyes. She inhaled and exhaled, and practiced her new relaxation techniques. She focused on the sounds and smells around her. Her body relaxed.

She couldn't give into unreasonable anxiety. She'd managed to escape her old life and done her time. She refused to live in its shadow.

****

In the week since Meg arrived, Simon discovered two things.

One, his tenant was not a middle-aged lady like he'd thought. Oh no. She was the woman he first spotted on the cliff—young, exuberant, and sexy as hell in a bathing suit. She walked every day this past week from the house across the way to his beach. He admired the sway of her hips each time. Despite her obvious hesitancy due to the cold, each day she'd ventured a little deeper into the water. Every time she retreated or shrieked at the temperature, he'd laughed, much to his dismay.

Two, he'd become a creature of habit. She destroyed his routine. He used the beach first thing each morning or as soon as he returned from work. But with her around, dancing and cavorting in the water at random times, he'd been thrown off his schedule. He wouldn't risk running into her. As a result, he spent a lot of time at his window. Staring at the beach.

In the future, he'd have to be more specific with his realtor about the type of tenant he'd allow. In the meantime, he needed to determine how to get her off his damn beach.

He looked outside and didn't see her. Screw it. He'd take a chance, run and take a quick swim and be home before she arrived. The ocean called to him. It drove him crazy to stay away. Before he changed his mind, he put on his trunks, grabbed a towel, and raced to the beach.

As his legs hit the water, he sucked in a sharp breath. The water was cold, colder than the last time he was here. As he waded deeper, his stomach shivered, and he plunged beneath the surface. He swam leisurely, coming up for air as necessary. He enjoyed the weightlessness and silence below the surface. Finally, he dunked once more, held his breath as long as possible, and shot out of the water.

An ear-splitting shriek greeted him as water sluiced off his body.

With a curse, he yanked his hair in front of his face, sank to his neck in the water, and searched for the owner of the offensive lungs.

Meg.

She stood on the shore and quaked as if she'd seen

a monster.

As if she'd seen his face.

He stifled an oath, swam backward, and placed distance between them. A long period of silence stretched between her shriek and now. Someone needed to say something. Anything.

"Sorry," she yelled as she approached the water's edge. "I didn't mean to scream."

"I won't hurt you," he called.

"I…I know. You startled me. I didn't expect you to be here." She looked along the shoreline, rubbed her arms, and shifted from one foot to the other. "Do you come here often?"

"Most days."

She turned as if ready to leave. He called out to her. "You're welcome to swim, you know."

With a pause, she glanced at him, eyes wide. "Thanks, maybe another time."

His pulse pounded as she raced along the path and out of sight. Spots speckled his vision. She could have at least pretended.

No longer aware of the cold, he stalked from the ocean and dried off before he headed home. Inside his bathroom, he turned on the shower and avoided the mirror. He didn't need to see his reflection to know how awful he looked.

No wonder she'd screamed.

So much for swimming.

****

So much for swimming. And for being friendly. Meg lay curled in the middle of her bed.

A man swam in her ocean. No, it wasn't *her* ocean. She'd gotten used to the privacy, but it didn't mean she owned the place. If anyone did, it was her landlord, although she suspected he was too old to use it.

She sat up with a start. Was *he* her landlord?

He'd told her she could swim. Who else would give permission *but* her landlord? It wasn't possible. He was too young. He didn't fit her image of a recluse. The damn realtor never mentioned he was close to her age. No, he must be a trespasser, or a neighbor with permission to use the beach.

Her face burned. She should have been prepared. She shouldn't have been shocked to see him in the water. It was why she'd shrieked like a schoolgirl. Her heart pounded so hard she struggled to get her breath or form sentences. Even when he'd told her he wouldn't hurt her. Even when he'd invited her to swim, too.

His ebony hair covered his face. She couldn't see his features, but his body? Broad shoulders, sculpted muscles, powerful arms. He was built better than any of the wealthy, Hollywood men she'd once known. There was a natural fluidity about him. It made her think he didn't get those muscles from a gym. Of course, it was pure conjecture. But still.

She tamped her curiosity. At one point in her life that kind of man had intrigued her, hopelessly attracted her. Tempted her to seduce him. But that was the old Meg. The before-that-night Meg. The one who acted first and thought later. The one who gave little thought to who, in particular, she spent time with, male or female. The new Meg? Well, she was much more careful about whom she associated with and the reputation she cultivated. She knew first-hand the effect of guilt by association. Been there, done that. No need for an encore.

Chapter Three

That afternoon, Meg drove into town to the library. Housed in a stately red brick building, it was off of the main street, across from the Town Hall and adjacent to the Post Office.

"I'd like to get a library card," she said to the young woman behind the counter. "And to see if you might have any job openings."

The woman looked about her age, with blonde hair and glasses. She smiled at Meg's request. "Sure, fill out this form, and I'll print it right now. As for job openings, I'm not sure, but I can ask and let you know."

Meg filled out the form and handed it to the librarian, who frowned for a moment and glanced between Meg and her form. Meg's stomach clenched. Did she recognize her? Or did she frown at the "yes" answer to "Do you have a criminal record?" It didn't matter. She had to be honest on the paperwork.

"You live in The Gatehouse? I knew Simon rented it, but I didn't know to whom."

Not another warning. Her stomach unclenched. "Yes, I'm here for the next three months. Maybe longer."

"You know, he has books delivered once a month at The Guesthouse. If you'd like, I can add yours to the delivery truck."

"It's nice of you to offer delivery to the elderly."

The librarian disagreed. "He's not elderly, unless you think I am. We went to school together and used to be great friends. Still are, although we don't see each other in person. We email. Oh, I'm Claire."

She held out her hand, and Meg shook it. "Oh, I guess I thought he was elderly because of his handwriting. I'm kind of embarrassed."

"Don't worry about it. I'm kind of surprised he rented to someone as young as you. He told me he'd instructed the leasing company only to offer it to elderly singles." She leaned forward and winked. "Between you and me, I'm glad he reconsidered. He needs to get out more, and he's the most handsome man I've ever met." She showed off her hand with a wedding ring on it. "Other than my husband, of course."

"Really?"

"Ebony hair, broad shoulders, abs to die for. Of course, the accident affected him, but oh you should have seen him in high school. We all drooled."

"Wait...it's...Oh." Holy cow. He was the Greek god. The one she'd screamed at.

Claire's friendliness lessened. She gave Meg a wary gaze. "Don't use his looks to judge him. He's the kindest man I've ever known."

"No, I wasn't. I mean, I haven't seen him up close. Just from a distance, as he swam in the ocean. We both keep to ourselves."

Claire appraised her with a glance. "Hmm. Well, here's your card. Feel free to browse. If you want delivery, let me know."

Meg left the main desk with the distinct impression she'd offended Claire. Which was a shame, when she thought about it. Claire appeared to be a potential friend, and maybe she could help her get a job here. As she perused the shelves and collected a stack of books to borrow, her mind whirled. Simon, her landlord, was the swimmer? Or was it possible the swimmer was another dark-haired, muscular guy—and if so, what did they feed these people, because what were the chances one town produced two such gorgeous men? What did Claire mean about his looks and an accident? She hadn't noticed anything wrong with him, although she'd been far away.

Simon was kind, according to Claire. Her chest expanded. At some point, she'd have to interact with her landlord. She'd be a lot more comfortable if she knew he was a kind man. The "It" crowd she associated with in the past was catty, superficial, and judgmental.

The next time she came to the library, she'd have to make a better effort to befriend Claire, to convince her she didn't judge people by their looks. The old Meg was well and truly buried.

****

Simon opened his email to find a new message from Claire.

"I met your tenant today. You didn't tell me she was our age! She seems nice. Do you have her phone number? I want to invite her over for coffee."

Simon shook his head and responded. "Oh. You didn't ask. Okay. Yes. Why?"

He was difficult on purpose. Claire was one of his oldest friends. They'd both gone away to college and returned, although for different reasons. His family's wealth never fazed her; she was the only one who continued to try to get him into the world. He admired her useless tenacity.

Scrolling through his other emails, he responded to clients and students and sent inquiries to contractors over the next few hours. None of his projects inspired him. Not even the project he worked on for Claire. Especially that one, truth be told. All he saw when he looked at the drawings were plants and flowers. They didn't speak to him, didn't provide dimension, offer a creative outlet, or touch his soul. They didn't convince him to bear the scrutiny he'd receive if he provided alternate plans to Claire for the town's open land. He already regretted agreeing to design the land into a community park.

Meg distracted him from all of it.

She'd run away from him. Despite her actions, he thought about her all day. It was annoying.

He didn't let Claire see him. Why in the world would he interact with a complete stranger, regardless of how pretty she was? Because the sound of her voice, other than the shriek, intrigued him. Because he needed to thank her for the zucchini bread. Because he'd scared her. Because he was a complete idiot.

His email dinged, and he opened Claire's response.

"Because."

Annoying female. His mouse hovered over the trash icon. What if Claire didn't take no for an answer and came over to his house to get Meg's number? She often went to great lengths to get what she wanted. And he could further imagine Claire deciding he needed a visitor. Or several. She would shatter his seclusion and peace. He responded.

"410-555-4819"

A moment later, she responded.

"☺"

With a sigh, he stalked toward the old mansion.

****

Meg jumped when her phone rang. When her presence, and that of her friends, was considered a boon, her phone rang non-stop with A-list friends who invited her to all the latest parties, clubs, and social events of the season. Texts and calls besieged her all day and all night. Afterward, paparazzi chased her for a scoop, and "friends" offered to "help" her, when all they wanted was gossip. Nowadays, her new phone with her new number rarely rang, other than her father's once-a-month call to check in. Lately, her old friend, Vanessa, started calling her. She didn't know how she'd gotten her number. After what happened between her, Mackenzie, and Vanessa, she had no desire to talk to anyone from her old life. She adjusted to the silence of her cottage, and when it overwhelmed her, turned on music. But the waves provided a soothing background noise, and most days, she enjoyed the peace and quiet. When the ringing phone shattered her quiet, it took her a moment to reach it. Since it was neither her father nor Vanessa, she answered.

"Hello?"

"Hi, Meg? This is Claire. From the library. I wondered, since you're new in town, if you wanted to get together for coffee sometime."

Meg pulled the phone away from her ear and stared at it before she returned it to her ear. She knew nothing about Claire. Could she trust her? Should she? If she said no, would she get a reputation for being aloof? She wasn't, she was careful. And thinking way too much. This was coffee. "Yeah, coffee sounds fun. How about tomorrow?"

"I don't have to be at work until one. How about we meet at nine at Rosie's," Claire said. "Unless nine is too early?"

When one left clubs at four in the morning, nine was still considered nighttime. But now she rose early. "No, nine is fine. Where is it?"

"In the center of town, on Main Street. You can't miss it."

Meg hung up. It seemed she'd made a friend. Maybe.

Chapter Four

It shouldn't be this complicated to get ready to meet Claire for coffee. Except it was difficult. She didn't know what impression she might give based on what she wore.

In the past, she always wore custom-made outfits. Designers paid her and her friends to draw attention to themselves. It added to her aura and helped seal her reputation—in a negative fashion. Starting fresh here, she wanted to fit in for the right reasons. After an agonizing twenty minutes, she settled on a light-washed pair of Calvin Klein jeans and an emerald silk blouse with black ballet flats. She left her hair loose, added a touch of makeup and simple silver knot earrings. It would have to do.

Inside the busy café, after a few moments of searching, Meg spotted Claire seated in a corner booth.

"I hope you didn't wait long," she said, and slid across from her. The waitress appeared with a carafe of coffee. "I'd prefer tea if you don't mind."

"Don't worry, I just got here," said Claire. "I'm glad you said yes. It's not often I get to meet people my own age."

"There aren't many people our age around here?" Meg thanked the waitress for her mug of hot water and added a tea bag and sugar.

"A lot of the people I went to school with moved

away. Only a few of us came home—Simon, me, Chelsea, Tom, Lauren, and Mark. We don't get a lot of newcomers who don't already have families. What made you choose Gull's Point?"

Another point on the map as far from LA as she could get. "I wanted quiet. And I love the water."

Claire fixed her gaze on Meg as she handed her a breakfast menu. "Did anything in particular make you pick here?"

Other than it was unlikely anyone here mingled with the vapid, high-society crowd she'd previously been with? Meg remained silent, but smiled to take away what might be perceived as rudeness.

Claire nodded. "Okay, I'll try to restrain my 'small-town nosiness'."

A man walked next to their table holding his phone like a camera. Meg turned her face away before she sipped her tea.

"So how are the books you borrowed?"

Meg nodded. "I started Mary Higgins Clark's latest mystery."

"Oh, I loved it! The bad guy was a total surprise to me. What else have you done, other than read?"

"I've gone to the beach. The water is cold, but I love it. Oh, and I decorated a little for fall—mums and cornstalks, for the most part. If I plan to live here for a few months, I want the place to feel like home. It doesn't sound like much, I know. I still have to settle in and figure out what comes next. I need to find a job." Meg held her breath. She never revealed too much information to people she didn't know, but she needed a job to repay her debt to Mr. Adams.

"Simon likes to swim in the cold, too. I can't

23

understand either of you. Why do you like water that makes you turn blue?"

Relieved Claire didn't press her for more details about her future, Meg cracked a smile. "Well, I can't say I like it. More like play at the edge of the water like an over-sugared child. But the water is refreshing." The man with the cellphone returned from the restroom. Meg watched him until he passed. The last thing she needed was to appear in a stranger's photo.

"I think Simon finds it therapeutic. I find it cold. I won't go near the water after August. If you're still here for Memorial Day, though, you'll have to join us for the big bonfire. Everyone goes to the beach, and there's music and dancing and of course, a fire. My husband and I love it."

"Oh, right, you're married."

"Two years in May." She held out her hand, and Meg admired her gold braided wedding ring. "How about you?"

"Nope, haven't met the right guy yet." For now, she refrained from telling Claire how many "not right" guys she'd been linked with, although the numbers in the papers were inflated for shock value.

"There aren't a lot of single men here. I can try to introduce you..."

Meg held up her hand. "I didn't come here because of single men. I like my independence. It's one of the reasons I didn't choose a big city to live in."

"Speaking of fall decorations," Claire said, with a change of subject, "do you like craft projects? Because I found this super easy DIY project to turn jars into candleholders. You use autumn leaves. I thought it sounded like a fun activity. I have a few other friends who craft as well. Want to join us?"

Talk about reinvention. "I've never done it before. Is it difficult?"

"Not at all. My friends and I wanted to try something new. Some of us are better than others, but we always laugh. And there's wine."

"Sounds fun. When is it?"

"Friday evening. Are you free?"

Meg gaped in shock. Making friends was never this easy. "I'm free all the time."

Claire removed a pen from her purse and wrote her address on the napkin. After Meg chatted with Claire a little more, they left Rosie's.

Claire hugged her as they parted. "I'll let you know if the library needs any extra help."

"Fantastic."

Claire smiled. "I look forward to getting to know you better."

On her drive home, Meg forced her doubts to recede. Unlike her friends in the past, Claire didn't spend time with her because of her money or her connections. The two women had things in common so it could be the start of a real friendship.

Claire wanted to get to know her better, but Meg didn't have to tell her everything.

****

Later that day, Meg explored farther along the drive. A light breeze blew leaves already on the ground into swirls of color. She took a detour toward the water, wondering if Simon swam, but she didn't see anyone and continued past The Guesthouse, Simon's home. The drive curved around to the left and down a hill. As she came to the crest, below her sat the mansion whose roofline she'd seen in the distance.

Or what was left of it.

The stone footprint of the original building was visible. What hadn't burned collapsed in on itself, and the stone foundation was filled with debris. Whatever destroyed the building happened a long time ago, as vegetation took over and sprouted between scorched boards and beams. Vines, twisted around and over and through, created life where destruction loomed. It was haunting and beautiful.

Intrigued, she continued to explore. As she got closer, the pounding of a hammer echoed around her. Her steps slowed as she searched for the noise. She walked around the outside of the building. Simon knelt on the ground about twenty feet away. His shirt was off. His muscles—glorious muscles actors in Hollywood paid big bucks to a trainer to get—bunched as he hammered. She admired his muscles and their play beneath his skin as he worked. It wasn't until she stepped closer she noticed his back was covered in scars.

She winced at the puckered scar tissue crisscrossed over most of his back. The patterns of scars reminded her of a map. She cringed at the thought of the pain they must have caused, as their pattern and texture intrigued her. While it was obvious the scars weren't new—they blended in with the rest of his bronze skin—the extensiveness of them chilled her. What happened? She swallowed and imagined how painful the injury must have been. Her hand rose reflexively to smooth away the hurt before she dropped it to her side and made a fist. She didn't know him well enough.

She remained where she was and watched him. It

looked like he built a box. He handled the hammer awkwardly, his hands not able to fully clasp the grip, but he was occupied, and she didn't want to disturb his concentration. When he cursed, she jumped. The movement must have caught his eye, because he swung around for a second before he jerked his face away from her.

"What are you doing here?" he shouted, still turned away from her.

A racing heart at his harsh tone replaced her momentary curiosity over his refusal to look at her. She retreated farther. "I…I'm sorry. I t-took a walk, and I heard noise."

He muttered a litany of curses before he dropped his chin to his chest and fell silent, continuing to hide his face.

Why wouldn't he look at her? If he kept his scarred back to her, what must his front look like?

"Never mind," he said in a more even tone. "Don't apologize."

"I didn't mean to disturb you." She stopped her retreat.

"Is there something you need?"

He faced away from her, and she continued to wonder why he didn't look at her.

"What are you doing?"

"Building another planter."

"This place is beautiful." The wide open space soothed her soul.

A laugh, which sounded more like a bark, escaped from him. She jumped at the sudden sound. "You have a strange sense of beauty."

"Maybe so. But I love how the new growth has

taken over, softening the destruction, maybe beautifying it. I bet this place will be gorgeous when you're done with it."

He grunted. She could take a hint.

"I'll let you return to work." She walked away.

"Wait."

Meg stopped.

"You can walk around the property if you want. Don't climb through the building. I don't want you to get hurt."

She accepted his offer to explore the property. One area was well-cultivated, with the beginnings of gardens. There was an order to it, although in the autumn it was hard to visualize. Still, the plants and bushes appeared to have a purpose, unlike the rest of the place, which was filled with overgrown garden paths, lookouts over the water, and brambly woods. The place was wild, and she loved it. After a few minutes, the hammering and cursing continued. Finding a large boulder overlooking the ocean, she climbed on top and observed the waves crash upon the rocks below.

Her landlord was an enigma. He was scarred, yet he cultivated beauty. Right now, he was frustrated. Anyone could tell from listening to him. Yet when he'd realized she was there, she'd sensed fear. And regret after he'd yelled.

More than that? She had no idea.

****

He'd seen movement from the corner of his eye and assumed the wind had blown a branch, or maybe a squirrel ran up a tree. He hadn't expected a person. He kept an eye on her on the rock as he hammered—or dropped—nails. His damn hands wouldn't allow him a

28

firm hold on the nails, and he spent half his time securing them enough to hit them with the hammer, without them bouncing off the wood, bending, and landing on the ground. This was why he was a landscape architect, not a carpenter.

In actuality, he'd chosen his profession long before the fire. Every day, he came here for a couple of hours and tried to bang nails into wood to assemble a box frame to plant seedlings. Or dig holes to plant shrubs and trees. Or furrow the ground to plant bulbs.

It was a lost cause. But his landscape projects for his clients, while profitable, didn't fill the empty space inside of him. Even his students didn't do it for him.

He thought maybe if he brought to life the ideas floating in his mind and planted them here, it might jigger an idea in his brain and renew his soul. Too much time in front of a computer, not enough time in the soil. But as far as he could tell, there were two problems with his idea. One, his damaged hands made it difficult to do a lot of what he wanted to do. Two, this place conjured memories he'd rather forget. Living here didn't bother him. Digging in the actual soil did.

He knew the solution. Hire gardeners to bring his ideas to life. There was a certain satisfaction he got from digging in the soil, however clumsy he might be. He wasn't ready to give up. At some point he'd give in and hire a crew to help him. But until then, he did it on his own.

And then she'd appeared.

He'd been a prisoner, trapped under a microscope. No matter which way he stood, she'd see his monstrous scars. He turned away from her. Better for her to see his back than his ruin of a face. But she didn't react, or at least her voice remained neutral.

And he'd been rude.

Now, twenty minutes after she climbed off the rock and, he assumed, went home, guilt washed through him. He'd have to find a better way to apologize. Because he'd scared her. The volume of her voice told him she'd moved away from him after he yelled at her. Unless she'd moved away because of his scars. But he didn't think so. Hell, he didn't know. He owed her an apology either way.

His hands ached and as much as he wanted to continue, he needed to stop. It was one thing to be an idiot. It was another to be reckless. Standing, he stretched his tired muscles, put his tools away, pulled his shirt on, and scanned the area. He didn't see her. Sticking to the shadows, he went home and hoped he'd make it before she noticed him.

Inside, he spotted the plate Meg used for the zucchini bread on his drying rack. Maybe he could return it with a thank you gift of his own added as an apology. She'd given it to him with delicious bread, but he didn't bake. His cooking skills, well, they were fine for sustenance as a bachelor, but he doubted she'd appreciate them.

He remembered something she'd said earlier, and he went into his office. A few minutes later, he attached a paper to the plate and left it on her porch with his own note. He didn't ring the bell.

Chapter Five

Meg noticed the plate next to the welcome mat as she locked her front door that night. An envelope was taped to it. She opened the door a crack and peeked around. When she didn't see anyone, she opened the door wider. She waited and listened, not expecting photographers to lurk in the bushes, but unable to make a complete break from the habit. Waves lapped in the distance. She locked the door behind her and brought the plate into the kitchen.

She opened the envelope and extracted an embossed notecard with the familiar almost illegible handwriting on it. Squinting, she deciphered his note.

Zucchini bread was excellent. Thank you. I'm not a baker, but I thought you might like the attached.

The handwriting might be the same, but the note was much nicer. He'd signed it this time. She moved the note aside and looked at the plate again. There was another piece of paper, folded. When she opened it, she gasped.

It was a graphic representation of his proposed plans for the mansion grounds, done with some sort of computer software. What she'd thought was beautiful today was nothing compared to what Simon gave her. The destroyed mansion with the vines was still there, but whereas today she'd seen the beginnings of gardens, this rendering showed them planted and in

31

bloom. They were stunning.

He'd given her his vision.

She rushed into the kitchen and found the phone number she'd taped to the inside of a cabinet. He answered on the third ring.

"The drawing is lovely," she said.

Silence stretched on the other end. For a moment, Meg thought he hung up.

He cleared his throat. "I'm glad you like it."

"Thank you."

"You're welcome."

She took a lock of her hair between her fingers and fiddled with it. This was the most awkward conversation ever.

"I'm glad you found it," he said, jumping in.

"I was locking the door and happened to look down."

"It's good you lock your doors. And...let me know if you need anything—light bulbs, keys, whatever. I can order them for you."

"I always lock my doors. I've got everything I need right now, but thank you."

"I'll let you go. It's late."

It was eight thirty. "Wait, I wanted to ask you a question."

"Yes?"

"Do you plan to make the grounds look like your rendering?"

"It's one version. I'm not sure what it will look like when I'm finished."

"Have you worked on the garden for a long time?"

More silence greeted her question. "About five years."

"But how can you work on it if you haven't decided what it will look like?"

"Have a good evening."

She disconnected the phone, more confused than ever. A reclusive landlord who avoided her. A man who designed gardens without knowing their final outcome. A house in disrepair for five years, without any plans for repair. What kind of man did she rent from?

****

Meg listened to, but didn't watch, the TV as she got ready for Claire's craft group and paused when the weather forecaster talked about an incoming storm this weekend. "Strong winds, heavy rains, and low temperatures make this a storm to watch and prepare for," he said.

"Great," she said as she rummaged through her closet and considered what to wear. "What the heck do you wear to make crafts, other than a smock?" With a quick reminder she didn't want friends who judged her by her clothes, she settled for the outfit she wore right now—jeans and a pale blue sweater with sneakers. As for a smock? She tucked an old shirt into her purse and hoped she wouldn't get messy enough to need it. She grabbed a box of fudge she'd purchased to thank Claire for the invite and raced from the house.

Claire's house was an adorable cottage off the main road of town, about ten minutes away. It looked like the subject of a New England postcard—white clapboard, red shutters, wide front porch.

Claire met her at the door. "Hey, you brought chocolate! You are definitely welcome!" She put her arm around Meg and drew her inside. "Laura, Kelsey, Charlene, this is Meg. She's new to town."

The women smiled. Meg wondered what they thought. Were they friendly? Did they plan to give the newbie a hard time? Was she overreacting?

An hour later Meg blew her hair out of her face in frustration. "I think I did this wrong." She meant to say it in her head, but Laura, seated across the table, heard, and looked over. "Oh no, why?" Laura asked.

Meg swallowed. Time to determine what these ladies thought of her. She cradled a gooey goopy mess. "Because *this* does not look like *yours*." She pointed to Laura's bell jar, which was covered with faux autumn leaves placed with precision. Laura's lips quivered, and she gave away the laugh she tried without success to hide.

"Oh, it's not bad." Laura's voice squeaked, and she turned away. Her shoulders shook.

Meg thought about feeling offended, but in all honesty, there was no way she could. She laughed, too, and pretty soon everyone in the entire dining room joined in.

"Here, let me see if I can help you fix it." Claire peered over Meg's shoulder.

"I'm pretty sure we should just call time of death and be done with it." Meg rubbed her fingers together in an attempt to get rid of the excess glue stuck to them.

"You know what this needs?" Kelsey said.

"Throwing away?" Meg asked.

"Wine." Kelsey handed her a glass, and Charlene offered her the box of fudge.

Meg exhaled, put the glass off to the side, and grabbed the chocolate. "You are my people."

Everyone nodded, and Meg walked to the window, drink and chocolate in hand. The window faced the small backyard. Flowerbeds surrounded it. These women were polar opposites of her old friends.

"You should see it in the summer," Charlene said as she joined her. "She has the most beautiful garden."

"Thanks, Char," Claire said. She pointed to the left of the yard. "In the summer I have marsh marigolds and shooting stars and great white trillium. Obviously gone now. Over there is my moon garden."

"What's a moon garden?" Meg asked.

"The flowers bloom and give off a fragrance at night. It's amazing."

"Everything sounds beautiful."

"Simon helped me design it," Claire said. "The trees and shrubs, too."

Meg's heartbeat quickened. "Like, he came over and laid it out?"

Claire shook her head. "Yeah, right. No, computer. His standard M.O. these days."

The other women exchanged looks. Everyone except Meg finished their crafts, and the other women packed their things to leave.

"I hope you'll join us next time," said Laura.

"After this?" Meg held up her failed jar.

"Especially after that." Charlene grinned.

The women said their goodbyes, and Meg stood with Claire and watched them leave. When they'd piled into their cars, she turned to Claire. "Speaking of Simon, I had an interesting interaction with him the other day."

"Oh really?" Claire stared, and Meg's cheeks heated. She sat at the table and motioned for Meg to join her. Meg described her meeting with Simon at the mansion and his follow-up "gift" and phone call.

"I don't know what to make of it."

Claire burst out laughing. "I'm sorry, I know you're confused. What can I tell you?"

"Why is he reclusive?"

Claire sighed. "He was badly injured in the fire that destroyed the mansion."

"How awful. What happened?"

Claire shifted in her chair. "There was a party and...I don't want to speak out of turn. Did you know he's a world-renowned landscape architect?"

Meg couldn't imagine what had happened to Simon.

"He designs, plans, and manages land. He's designed parks, college campuses, and resorts. He teaches too, online. Look him up—Simon McAlter. He's devoted his life to beauty. I think the injuries damaged his psyche. I think it's hard to have a job that deals with beauty when he feels hideous. I know it sounds girlie and superficial, but it's the only thing I can think of. Anyway, he's hidden away. He still works, but remotely."

"How awful." Maybe it was why he hid his face. "He doesn't see anybody?"

"He lost his parents in the fire. Many of the townspeople rejected him because of his scars, unfortunately. He's pushed most of his friends away. He pushed me away, too, but I'm stubborn." She grinned. "He sounds like he might be softening a little."

Meg snorted. "He speaks to me only when necessary."

"Still. I see a spark of interest from you whenever his name is mentioned."

Meg shivered. The thought of getting close to a

man who was "world-renowned." She wasn't sure she was ready.

Claire's phone buzzed. "My husband texted me. He's the editor of our local paper. He says we're getting a storm. Ugh, our harvest festival and book fair is this weekend," Claire said. "I hope the storm holds off until afterward."

"Yeah, I heard about it."

"Make sure you're prepared. Fall storms can be unpredictable, and you're kind of isolated there."

Chapter Six

Simon signed off the call with his three CAST colleagues and college friends—Caleb, Alexander, and Ted. Each was an expert in, and had made fortunes in, their chosen career fields—he in landscape architecture, Caleb in media, Alexander in architecture, and Ted in computer security. Today's call centered around their desire to diversify. After an hour and a half poring over spreadsheets, forecasts, and other financials, Simon's brain hurt.

Working in the garden would be a welcome relief. His computer chat pinged.

"Meg is awesome."

He thrummed his fingers on his mahogany desk. *Here we go.*

"You should get to know her."

"I do know her. She's my tenant."

"You know what I mean."

He brushed his hair out of his face, and wished he had the nerve to cut it. "What do you suggest I do?"

"Ask her out."

He choked on his own breath. "Funny."

"Seriously, all my friends loved her. She's sweet and has a self-deprecating sense of humor."

"Great. You ask her out."

"I will, but I think you should, too."

He swung around and stared out the window. He

could already predict the results of asking Meg on a date. His face, her screams, interactions with the townspeople, taking chances...and those were only his immediate thoughts.

But her voice was lovely. On the phone, he'd admired the velvety tone, like a smooth aged whiskey, at least when she didn't scream in fear. He missed in-person conversations. His conversations with Claire and his college friends weren't in person. He opened and closed his hands as much as he was able. He missed touching people, the feel of skin, the whisper of breath. The sight of his reddened hands made him scoff. Who would ever want to touch him?

He shut off his computer. Asking her on a date would be reckless, a trait he hadn't been able to abide since the night seven years ago.

Never again.

****

Gray skies arrived the next day on wind that blew leaves from the trees and created rainbow spirals, but the rains held off. Main Street was awash in yellow, orange, and red foliage. With the street closed off to cars, local famers sold pumpkins, hot apple cider, and donuts in tents in the middle of the road. The town's storekeepers held sidewalk sales to take advantage of the influx of tourists. Children with powdered sugar faces ran around and local newspaper photographers snapped autumn celebration photos. Cornstalks, hay bales, pumpkins, and gourds decorated the library, and people from all over town visited the book fair.

Meg marveled at the activity—she was more familiar with the glitzy, glamorous shows of Hollywood, where everyone hired professional decorators to attain the "right" look—and she enjoyed the holiday spirit. Shopkeepers waved as she wove her way around the customers and wandered toward the library. Once there, she waded through tables piled high with books, on her way to find Claire. She spotted her across the room and wended her way toward her.

"Hi." She looked around and rested her hand on her purse strap. "You got a great turnout." People squished past each other and stood in line ten deep to pay for their purchases.

"Yeah, we did. I'm glad the storm held off. Thanks for stopping by today."

Meg smiled at her new friend. "I love this. So many things to see and do. Everyone is genuine—not a single air kiss to be seen."

Claire raised her eyebrows. "Are we different from where you used to live?"

Well, she'd lived in three places before here, but Meg knew Claire meant California. "From what I've seen so far, yes. You're more genuine. People are here today because they'll have a great time, not because they want to be seen…"

As a mob of people swarmed Claire, Meg waved goodbye and maneuvered her way through the crowd. When she found the section with women's fiction and literature, she breathed a sigh of relief. Without all the kids running around, it was a little quieter, a little calmer.

Bins decorated with autumn leaves were stacked on tables like mini bookshelves. Meg browsed through all of them and chose two novels by well-known authors. In the biography section, she found three of her favorite historical figures—Nelson Mandela, Lola Montez, and

Ruth Bader Ginsburg—and grabbed those as well. Satisfied, she returned to the front room of the library to pay for her purchases.

When Claire inventoried her purchases, she frowned.

"What's the problem?"

"I get the literature. They have fascinating stories and deep characters. But biographies?"

Meg shrugged. She'd learned to appreciate a variety of genres from the prison library. "I love learning about people who followed their dreams and made a difference. Don't worry, I like escapism as much as the next person. You should see the horror movies I watch."

With a last wave to her friend, Meg left the book fair and wandered the streets of town, taking in the sales and harvest activities. She stopped at a few stores and offices to ask about employment, but there were few openings available. People were friendly. After a simple "Hello," most left her alone. The wind chilled her, and she returned home.

That night, after she made an omelet for dinner, she curled up in bed with the biography of Nelson Mandela. Outside, the wind increased, and rain fell, but inside was warm and safe. A good book, a warm blanket, and a cozy house—it was the best way to weather the storm—and she drifted off to sleep.

She swam in the ocean, water splashing against her skin, except no matter how hard she kicked, she didn't move forward. The water was cold, but she didn't shiver. The waves didn't make the gentle "lapping sound." No, these waves crashed over and over again. She struggled against the pull of the

41

current. She shouldn't swim in treacherous waters. It wasn't safe. But no matter how hard she kicked, she couldn't get to the shore. She turned a page in her book, and Winnie Mandela crawled off the page and swam alongside her. It was nighttime, but a light flashed on and off, like a strobe light in a dance hall, which made her feel as if she were in an old-time black and white movie.

A loud crash woke her. Her heart pounded as she sat up in bed. Lightheaded from the quick movement, she squinted at the darkness in the room, illuminated slightly by the light from her nightstand. She gripped the blankets and struggled to get her bearings. A drip on her face made her look up. Lightning flashed and illuminated the room. A loud, rumbling boom of thunder shook the wall. Water leaked from the ceiling. It had already made a puddle at the end of her bed. Rain pelted the windowpanes. She loved storms, but this one was wilder than anything she'd experienced in California. She climbed out of bed and went into the kitchen to look for a bowl to catch the dripping water. A cold wind blew through the room, and rain sprayed her face. She turned on the light. More puddles on the kitchen floor revealed a second leak.

The kitchen was freezing, with a crosswind whistling through the house. With a start, she realized why: a tree branch stuck through the window.

Her body tensed. "Crap." The house reminded her of Swiss cheese, and not in a tasty sandwich-enhancer kind of way. Was it sturdy enough not to collapse on her? There was no way to remove the branch without going outside, and she couldn't do anything at two in the morning in the middle of a storm. There was no telling what might fall on her if she left the house. Her teeth chattered as wind blew rain against her body. Rushing into the bathroom, she removed the plastic shower curtain. In the kitchen, she rummaged in a drawer for duct tape. An errant thought penetrated her panic. For all his oddities, Simon supplied The Gatehouse well.

Balanced on a kitchen chair, she taped the shower curtain over the window.

"What are you doing?" A man's voice came from behind her.

She screamed. The chair toppled. Strong arms caught and held her as she struggled to leap out of them, much like her heart thumped wildly against her breast. Twisting, she came face to face with Simon. Her screams died in her throat. Despite deep scars bracketing them, he possessed the most beautiful eyes she'd ever seen—a deep gray edged in black with flecks of silver. His scars were arrows, pointing to them and reminded her of the Milky Way.

"How about we save the 'fear of the monster' for after we get you to safety," he said through gritted teeth. With a quick step in retreat, he swung away so his hair covered his face again. "I won't hurt you. Relax." He deposited her on her feet in a rush.

"I…I'm sorry, you startled me. I didn't expect you to be in my house. What are you doing here?" Her heart raced in her chest, and her voice stuttered.

"The branch through your window?" He pointed, and she followed the line of his muscular arm to his scarred fingers, curved from taut, puckered skin. "It's attached to a large tree that crashed when it destroyed the rest of your living room. The sound woke me, and I

43

came over to make sure you were okay. I'm surprised you didn't hear it."

Her jaw dropped, but she couldn't ignore the damage. Simon shifted and turned away from her again.

"I heard a boom, but I thought it was thunder. I was still half asleep and wet from the rain."

Simon stiffened. "What do you mean you were wet from the rain?"

"There's a leak over my bed. I came in here to get a bowl, and I stepped in this puddle"—she pointed to the middle of the floor—"and I was cold and found the window."

"A clever temporary solution." He pointed at her repair job. "But you've got problems a shower curtain can't fix. Go pack a bag. You'll stay at my house."

"Why?"

He sighed. "You can't stay here. It's not safe. You won't have to see me at all—I've got extra bedrooms. And my house is not in pieces right now, this one is.

He looked around. "Go get your things so we can leave."

The lights flickered and went out.

He turned on the flashlight on his phone. "Come with me." He walked toward her living room. She followed. Her mouth dropped when she entered the room. It looked like the open side of a dollhouse—rain slanted into the room through dripping branches covered with pieces of siding. Broken glass littered the floor. The wind blew her hair in her face and pressed her nightshirt against her body. She looked as he turned his light toward her. She gave him a great view, but she wondered if he'd noticed. Then she wondered why her thoughts strayed there when the house was collapsing around her.

"Now do you understand why you can't stay here? Go get your things," he repeated.

She returned to her bedroom, grabbed a duffle bag, and opened drawers. She packed enough for three days, changed into warm and dry clothes, added her books, and returned to the kitchen where Simon waited.

"Do you have a jacket?"

She pointed toward the now-destroyed living room, where the coat closet was. Shaking his head, he removed his sheepskin and handed it to her. Underneath the coat, his flannel plaid shirt stretched across his chest and hung, untucked, over jeans mottled with water.

"Wait, you need this," she said.

"I'll be fine."

The jacket was at least three times too large for her and hung to her knees. She rolled the sleeves in order for her to have use of her hands. It was warm and infused with the scents of pine and sawdust and the ocean. She inhaled and wrapped it close. He lifted her duffle and motioned for her to follow him.

Outside, the wind whipped her breath away. The rain mixed with the surf stung her cheeks. Bending forward, she struggled to make any headway. Simon must have realized her difficulty, because he swung the duffle over his shoulder and wrapped his arms around her. He tucked her into his side and forced his way through the booming thunder and slashing rain to his house.

Although his house was only a hundred yards down the dirt road, the storm made it difficult for him to walk on his own, much less carry her bag and direct her. But he forged ahead as if it were nothing. This close to him should have made her nervous. He hadn't asked her permission. But his arms protected her, more than all the money her father showered on her growing up. His broad torso sheltered her, his heartbeat lulled her, and his warmth cocooned her. It was like being in a bubble. Despite the raging storm, she burrowed into him. A tremor ran through him, and she thought he must be cold. As she was about to ask, he jostled her as he walked up the steps to his porch.

"You can let go of me."

He ignored her. Or maybe he didn't hear her. Either way, he kept a firm grip on her as he opened the door and made his way inside. Only when they were inside the front hall did he drop the duffle and release her. He waited to make sure her feet were planted on the floor before he let go.

The sudden space between them jarred her. The lights were off—had he lost electricity, too?—and she could only see his shadow as he strode along the hallway. She stood frozen in place, not sure whether to follow him or stay behind. Lightning flashed, illuminating his body, arm beckoning, and she followed.

In the kitchen, he turned on the light, but visibility wasn't much better as the bulbs were dim. Still, she glimpsed his wet hair plastered to the sides of his face, which he managed to keep turned away from her. He strode to the stove, filled the kettle with water, and set it on the flame to heat. Despite his scarred hands, he grabbed two mugs from the cabinet, along with tea bags and sugar. His movements were spare and sure. Meg suspected he could have done this in the pitch black. Once the water heated, he kept his face averted and held out his hand. "Let me hang up the jacket," he said.

She removed it, and he left the room, returning after a few seconds. Grabbing her bag again, he motioned her to follow him, and led her upstairs. He opened the first door on the left and waved her inside, again keeping his face turned away from her.

"You can stay in here." When she opened her mouth to speak, he interrupted. "I won't bother you. Get yourself settled and come downstairs for tea."

Before she could respond, he dropped her bag on the floor, left the room, and shut the door behind him. Exhaustion licked around the edges of her consciousness, but she fought it. He'd told her to join him for tea. What she wanted was to ignore him and go to bed.

A knock on her door startled her.

"Meg? I have your tea."

She opened the door. Simon stood there, hand outstretched and face turned partially away from her. His hair dried into a curtain to block his scars. She reached for the tea. Her fingers brushed his and sent a jolt of electricity through her arm. He must have felt it, too, because he looked at her hand.

"Thank you."

He turned without a word and walked down the stairs. His jeans sculpted his butt and emphasized the muscles in his thighs. She bit her lip at the unexpected thought. At the bottom of the staircase, he called to her. "Sleep as long as you want in the morning. I won't disturb you."

"Goodnight."

She shut the door and leaned against it. Exhaustion swept through her, and she couldn't resist the bed across the room. As she sank into it, she wrestled with the Simon enigma. But the only thing she could focus on was how she'd felt in his arms, and her emptiness when he'd let her go.

Chapter Seven

Simon sat at his kitchen table at seven the following morning, chin propped in his hands. The scent of coffee wafted under his nose as he summoned energy for the day. He'd tossed and turned most of last night, unable to shake the desire to hold Meg in his arms.

He snorted and looked behind him, as if he expected her to appear. But it was early. He figured he still had time to sit and drink his coffee before she came into the kitchen. She was exhausted. From the way she relaxed into his arms, he was surprised she didn't fall asleep on the walk between the two houses.

His brain was obviously addled because he couldn't understand her. She jumped and screamed each time she saw him, yet she'd settled into him like she belonged there. He hardened at the memory of how she burrowed into him. Her lemony scent permeated his jacket, and he shifted in his seat.

This train of thought was useless and set him up for disappointment. He finished his coffee and retreated into his office for the morning. He could prep his online lessons for his students and review the CAST investment portfolio. While the storm had lessened, rain still pattered against the windowpanes, and the wind still blew leaves in swirls outside. Repairs to The Gatehouse would have to wait at least another day.

Today, he'd make himself scarce. She'd probably sleep most of the day away.

Soft footsteps tapped in the hallway, and he glanced at the clock in surprise. Seven thirty. She was either an early riser or she didn't sleep well. Maybe he'd given her nightmares. Great.

He had answered one more email when a timid knock at his door interrupted him. He frowned. She knocked again, a little louder this time. He double-checked that the curtains were drawn and turned away from the door, before he called, "Enter."

"I made myself breakfast. I thought you might like some, too." Reflected in the computer, she walked toward his desk with a plate and a glass of orange juice.

"I hope you don't mind. I wasn't sure what you wanted for breakfast or how you like your eggs, or how many eggs you might eat, so I scrambled four of them. I—"

"Meg."

"Yes?"

"Stop talking."

She paused. "I talk too much when I'm nervous."

His chest tightened. She was afraid of him? "There's nothing to be nervous about. Thank you for making me breakfast."

The breath she expelled was loud enough for him to hear and with her drooping shoulders, she reminded him of a deflated balloon. "I looked in your cupboards—I swear I didn't snoop. I hope it's okay—but I couldn't tell what you liked to eat, and I thought maybe you'd eaten already and—"

"Meg."

"Yes?"

"You're doing it again."

She wrapped her arms around her middle, and an unexpected desire to hold her overpowered him. Which was stupid, because if she were this nervous halfway across the room from him, he suspected he'd send her into shock if he turned toward her in the light of day.

"Sorry. Again. I'll let you get to work."

Before he could stop her, she'd slipped out of his office and shut the door behind her. He took a bite of the eggs, restraining a groan at their buttery goodness. He half rose to call her but stopped and sat in his chair.

****

Meg glanced around the kitchen. It was her favorite room in the house. A pretty ridiculous decision to make, since she'd only seen it, Simon's office, and her bedroom. But it was large and functional, yet warm. She could picture a family here—the adults cooking together on the top-of-the-line stainless appliances, the kids working on homework or playing at the maple-and-white-painted kitchen table, pets running underfoot and sliding across the stone floor. Through the bare windows, rain slanted across the backyard, multi-colored leaves blew in circles, and in the distance, the storm whipped the frothy surf. On a sunny day, it would be beautiful.

She cleaned the kitchen and returned upstairs to grab her book. In the living room, she found a window seat, tucked beneath deep green velvet drapes. The green-and-blue-striped silk cushion was comfy, and soft blue chenille pillows offered the perfect propping necessary to read. She sank against them, stretched her legs, and opened her book.

Thunder made her screech, and she knocked a

pillow to the carpet. As she bent to grab it, her phone rang.

"Hey, I thought I'd check in with you because of the storm," Claire said. "Are you okay?"

"Yeah, I'm fine, although my house isn't." She filled in Claire on what happened last night.

"Wait, you mean to tell me you're staying with my friend, the recluse?"

Meg nodded. "He insisted on it."

"Put him on the phone. I need to make sure he's still the same man I knew yesterday."

"He's holed up in his office. I already disturbed him once this morning. I don't want to do it again."

"Fine, I'll talk to him later. What are your plans with Simon after he's done working?"

"Claire, he doesn't need to entertain me. It's enough he rescued me. I'm not his guest, just a refugee from the storm."

"Oh my God, you sound like him. You two are perfect together."

Meg's cheeks reddened. She looked around to make sure Simon wasn't there to see. "How did you guys survive the storm? Do you need anything?"

"We're fine. Property has some damage, though. I'm hanging at home. Tom's also in his office, reporting on the storm. I'd invite you over except I don't think all the roads are passable. Do you like him?"

So much for a new topic of conversation. She lowered her voice, not wanting him to overhear her conversation. "I don't know him well at all."

"No, but you sound a lot more relaxed than I'd expect you to sound."

"He's considerate."

"We'll talk about it after you've spent more time with him."

Meg hung up the phone to the sound of Claire's laughter.

Her voice sounded defensive, even to her own ears. Did she like him? She didn't know him well enough, and she refused to judge a person without knowing them well. But those sparks of attraction? No one ignited them in her in years. Scars ravaged his body, but they didn't turn her off. They were marks of survival. He was huge, but his size didn't frighten her. His shoulders spanned almost twice her width, and on tiptoe, she barely reached them. His powerful muscles beneath his sweater last night tempted her. The men she was used to were rich playboys who focused on wealth, surface finery, and reputation. Their muscles never made her feel safe and protected. Not to mention those men possessed certain expectations of the women they associated with or helped. What did Simon expect of her?

Chapter Eight

"So what do you think?"

Simon regretted answering his phone as soon as Claire's knowing voice came across the line. "About what?"

"God, you were never this thick in high school! About Meg?"

"She makes a damn fine breakfast." Welcome to the fifties, he thought as he rubbed his neck.

"She cooked for you? Did you ask her to?"

"What the hell, Claire? Of course I didn't ask her to. She did it on her own." He swore he could hear the gears in Claire's mind turn. Unfortunately, he had no idea what the gears signaled.

"She likes you."

His feet slipped off the desk where he'd propped them and slammed to the floor. "Did she say she did?" Great, now he sounded like a teenager.

Claire made a tsking sound. "Of course she didn't tell me. She keeps things quieter than you do, which says a lot. But women don't cook for men they don't like."

Pressure built in his chest. Simon couldn't tell if it was from disappointment or excitement. Neither, probably. Better chance it was heartburn. Scrambled eggs were a known cause, weren't they? "Claire, she's staying in my house. She made me breakfast as a thank you. Like the zucchini bread."

"What zucchini bread?"

Damn. He covered his face with his hands and counted to...oh hell, better get it over with. He told her about the zucchini bread and listened to her giggles.

"She likes you."

"No, she doesn't. You'd know if you saw how she jumps every time she sees me." He couldn't bring himself to tell Claire how Meg screamed.

"You're overreacting, as usual. The only person with an issue about your scars is you. Ask her to go for a walk together."

She hung up before he could respond, and he looked at the clock on his computer. Maybe he should go talk to her. But what was he supposed to say? Was Claire right about him making a bigger deal about his scars than other people? He shuddered at his image reflected in his computer monitor. How could a woman *not* react to them? But Meg appeared different. Maybe she wouldn't mind them. He swallowed. It had been a couple of hours. He should check on her, like any good host.

****

Meg was curled in the window seat reading when the lights dimmed, and Simon walked in. What was it with him and lights? Was he hiding his scars? He stopped halfway across the room and moved his head so his hair blocked her view of his face. Her hands itched for a pair of scissors right about now.

She put her book aside and waited for him to speak.

"What are you reading?" He nodded toward the book next to her.

"A biography of Nelson Mandela."

"Really?"

Disbelief oozed from his tone of voice. Another person with preconceived notions about her. She showed it to him.

"With you curled against the window, I assumed you read Brontë or Yeats. Or a romance. Nelson Mandela never entered my mind."

"Why not?" She'd grown to expect people's expectations of her at home. Truth be told, she hadn't done much to dissuade them. But here, she was trying to make a fresh start. She clenched her teeth.

He stuffed his hands in his pockets. Silence stretched. "I realized you might want to do laundry soon. I'll show you where the machines are."

Laundry. He came to talk to her about laundry? Loosening her jaw, she hopped off the seat and followed him into the basement. "Here they are. Detergent is there. Use whatever you like."

The basement was dark and old, but the machines were new. She shivered and headed upstairs.

"Don't tell me you don't like basements."

She smiled. "Okay, I won't." It was more than basements; it was any dark, enclosed space. Now free, she hated confinement. She returned alone to her reading nook. Her phone rang once again. Vanessa's name popped on the screen. She ignored the call. Mackenzie never tried to reach her. Why was Vanessa so persistent? As usual, she didn't leave a message.

Later, when her stomach rumbled, she searched for lunch and found Simon in the kitchen. Once again, the lights were dim.

"I'll be out of your way in a minute," he said and

turned away from her.

"You don't have to go."

"You're uncomfortable around me."

She walked toward him and stopped two feet away. He stood at the counter next to the sink, his back to her, hands gripping the edge. His knuckles were white, and his arms were braced. Tension rolled off him.

"No, I'm uncomfortable when you sneak up on me, or when you arrive without warning inside my house in the middle of the night." His shoulders relaxed. "I'm not uncomfortable around you here. You belong here."

He nodded but sidestepped around her and carried his plate to the door. "I'll be in my office if you need anything."

As he left, she noticed a plate on the counter, with a sandwich, sliced on the diagonal, and chips. He'd made her lunch.

****

He hoped she liked turkey.

Should he have made her a sandwich? He'd made one for himself. It would have been rude not to. Maybe he should have given her a choice. He banged his hand on the desk. This wasn't a damn restaurant. She was his guest, though, and options were nice. Leaving her to eat alone wasn't high on Miss Manners' list either.

He groaned, staring at the computer screen and the drawings he'd worked on all morning. The town owned twenty acres of open space. People who grew up here wanted to preserve it; a developer from Baltimore wanted to build townhomes and a golf course. Claire, who sat on the subcommittee in her capacity as a library employee, had asked Simon to help the townspeople preserve the land and create a proposal to present to the town council. He hated the idea of helping the town, the same town that saw his scars and ran the other way. But he was doing this for Claire.

His design met every single criterion she requested: meditative, native to the area, environmentally friendly. And it was cold and lifeless. He scrolled through other projects and looked at comments from other clients. They all suffered from the same problem. No warmth, no emotion. His clients had complained, and one wrote him a letter expressing dissatisfaction. Frowning, he searched through one after another until he found ones he liked. Three years ago.

The worst part was he didn't know how to fix it.

He pushed away from his desk and strode to the window. Outside, the rain splattered against the house, the wind swirled, and the waves crashed against the rocks. A drawn out scratch against the side of the house—high pitched enough to make his teeth ache—diverted his attention. A moment later, a loud boom made him jump. The house rattled, and his muscles tensed. He looked around, a foolish gesture since he couldn't see what happened. It was useless to peer out the window as well. Outside his door, he ran into Meg, who was poised to knock. He grasped her upper arms to keep her on her feet and turned his face so his hair covered it.

"What was that?" she asked, face pale.

"I'm not sure," he said. The scratching was no longer audible. He led her on a quick tour of the lower and upper floors of the house, but found nothing out of place. Simon entered the mudroom, dimmed the lights, and put on his coat.

"Shouldn't you wait until the storm lessens?"

"I need to check for damage. Whatever made that boom might have destroyed property that needs to be fixed."

"In this storm?"

He turned halfway toward her, until he could see her from the corner of his eye. "Only if necessary."

"I'll come with you." She reached for a jacket on one of the hooks on the wall, but he stopped her. Her hand was small compared to his, despite his inability to flatten his fingers, and dwarfed her own. Her skin was soft. She stilled but didn't yank her hand away, or scream. Progress.

"You stay inside. If I need help I'll come get you."

He thought she'd protest, but she nodded and stepped away from him. After he zipped his coat, pulled his hood over his head, and put on his boots, he stopped at the outside door. "Make sure you close this tight behind me. Lock it if necessary so the wind doesn't blow it open." He waited for the click of the door behind him before he walked outside.

The wind wasn't as strong as last night. A lack of luggage made it easier to walk. He circled the perimeter of the house until he found the fallen tree that caused all the noise. The smell led him to it. A large balsam tree had been uprooted, and the sweet, woodsy scent combined with the rain surrounded him. He shook his head at the loss of a beautiful tree. He'd miss its majesty. He remembered a design with balsam trees he'd created years ago for a client because they gave off such an intense aroma. The design didn't lack feeling. He burrowed farther into his coat and shook off the memory. Walking around the large uprooted tree, he noted damaged siding—the cause of the scratching sound—but nothing needed immediate repairs. As he turned to go, his foot caught on a branch. He pitched forward onto the wet ground. Branches tore his face, and the rocky earth jolted him as he braced his hands beneath him. For a moment, he lay where he'd landed. When he caught his breath, he climbed to his feet, wincing at the pulls and stings. *Clumsy idiot.* He turned to the house. The door opened as he reached for the knob. He averted his face.

"What happened?

Her voice was high, and she leaned toward him as he entered the mudroom.

"Nothing."

"There's blood on your hands." She reached toward him.

He jerked away. "It doesn't matter!"

She retreated and wrapped her hands around her stomach. Great, he'd scared her. Again. He already looked like a monster. Now he sounded like one, too. He took a deep breath and spoke, modulating his voice.

"It's just a few scratches."

She nodded, not taking her gaze off him.

He shucked his coat, wincing as it slid across his hands. In the dim light, the scrapes and pieces of wood, leaves, and dirt embedded in them were visible. A towel passed his line of vision as Meg handed it to him.

"Thanks." He was soaked and filthy, and a single towel wasn't much use. He dried his hair before he dabbed at the rest of him.

"You might want to change out of the wet stuff and clean yourself off."

"I will." Leaving as much as possible in the mudroom, he went upstairs, Meg at his heels. At the door to his bedroom, he paused. "I've got it from here," he said. She reminded him of a puppy, following him around.

She squeaked. "Let me know if you need anything."

With a nod, he entered his room and closed the door behind him. He only turned on the light after the lockset clicked shut. Her retreating footsteps echoed outside in the hallway. Removing his wet clothes—he seemed to accumulate a lot of them—he showered and put on a dry hooded sweatshirt and blue jeans. His hands stung like a sonofabitch, and his fingers fumbled more than usual. Dry and dressed after much too long, he looked in the mirror to assess the damage. Pushing his hair away from his face, he took a deep breath before he examined his features. All the old scars were still there, of course. There were a few scrapes on his forehead and chin, but they weren't horrible. He cleaned them and treated them with antibiotic ointment before he moved on to his hands.

They were much worse. When he'd fallen, he'd tried to catch himself, and the brunt of the damage was to his palms. He ran them under water to clean them off, but the water did nothing for the splinters and dirt embedded under the skin. He tried to remove them, but fine motor skills were no longer his forte. He couldn't work the tweezers. He groaned. He'd have to let everything work its way to the surface over time. He'd be in pain for days. There might be infection. Just what he didn't need, considering.

Adjusting his hood, he left the bedroom, and stopped when Meg poked her head out of her doorway. The dim light in the hall made it difficult to see, but bright light from her room made a yellow swatch across the hall floor, which he avoided.

"Is everything okay?"

"Basically."

"What do you mean?"

"Most of the scratches are superficial and will heal fine. There are splinters in my hands…" He stopped midsentence.

"May I see?"

Her voice was gentle, and she didn't reach for him. Instead, she kept her hands still, as if she waited for him to agree. There was no need for her to help. He'd managed before, and he'd manage again. But then why did he hold his mangled hands into the light?

She took first one hand and then the other, turned them palm up and examined them. Her touch was feather-light and gentle. Despite the scars that masked much of the sensation in his hands, the contact made his entire body seize. Blood rushed in his ears. His heart skipped a few beats. No one touched him. Ever. Not since the fire. Meg's touch was different from the doctors and nurses who had healed him. He closed his eyes and let awareness wash over him. A noise made him open them. Keeping the rest of his body shrouded in the dimness of the hallway, and his head tilted so his hair covered his face, he noticed tears on her lashes as she examined his hands.

He frowned. "You're crying."

"No I'm not. Dirt from your hands got in my eyes."

He raised an eyebrow. "You can defy gravity?"

She nodded. She still didn't let go of his hand, nor did she meet his gaze.

"This must hurt," she whispered.

He shrugged. "I've felt worse."

"I have, too, but it doesn't make this any better." She examined them again. "You can't leave them like this. I can help, but I need light."

Not a surprise. She needed light in order to administer first aid. His chest tightened. The question was, would he let her?

His hands were stiff, and the pain made him wince. They needed to be cleaned and bandaged, and he couldn't do it. Not to mention the risk of infection. The only thing he could control was whether or not to show her how much he didn't want her to do this. He needed to preserve his dignity. He straightened his spine and walked into her bedroom.

Her bed was made, the blue and white striped handmade quilt smooth. Her duffle rested on the hardwood floor at the end of the bed. He sat on the blue silk armchair next to the window and rested his hands, palms on his knees. When he tipped his head, his hair fell around his face, although the antibiotic ointment made some of the strands stick to his cheek. It didn't provide as effective a curtain as usual. At least he had the hood.

She walked past him into the bathroom. When she returned, she knelt next to him, her face away from him, as if she knew he didn't want her to look at him.

"I'll try not to hurt you."

"Do what you have to do."

She stilled for a moment, nodded, and took his hand in hers. Her soft hand cradled his, brushed against his scarred skin, and sent swaths of heat and desire straight into his heart. The whisper of her breath against his wrist made him shiver. He clenched his muscles against the impulse. The rush of fabric against fabric, where her arm touched his, filled his ears. What would happen if he took her in his arms?

But she got to work, and his desire dissipated. He gritted his teeth against the pain as she extracted pieces of dirt and splinters, alternating between a needle and tweezers. With every movement, she apologized, until he wasn't sure who suffered more, him or her.

"Meg. I know you're not trying to hurt me." His voice croaked. He cleared it, needing to lighten the tension in the room. "You're not, right?"

She straightened. Her soft laugh told him he'd accomplished his goal.

To distract himself, he studied her. Kind of ironic, given how he hated to be stared at. Auburn hair curled at her shoulders. The light created streaks of red and gold. Despite the bulky sweater she wore, he could see the outline of her torso, which gave a hint of delicacy through the wool. Her wrists were fine-boned, and her movements were quick. He lost track of time as he studied her hair and wondered what it would feel like to run his fingers through the strands, to have them brush against his face. Would her hair feel coarse like his or as silky as it looked?

"I'm finished," she said.

He startled before he pulled away.

"I think it will heal without too much difficulty."

The irony of her statement made him laugh. She bandaged both of his hands. They resembled oven mitts. As she rose, he stopped her.

"Thank you."

"You're welcome. I can change the bandages later."

Walking past him, she placed her hand on his shoulder. Her touch sent shivers along his spine and heated his neck.

This wouldn't do.

Chapter Nine

How could she have been so insensitive? Telling him his hands would heal without difficulty, when they were already scarred? She groaned. He'd laughed, but she wasn't sure if it was in humor or embarrassment. Even now, the sound sent shivers along her spine. Her palms tingled, and the weight of his hands still haunted her. For all their scars, they were good, strong hands. Large, with curved fingers unable to straighten, clean nails. They conveyed strength despite the pain his injury must have caused. As she'd cleaned them, she'd gotten a glimpse of his wrists beneath his long sleeves. Solid, tanned skin, lightly dusted with dark hair, and more scars running beneath his sleeve. She'd bet his arms were muscular. He fascinated her. Each time she was in his presence, she wanted to know more. For the first time, Meg was thankful for his hair hiding his face. Otherwise, she might have been tempted to…what? Peek? Touch?

She didn't know, and her lack of knowledge scared her. He was secretive and short-tempered. Yet at times she glimpsed kindness. She didn't know what to make of him. She'd kept her back turned while she worked on his hands as much for her own composure as for his. She didn't want him to see her nerves. Despite them, though, her attraction grew.

How could she be attracted to a man she barely

knew? Everything she'd seen intrigued her and left her hungry for more. She wasn't like the girls she'd socialized with, after anything with a penis, even if the paparazzi reported lies. She'd never been comfortable hooking up with random strangers just because they were wealthy or handsome or famous. She wanted to get to know them first. Most of them never wanted more than a quick lay.

She looked around her bedroom. Whoever decorated it had good—and expensive—taste. The large blue and white geometric wool area rug at the foot of the bed was soft beneath her feet, and she buried her toes in the nap. Curious about the rest of the house, she explored its rooms. Simon returned to somewhere—his office, she suspected—and she was alone. Would Simon mind? He'd told her to make herself at home. She was curious about his home, as well as the man in it, and until things returned to normal from the storm, she couldn't look for a job.

The foyer, his entry to his lair, was dim, and she brightened the lights as she entered. Unlike the man, it was ordinary, with a slate floor and a red Oriental area rug, and gave way to a symmetrical house with a mahogany staircase leading to the second floor.

But that was where "ordinary" ended.

Across from the front door was a wall. Most people hung a mirror there, to enable last minute primping before leaving. But instead, Simon hung a large photo of the sea in the middle of a storm—frothy waves crashed against the cliffs. Meg recognized the beach she'd gone to for the past few weeks. Did he take the photo or did someone else?

Beneath the photo was a small, black lacquer table

with a bowl of smooth rocks at its center. She dipped her hand in and ran them through her fingers. They were cool against her skin and soothed her.

Turning to her right, Meg entered the living room. A large fieldstone fireplace dominated the room. White wood cabinets surrounded it. Large floor-to-ceiling windows at the front and back of the house let in plenty of natural light on a sunny day if the curtains were opened. Ironic for a man who dimmed each room as he entered. Dark cherry wood furniture contrasted with the white wood built-ins, and neutral colors provided peace. Meg imagined sitting on the beige velvet sofa with a cup of hot tea and a roaring fire. But what did Simon do? Did he sit here and brood into the fireplace? She could picture it.

Crossing the foyer once again, she entered the dining room. This room was modern. She wrinkled her nose.

"You don't approve?" he asked as he dimmed the lights.

She screeched.

Simon muttered a curse. "I didn't mean to startle you."

"I think you like it."

"Perks of being light on your feet, I guess."

She shook her head. "The room is stunning. It's…a little stark for my taste." The walls were painted a dove gray, with a white marble fireplace, and a gray and green Aubusson rug on the floor. A black marble rectangular table with eight high-backed chairs upholstered in pale gray and deep green. In the center of the table was a bowl of flowers. "I love the flowers, though."

He nodded and crossed his arms over his chest as he studied the room. "Mm, you may be right about the starkness. I decorated this room a few years ago, when I wasn't as cheerful as I am now."

Meg coughed.

He spun, his entire body angled toward her as he kept his face in shadow. "Are you laughing at me?"

She bit her lip and cleared her throat a few times. "Me? I got something caught in my throat."

His jaw twitched. She glimpsed the flex of muscle on the side of his neck. His shoulders straightened. "I can't believe you don't think I'm cheerful." His husky tone of voice made her take a chance.

"I can't believe you think you are," she said.

"I'm smiling now."

"Only because you're laughing at me," she said.

He crossed one foot over the other and leaned against the wall. "I don't call this laughing."

"And I don't call you cheerful, so I think we're even."

He snorted.

"I hope you don't mind if I explored," she said. "I was curious." She'd never again take for granted space or spread-out living quarters.

"I can give you a tour if you'd like." He waved her through the doorway between the dining room and kitchen, dimmed the lights and followed her inside. "We already know you don't like the dining room." Ignoring her protest, he continued, "You made breakfast here this morning. What do you think of the kitchen?"

"It might be my favorite room, or at least it was until I found the living room. It's warm and homey. The appliances are terrific. Do you cook?"

He nodded. "My mother insisted I learn. Our cook used to give me lessons every day after school."

"You had a cook?" Maybe they were more alike than she thought.

Simon leaned against the counter. "A housekeeper and butler, too. Plus other staff. Some of them used to live here."

"And they don't now?"

The cords on his neck tightened. "I don't need all of the staff for me, now, do I?"

She looked around the kitchen. "I guess not. But this kitchen begs to be used. I don't think I could *not* cook if it were mine."

He leaned against the counter next to her. His warmth permeated the space between them, though they didn't touch. "Feel free to use it as much as you want while you're here. And if you need a taster, I'll suffer through it."

"For your comment, I might poison you."

"Good luck. Iron stomach." He patted his flat abs.

Meg swallowed, throat dry. Her hand lifted, as if it, too, longed to touch him. She made a fist and let it drop to her side.

"I don't get you," Simon said. He pushed off the counter and dragged his hand along the counter.

What would it feel like for him to caress her with those hands? She stopped short. *Focus.* "What?"

"I don't get you. Most people would shout to prove me wrong, swear they're good cooks."

"I learned a long time ago people will judge me regardless of what I do. It's not my responsibility to prove myself to anyone."

He straightened his shoulders and paused, as usual not letting her see his face, but still somehow focused on her. "So noted." He pointed toward the left. "That way is my office. But through here is the sitting room where you read earlier."

She walked with him through a short, dark hallway, past the closed door of his office, and into the zebra-wood-paneled room she'd sat in earlier. Meg strode right to the window seat, pushed open the curtain and ran her hand over the green and blue striped seat cushion.

"I can tell from your reaction you like this room." His tone teased her.

"I'm surprised I do."

He cocked his head to the side. "Why?"

She walked to the middle of the room and turned in a slow circle. "You've got to admit, this is a somber room. I like light and airy ones, but this one is cozy and just about perfect."

"Only 'just about?' "

"Come on, I need to leave you room to grow." She winked and turned away, needing distance between them.

"I appreciate your consideration."

"Anytime. But in all seriousness, why did you make this room so welcoming?"

He stared at the green and blue rug and thrust his hands behind him. "I wanted a hideaway, a place where I could retreat from the world."

How many times had she wanted the same thing? Meg noted the heavy drapes, dark furniture, and soft textures. "I get it."

This time, when he raised his head, she was ready.

His face was shadowed from the hood, but their gazes met. For a moment, relief flashed, before it gave way to something else. He looked away.

"We have the rooms upstairs left," he said, his voice gruff. "Come on."

His long strides took him out of the room so fast Meg jogged to keep pace with him. At the bottom of the hand-carved mahogany stairs, he paused, and she skidded to a halt. Nodding, he climbed. He skipped his room and hers but opened the other two doors.

They must have been meant to be bedrooms, but Simon converted them. One was an exercise room, with state-of-the art equipment. Meg paused, not sure which surprised her more—the idea of a home gym or the well-lit room with many mirrors.

She turned toward him, eyebrows raised.

Keeping well out of the light and turning his face away from her, he leaned against the wall. "I needed the equipment for physical therapy, and I kept it."

Now it made sense. "Oh, I see." Since he lived alone, she assumed he didn't mind the brightness.

The other room was a TV room. It reminded her of the screening rooms she'd seen in her friends' mansions in California, with a wall-sized flat screen, leather reclining sofas, and shades to cover the windows.

"A man cave!"

His snort burst from his lips. She jumped. He put a hand on her arm as if to apologize, but before she could say anything, he removed it and walked to the other side of the room. She could still feel its imprint, like a brand.

"Everyone needs one," he said.

"True. I should get out of yours. Don't want to

contaminate it or anything." She stepped into the hallway and waited for him to join her.

"You should feel free to make yourself comfortable anywhere, even my 'man cave.' "

"Thanks, but there's a TV downstairs I can watch. You're entitled to the freedom of your own private space." She walked toward the stairs. His gaze burned into her back. Halfway down the steps, his footsteps echoed behind her.

"How about I make us dinner?" She let the question hang in the air, not looking at him.

"You don't have to cook for me. I told you I learned a long time ago."

"I know, but you're working, your hands are bandaged, and I have time. Have any preferences?"

"Whatever you want to make is fine with me."

"I'll let you know when it's ready. Whatever 'it' turns out to be."

"I look forward to it."

He retreated to his office, she to the kitchen. She wondered if he'd join her for dinner or eat on his own as he'd done that afternoon.

****

He should make a plate and eat dinner in the office, he thought as he watched her from the doorway. She stood at the stove. Her auburn hair glowed fiery red from the overhead light. An off-key tune came from her lips. She swayed to whatever song she thought she hummed, and the movement of her hips made it hard to breathe. His fingers itched to touch her hair. His lips tingled at the thought of silencing her God-awful tune with his mouth. If he'd thought the fire made his nerve endings useless, it was time to rethink his assumption.

She turned and startled when she noticed him. Her reaction was one alternative to a cold shower. He focused on her feet encased in pink fluffy socks.

"Didn't mean to scare you."

"You don't."

What the hell? Every time she saw him she jumped. Like everyone else. He'd done a decent job of keeping hidden from her when she lived in The Gatehouse. Sharing the same house, though, made it impossible. He raised his head for a moment.

"Why did you jump?"

She lowered the flame on the stove and turned toward him. She stared, and he looked at the ground. The toes of her socks were dotted with orange and purple spots.

"I didn't expect you to be there. You startled me," she said. "But you don't scare me."

He clenched his jaw so tight, it ached. Did she mean what he thought she did? He raised his gaze an inch at a time until he met hers once again. Her expression was open, warm. Was it possible? He swung his hair across his face once again. "What are you making?"

"Crab cakes, corn soup, and bread. Well, I heated the bread, I didn't make it from scratch."

"Sounds good. Smells better."

"It'll be ready in about three minutes if you want to sit."

He shook his head, but before he could speak, she asked. "You're not eating in the office again, are you?"

"That would be rude. I was about to offer to set the table."

He reached around her to get soup bowls, and she

stilled. This close, her body heat surrounded him, her citrus perfume taunted him. He inhaled. But she stiffened, and he moved away to set the table. Not being afraid of him and wanting to be close to him were two different things.

"Before we sit, let me remove those big bandages from your hands," she said. "It will be easier for you to eat."

He looked at his hands, unable to believe he'd forgotten about the wrappings. Then he eyed the food she'd made. Nothing required fine motor skills to eat. Did she plan this particular meal on purpose? She walked over to the table and sat across from him. He held out his hands.

She unwrapped the bandages and examined his hands before she returned to the stove and retrieved the soup and the bread. "They look better already. How do they feel?"

He flexed and curled his fingers as much as he was able to. "Not bad." He tasted the soup. "You put my cook, and me, to shame."

She blushed. "Thanks. I cook for myself all the time now and before…" She waved away her spoon and her thought.

Or tried to. "Before?"

"It gave me a nice break."

It was an odd way of phrasing things.

"Break from what?"

She looked like she wanted to squirm out of her seat, and he realized he shouldn't have pushed.

"Never mind," he said. It was a long time since he shared a meal with anyone. His conversational skills needed work.

He walked to the fridge and asked, "What do you want to drink?"

"Water, please."

He returned with a beer for him and the requested glass of water.

"You're welcome to have one, too." He tilted the beer bottle.

"No thanks. Did you get a lot of work done today?"

"No. I'm still struggling over a design my client wants. Not to mention, it's hard to type with oven mitts."

"Why?"

"Lack of finger movement?"

She rolled her eyes. "No, I meant, why are you struggling with the design?"

He leaned forward, not used to talking things over with anyone. He struggled to find the right words. "It's got all the physical elements they want. I...I don't know. It doesn't...there's something missing."

"How can you tell?"

He ran his hand across the smooth wood of the table. "I can't get the emotion right. I know it sounds weird—plants conveying emotion—but my designs? They used to. And now. Well, they don't."

"Have you worked on it long?"

He tore off a piece of bread. "About a month."

"Maybe you need a fresh perspective."

Her smile was beautiful, and he forgot to chew. Her skin pinked, and her lips parted a fraction. He couldn't look away. It took him a good thirty seconds to realize she cleared the table while he sat like an idiot and stared. But she didn't look away. Crashing into reality, he swallowed the piece of bread and helped her until the kitchen was cleaned, and there was nothing left to do. She paused in the doorway.

"It was nice eating with you," she said, before she ducked and left the kitchen.

Simon stood there and realized he hadn't hidden his face from her. He swallowed as he analyzed her words and reactions. She didn't appear to notice. Something in his chest loosened. He listened to her footsteps echo in the hall and wondered if he should call out to her. For the first time in as long as he could remember, he was hungry for companionship.

****

Meg leaned against the door to her room and listened. On the other side, the hallway was silent. He didn't follow her upstairs.

She slid to the floor and rested her elbows on her knees. Simon was not like the men she'd associated with before. His size might surprise her. His behavior might confuse her. But he wasn't a man who expected a return on his investment. Neither was Claire or her friends.

Why didn't she expect Simon to be different? Why didn't she wait for the other shoe to drop, for him to demand something from her? Because she hadn't made dinner for a man in years. The last time she'd done it, well, it was looked upon as quaint and old-fashioned and a little bourgeois. A cute trick, not to be repeated too often, unless it was in exchange for sex. After all, people who dined out in order to be seen didn't need a friend who could cook. What they needed was a friend to get them into clubs, provide them alcohol, drugs, and anything else they wanted. Or an alibi.

But Simon was different.

She sat straighter. She'd told him she wasn't afraid of him, and he'd shown her his face. She didn't pay attention to it because she was too nervous. When he stopped turning away from her, and looked at her, she saw something reflected in his gaze, a look she hadn't seen in a long time, if ever.

Chapter Ten

When the winds died and the rain stopped early the next morning, cool temperatures settled over the area, and skies lightened to a dove gray. The sun, such as it was, peeked above the horizon. Simon settled into his black leather desk chair, turned on jazz, and read emails. One was from Claire.

"Hey, checking in to see how you managed with the storm and how you're handling your new roomie. Let me know!"

She'd included a devil and a wicked smile emoji, and he was tempted to throw his computer across the room. But he refrained and read the email again. His "roomie" was too tempting. He massaged his hands as he considered whether or not to respond, but Claire was one of his closest friends. He couldn't blow her off, no matter how annoyed he might be at her teasing.

"Storm damage is minimal. 'Roomie' is a good cook."

Moving onto other emails, he sent estimates and design plans, answered inquiries from clients and vendors, and posed questions for CAST's next videoconference. An animal rescue organization looked for funding to update their shelter into a state-of-the-art facility. It was a small project, but Simon was concerned about how state-of-the-art the facility needed to be. Not that he didn't love animals, but he needed his concerns addressed before he gave the go-ahead.

Additionally, Claire needed help with the open-space project, and it was time he stepped in to see what he could do. He owed her, and CAST might also be able to lend its financial support. He composed another short email to his partners and attached a few newspaper articles, as well as his design plans, such as they were, and the bare-bones proposal accompanying it. Then he got to work on his students' assignments. His email pinged again.

"Well, you know, the way to a man's heart is through his stomach…in all seriousness, you're nice to her, right? I mean you don't expect her to cook for you, do you?"

He rolled his eyes.

"Actually, I treat her like my own private maid. Of course I'm nice! I only *look* like a monster, Claire; I don't *act* like one."

His phone rang a minute after he pressed, "Send."

"Simon MacAlter."

"It's Claire, and you're not a monster, so stop saying you are, and I know you're a nice guy, but sometimes you can be foreboding and bossy, and Meg is nice and needs friends, and you can't run all over her and expect her to be okay about it, you have to be gentle and if all she does is cook, well, you have an actual person to socialize with right now so you should watch a movie or go for a walk or—"

"Claire?"

"What?"

"Breathe."

She took a deep breath. "I don't want you to mess this up. I like her, Simon."

"I do, too. Not"—he held up his hand though she couldn't see—"as more than a tenant, though." His gut tightened. He ignored it. "And I am nice to her." Except for the times he'd yelled. But he'd apologized, and she'd forgiven him.

Then where was she now, and what was she doing?

"She's got plenty of spunk. She yells at me."

"What? I can't picture it."

"Because you know her well?"

She sighed. "Fine, but you have to tell me about this yelling thing you say she does. Because I don't believe you."

"Later. I've got to go now."

"Okay. But you could let loose a little and…"

Simon swallowed. "I don't let loose."

"I know. But you should. It won't hurt—"

"—Are you serious? You're telling *me* 'letting loose' won't hurt?"

Claire sighed on the other end of the phone. "Simon, there's a difference between letting loose and recklessness."

"Goodbye, Claire." He swiveled his chair to face the window. His heart pounded in his chest. His nostrils flared as he struggled to breathe. Loosen up and be social? After everything he'd been through? He let his head fall against the chair and covered his face with his hands. Images of masses of people dancing on the back lawn, the roaring bonfire situated too close to the house, the thrum of the music from the party years ago flashed through his mind. He pushed from his chair and banished the memories.

As his heart rate slowed, Claire's comment filtered through. "There's a difference between letting loose

81

and recklessness." She was right. Socializing with Meg was not the equivalent of an uncontrolled rave. He might, just might, have overreacted.

He swung around. Maybe he should suggest to Meg they do something together. *Yeah right. When you turn the lights off every time you enter a room? There's only one thing you do with a female in the dark.*

Before he thought too much about it or got cold feet, he left his office in search of Meg. She was curled in the window seat, but this time she was on her computer. He stood in the doorway and admired her. The light set off a multitude of colors in her hair—rust, brown, purple, copper—before he dimmed the lights and walked toward her.

"I'm going to your house to get rid of the fallen tree and wait for the tarps to be delivered."

"Do you want help?"

He swallowed. "No." He forced his body to relax as her face reddened. "Thank you. I'll come find you when I'm done. What are your plans today?"

She shrugged. "I need to find a job, but until people answer my email inquiries or the roads are cleared so I can search in person, there's not much I can do."

He left before he could say something he'd regret.

Chapter Eleven

Simon staggered home midday, hands burning, head aching, and frustrated. Things didn't go as planned. To start with, the downed tree was harder to deal with than he'd expected. He shouldn't have been surprised. He was a landscape architect, not a tree remover. A power saw with his hands? What the hell was he thinking? That was the problem. He wasn't. At least not the rational side of him. Pride overcame him. Because he wanted to prove he could do this on his own, hands be damned.

He should have called a tree removal service.

It took him hours to cut the tree into sections he could move. Tomorrow he'd cut it into firewood and stack it behind the house, but he couldn't bear to think about it now. He still needed to cover the gaping hole with a tarp, but it would have to wait until this afternoon. Maybe he should give in and hire someone.

The Gatehouse was Meg's home. As much as he liked her company, he needed her to return to her house and get on with his life.

Gingerly he removed his jacket and shoes and trudged upstairs. As he approached his bedroom, her door opened, and she peeked into the hallway.

"Hey, how did it go?"

The hallway was unlit, casting deep shadows along the dark red walls. He didn't have to worry about her seeing his face. The rest of him, however, was problematic. He leaned against the wall and forced his muscles to relax. He refused to give away how tired and sore he was.

"I removed the tree, and I'll cut it for firewood tomorrow. I'll have to go out this afternoon to cover the hole with a tarp."

She stared at him for a long moment. "And you're exhausted."

Dammit, she'd noticed. "Not unexpected."

"Why don't you let me help with the tarp?"

What, she was a mind reader now, too? His gaze roved her body as he stood straighter. "What exactly are you able to do?"

If he'd been less tired, he would have phrased it better. Or not said anything at all.

Sparks flashed in her blue eyes. She folded her arms in front of her—did she know her motions only accentuated her chest? Probably best not to mention it.

"Do not let my size fool you." She enunciated every word as if she dared him to interrupt her.

He knew better. Now. "You could stack the wood for firewood."

She nodded. "I'll do it tomorrow, but I'll help you with the tarp this afternoon, so get used to it." Meg turned to her room but stopped and looked over her shoulder. "And go take a quick soak in the tub. You look like you need it."

She pinned him with a glare. He wouldn't be surprised if she wanted to drown him.

****

Meg leaned against the door, shaking. Simon infuriated her. Did he think she was a helpless female

84

who couldn't do anything except sit and read all day? She blew her hair out of her face. Okay, since being in his house, it was all she'd done. But only because she hadn't yet found a job. She pushed away the worry unemployment caused her. Without a job or income, she didn't have money to repay Mr. Adams. She hated the hold he had over her. The sooner it was gone, the better. However, there was nothing she could do about it right now. When she went to the house later, she'd show Simon she could be useful.

He needed her, even if he didn't know it yet.

Anger gave way to sympathy as she pictured him standing in the hallway. He looked dead on his feet. He might have thought he fooled her, as he attempted to look nonchalant leaning against the wall. But she'd bet if the wall weren't there, he'd have fallen over onto the floor.

A half hour later, she was in the kitchen when heavy footsteps clattered on the stairs right before the kitchen lights dimmed. He poked his head inside the doorway. His hair hid everything other than the outline of his nose and jaw.

"I'm going over to fasten the tarp after I eat." He walked the rest of the way in and glanced through the window. "I want to make sure everything is covered in case it rains again."

By the time she'd poured him a glass of milk, he'd scarfed the sandwich she'd made him. He gulped the milk and walked toward the door. In the doorway he paused. His chest rose and fell, as if he'd taken a huge breath and let it go. Still not facing her, he said, "If you still want to help with the tarp, let's go."

Without a word, she zipped her coat and followed

him over to her house.

Simon lifted the ladder and rested it against the side of her house. Only then did she notice the extent of the damage. She moaned before she covered her mouth. The tree smashed a huge hole. Pine needles and small branches littered the yard. No wonder Simon was exhausted.

On the ground were folded tarps, boxes of nails, and a hammer. He grabbed the hammer and box of nails and thrust them in his pockets, then carried the tarp up the ladder. Meg held the ladder steady and waited for him to tell her what else she could do.

She watched him for ten minutes as he stood on the ladder, cursing and hammering in about equal measure as he struggled to cover the hole. But she didn't pay attention to the curses or the hammer or the lack of progress. No, she paid attention to his ass. Another five minutes, and he shucked his jacket, allowing her a better view to admire how his denim jeans hugged his backside in all the right ways. The worn denim emphasized his thigh muscles. Her mouth went dry, and she looked away.

In the past, she'd always been a sucker for a guy in a well-cut tux. Now she knew what she'd missed.

Granted, she'd never done manual labor before, but if this was how it was to be, she'd turn into Lumberjack Jane. As she waited at the base of the ladder, Simon's arm muscles flexed. She needed to stop staring. He wasn't her type. Of course, she didn't have a type anymore, not since she turned over a new leaf, but still. Moody, broody, and silent didn't seem what she should switch to. No matter how attractive she might find him, she had to stop.

Except…

His muscles were taut, his Henley stretched across them. When he bent his head, his hair swung to the side. He clenched his jaw. For every nail he pounded, he dropped three. Why did he insist on doing this work, when it was difficult? Was it pride? Fear of being seen? Something else? Her chest squeezed at his persistence and how hard he worked to overcome his difficulty. Other men might rail at the world for what happened, and what he could no longer do. Yet he never yelled at her or demanded she retrieve his dropped nails. He never asked her for help. He cursed in general and continued.

She snuck glances his way as he continued to attempt to fasten the tarp. Maybe it was time to worry less and take control of the situation.

She climbed the ladder. When he didn't stop or acknowledge her presence despite the rattle of the metal against the side of the house, she held out her hand. It hovered in midair until, with a deep breath, she lowered it onto his shoulder. He froze, and she forgot to breathe. Bone, muscle, and sinew flexed beneath her fingers. The soft material separating skin from skin contrasted with the hardness of his shoulder and overwhelmed her.

She wanted him. More than she'd ever wanted any other man, she wanted Simon. Her mind carried her to the day when he'd protected her from the storm. His spicy scent, mixed with the scent of the cut tree, filled her nostrils and warmth pooled in her belly.

"What are you doing?" His question sounded strangled.

What *was* she doing? Physical contact eliminated all thoughts other than a desire to be with him. She tried to remember why she'd come here in the first place.

He dropped another nail. Oh, right.

"Give me the nails."

"What?"

"Give me the nails. I'll hold them. You can hammer."

"I don't need your help."

"Please?" She kept her tone matter-of-fact, so as not to offend him.

His tension left him and without a word he clumsily dumped the nails he held into her hand. She cupped her hands together and held them out to Simon, waiting for him to pick a nail to use. He grabbed for one, but with his bent, stiff fingers, all he did was mix them around and scrape her skin. The contact tickled, but the sight of his scars made her pause. This was why it took him such a long time. She glanced at him and caught his expression a split second before he covered his face with his hair and looked away.

Pride.

His hands, with their scars, didn't have the fine motor skills to hold an individual nail in place, which meant if she were to help him, she'd have to do it while he hammered.

She blanched as she looked at his hammer. Could she trust him not to miss? Desire and compassion for this man combined. He'd gone out of his way to help her.

She trusted him.

The last time she'd helped a friend she'd lost everything. Maybe the consequences this time weren't as severe—worst case, she got bruised fingers. If it happened too often, she could tell him to stop. But did she want to sacrifice her own well-being for someone else again? There used to be a time when she'd never have given the question any thought. The answer would have been clear. But now?

With shaking hands, she held the nail in place and raised her shoulders to her ears as she waited in fear. Nothing happened. Movement to her left made her hold her breath. His large hand on hers made her jump. She might have squeaked, but she would never admit it. Pressure on her palm was firm but gentle. Her lips were pressed together, and she swallowed.

He moved her hand into the correct position.

"I won't hurt you." His voice was low and hoarse.

She stared at his thumb as he tilted her wrist and positioned her hand in the exact spot he wanted the nail. His touch sent tingles along her arm, and goose bumps formed. She wanted to twist her hand and hold onto his, but she'd drop the nail, and he'd probably curse at them again. She let him maneuver her fingers into their proper position. When he was satisfied, he placed his own hand over hers, so only the nail head showed. His scarred skin was warm against hers. With a quick set of taps, he hammered it into the wood before her goose bumps faded.

He'd protected her.

Chapter Twelve

He lay in his oversized, antique, four-poster bed that night with the biggest hard on he could remember. He hadn't been this close to a woman since his accident. He couldn't get the feel of her skin, the curve of her body, the smell of her, out of his mind. More important, he'd never had anyone help him before, never allowed it. But she'd made it look natural. Did she pity him? He didn't think so. She'd made it into a partnership. When she'd shown her own vulnerability, her fear of the hammer near her fingers, it opened the gates and allowed him to accept the help she offered.

It was official. He was attracted to her. Quite possibly more than attracted to her, but it was pointless to explore his feelings. His attraction was pointless as well. How could any woman want a man with scars like his? In disgust, he threw off the silk bed covers and strode naked to his bathroom. He stared at his reflection in the mirror.

The house had caught fire, and beams collapsed on top of him. The scars crisscrossed his face like a crooked tic-tac-toe board. His nose was bent, and his eyebrows looked like dashes. His hated long hair provided cover, but not enough. His chest was covered in burn scars. Same with his back. He reached a hand behind him and traced the bumps and ridges. His touch wouldn't turn on anyone. He sighed. No beauty awards for him. He'd have to rely on his personality. Unfortunately, most of the time she made him tongue-tied and cautious. Apparently, he wouldn't win any personality contests either.

What would Meg think if she saw his body and his scars? Would she think him horrific?

He was alive, and at this point in time, he appreciated it. But his life? He didn't know what to do about it, and he needed answers soon. Horticulture or planting gardens at the burned-out shell of a mansion hadn't inspired him in months. Claire's project didn't inspire him. Only Meg turned him on, and he couldn't understand her.

She ran hot and cold. One minute she challenged him. The next she was wary of him. The insecure part of him thought it was his face, but deep inside he thought it might be something else. In fact, there were a few times the past couple of days where he'd swear she found him attractive—it was a loaded silence, a hitch in her breath. Or maybe he imagined the whole damn thing. He was out of practice, he barely knew her, and he was clueless if he were honest.

Meg was gorgeous and still a mystery. He had no idea where she was from, but it wasn't from here. He could tell by her clothes. The cut and quality were not Gulls Point, Maine. They weren't catalog-over-the-Internet ordered. Sure, they were jeans and simple tops, but they were quality. He might not be a fashion expert, but he could identify well-made and bespoke items—his mother had owned enough of them. And these were. Why was she in this small town?

Simon paced the bedroom, and for the moment, gave into his desires. He longed to run his hands through her hair, feel her body beneath his, taste her lips. But in addition, he wanted to know her favorite music, books, and colors. He wanted to take her into the ocean and swim with her beyond the waves, collect shells and driftwood on the beach, and climb the rocks surrounding the inlet.

But it was years since he'd gotten what he wanted. And he'd learned not to put much faith in hope.

****

The next day, Simon found Meg in the kitchen. Her natural beauty smacked him in the chest. He stared. When he could pull his gaze away from her, he found breakfast made and lunch being prepared. She was cooking for him, like it was the most natural thing in the world. Flashes of Claire's warning not to force her to feed him brought him up short. Crap.

"You don't have to cook for me, you know," he said from the doorway.

She spun around, before he could hide his face. "Geez, I didn't hear you. Sorry. I have a plan." The smile she gave him stunned him into silence and lessened the effect of her flinch. "Do you want to hear what it is?"

He nodded. When she smiled, he'd give her anything she wanted.

"Maybe it's a good thing I took care of the food this morning, since you're too tired to speak." She walked toward him.

He moved his hair in front of his face again. Better she think he was tired than stunned by her beauty. The potential awkwardness made him shudder. Placing a plate of pancakes in front of him, she joined him with her own.

"As soon as you're ready to go outside and work again—I assume you want to clean the yard and cut the tree into firewood—I'll go with you and help, and we can have a picnic as a break. Unless your plans have changed…?"

Swallowing a mouthful of pancake, he washed it down with juice before he spoke. "The construction guys come today to start repair work on the house, but I planned to clean the yard."

Meg nodded. "Okay, my plan will work."

"You don't have to help, you know."

Meg arched a brow. "Kind of like you don't have to do the work yourself."

He frowned.

"It's the least I can do. You're kind enough to let me stay here."

He thought about arguing, but the prospect of an entire day with Meg enticed him too much. He nodded instead.

"Good. Claire was right."

"What did Claire say?" And why did she talk to Claire about him? His body ran hot and cold at all the possibilities.

"As long as I feed you, you'll let me get my way."

****

"No more chopping firewood until you eat," Meg called from the blanket she'd spread on the grass in the backyard. She'd done her best to find a spot without too much storm detritus. The gray wool blanket was scratchy, but a waterproof side kept the damp from seeping through.

Simon walked over as she unpacked the basket. He looked wary.

"I promise it's edible," she said.

He sat with a groan.

"Me, too," she said. "But we'll feel better after we eat."

"Promise?"

"I told you, it's edible."

She pulled chicken sandwiches, paper plates, and napkins from the basket. Opening a bottle of water, she handed it to him before she opened her own. She ignored his frown—based on yesterday, she'd known two things. One, his hands would be sore, and there was no way he'd be able to open the bottle without suffering. Two, it would take someone stronger than her to pull the admission out of him. She moved on.

He must have decided not to argue. Or maybe he saved it for later. Either way, he took a bite of the sandwich instead of stalking off. She chalked one in the win column.

"What made you decide on a picnic?" He looked around. "It's not picnic weather."

He was right. But in the backyard, they were sheltered from the ocean winds. "I like the fresh air. My friends and I used to picnic in this secluded spot on the beach. No one could find us there, no one knew it existed."

In her old life, she staked out secluded spots where the paparazzi couldn't find her. This was similar, except she didn't hide from anyone. She enjoyed the peace.

"I can't believe how much damage the storm did," she said. He wasn't much of a conversationalist, so she filled in.

"This one was pretty bad."

"I wonder what downtown looks like."

He looked away. "I have no idea."

Of course not, she thought. "I thought of planting flowers in the front garden," she said. "I was going to ask you first, because it's your house. But I'm glad I didn't yet. They'd have been destroyed."

He waved her concerns away. "You can plant anything you'd like. I've never gotten to it. But you're better off planting bulbs this time of year. Flowers should be planted in the spring."

"Your other tenants haven't wanted any flowers out front?"

"I never spoke to any of them."

"You mean you don't have picnics?" She laughed.

After a beat or two, he huffed. "Nope, you're the first."

She took another bite of her sandwich. "I'm honored."

His face lightened. He wiped his mouth and made to rise.

"Wait," she said. "There's dessert." She removed cookies from the basket. "I found these in your freezer and defrosted them."

"Claire sent them over one day. I love her chocolate chip cookies."

Meg took a bite. "Mm, me, too."

He swallowed the last of the cookie and put his garbage in the basket, facing away from her. "You relax. I'll get back to work."

"I'll be there as soon as I clean this stuff."

"Meg, you don't ha—"

"—Don't start with me, Simon."

Turning halfway toward her, he nodded. "Okay. You win."

****

When they finished cutting the tree and stacking the wood together and the sun set, he called it a day and packed his things. He expected Meg to leave ahead of him. But she waited, and he didn't know what to do. He supposed it made sense to walk with her. It wasn't far. They could leave together. They'd picnicked together this afternoon. Walking next to each other was nothing.

Except it was everything.

He didn't know what to say most of the day so he remained quiet. She didn't act like she minded too much. At least, he hoped she didn't. But now? If he thanked her for her help, it would draw attention to his need for it in the first place. He didn't want her to see what he wasn't.

But if he remained silent, he would appear ungrateful, and he appreciated so many things. For her assistance, without which he would still be on the roof hammering in the damned nails. For her beauty, which blinded him every time he looked at her. For her kindness, which surrounded him like a warm blanket. For her innate ability to know what he needed.

Despite everything, he'd never thanked her. God, she must think the worst of him. His lungs constricted at how careless he'd been with her. The desire to tell her his feelings overwhelmed him. She deserved that much, at least. And he needed to tell her.

He swallowed. "Thanks for your help today."

"You're welcome. I need to move into my house sometime. Preferably without a tree for a roommate."

His hand brushed against hers as they walked across the drive, and he sucked in a shaky breath. Her skin was smooth. He'd wanted to caress it yesterday each time he held her hand to ensure the hammer didn't hurt her. It was agony touching her and maintaining an unaffected façade. And now? A deep physical desire overtook him at the thought of being able to hold her hand, like a man held the hand of a woman he cared for.

Once inside, she sank onto the first sofa they came to and groaned.

"Why don't you go soak in the tub upstairs?" he asked. "I'll fix dinner."

She toed off her sneakers. "No, I'll do it. Give me a minute."

"Meg, you're exhausted. You're not my personal chef. Go upstairs. There are extra towels in the hall closet."

She rose and walked toward the stairs. Her hips swayed. Her jeans accentuated her butt. He reached for her, took a step forward, and fought the urge to ask to join her. He walked into the kitchen and thought about food. Every squeak of a pipe, muted sound of water, and footstep on the floor above reminded him of her, naked, in his tub.

When she walked in with her fresh-scrubbed skin, he focused on the pasta he'd cooked instead of her rosy cheeks or her wet hair. When it didn't work, he looked for something else to think about. The marinara sauce—including the spot he'd spilled on the tablecloth—the garlic flavor, the warm bread in the basket next to her. Anything else.

"Want to play a board game," he asked after they ate as he loaded the dishwasher.

She arched her brow. "You have board games?"

She was right. He lived alone. Why would he have board games? His throat constricted at the memories of playing games on rainy evenings with his housekeeper, after she'd finished for the day and come here to her home. He'd sneak out and join her. Instead of sending him home, she'd make cookies and challenge him to a game of Clue or Monopoly. Like everyone else, she was gone, too. Only the games remained, unused in the cabinet.

He concentrated on stacking the silverware and mumbled, "They're old."

Her hand on his arm, the second time she'd touched him on purpose, made him freeze.

"I didn't mean to be unkind," she said. "I commented more because I didn't see them when you gave me a tour. Not that you opened drawers and closets..."

Her hand was on his elbow. If he turned, he could take her in his arms... And she'd stopped talking, which meant she waited for an answer. He replayed her conversation in his mind, which he'd heard but not listened to due to the distraction of her lovely fingers. Right, board games.

"Most of the games are unused since I never have people over. Although I do play Scrabble online." He froze. Scrabble online didn't require dexterity. The board game version did.

She removed her hand.

He wanted to pull it back.

"Ah, so you're good?" she said. Her voice regained the cadence he noticed today. If he were optimistic, he might think she was comfortable with him.

He closed the dishwasher and wiped the counter. "Not bad."

"Let's play..." She paused. When he turned to

look, her gaze was focused on his hands.

Bracing himself on the counter, he took a deep breath. There was only one solution. "We can, if you don't mind helping me with the tiles." The words were easier to utter than he expected, but they still left a bitter taste in his mouth.

She moved closer. "Like the nails, but without the hammer." Her voice was gentle, and his skin warmed.

"I promise not to whack you with the tile holders."

She bumped against him, and he smiled. "I'll hold you to it," she said. She cleared her throat. "My grandma taught me. I haven't played in years, though."

"They're words. English. I doubt you forgot."

She laughed.

His insides warmed. "I'll take a quick shower," he said. "The game's under the window seat you love."

Simon raced through his shower and made it downstairs in less than ten minutes. Normally, he'd have brushed his hair away from his face to dry and keep it out of his way, but with her here, he let it fall forward, and the wet strands dripped on his T-shirt. He dimmed the lights in the living room, sat across from her, and arranged the board. It was tricky keeping his face from her. He focused on his tiles instead.

He was a sloppy player. Unable to grasp an individual tile, he dragged them around and scooped them. He'd be lucky if he didn't knock over his rack twelve times. Meg reached over and helped with his tiles. Their fingers touched and sent zings of attraction along his arms. It added a whole new challenge to the game.

"So, your grandma taught you to play?" He seized on the first question he could think of, his voice raspy.

"Yeah. She used it to learn English, and it became her favorite game. She taught it to me as soon as I could read." She made quick work of setting his tiles in the tray, taking care not to look at them.

"Where did she come from?"

"Russia."

"And you? Where do you come from?"

She knocked over her tiles. This was new. "Excuse me?"

"I was curious where you're from."

She fisted her hand and moved it to her lap. The unexpected motion drew his attention to her discomfort.

"Oh, um…California."

"Sorry, didn't mean to pry." He sighed. He'd ruined the easy mood.

"It's okay."

She was quiet for a little, and he focused on his tiles. When it was his turn, he indicated to Meg the tiles he wanted to use. Her hands brushed his. He wanted to grab them to his lips and kiss them. He refrained. She removed the tiles from the tray, and he pushed them onto the board. B-R-A-V-E.

Her hands stilled. "So Claire told me you were raised here," she said. "Have you lived here your entire life?"

His heartbeat raced. Why did Claire talk about him? She knew he didn't discuss his past. *Maybe it was why she mentioned it to Meg.* "No."

She played with her tiles before she put them on the board. A-V-O-I-D.

He wanted to laugh at the irony. Instead, he shook his head. He thought he heard her huff, but he couldn't be sure.

"I can see we're great conversationalists." Her voice was quiet.

"Well, maybe we should start with the easy stuff first," he said. "Like, what's your favorite color?"

She pulled away in disbelief. "Just one? Pfft. The color of the ocean in the morning. A gray-blue with gold highlights from the sun."

He pictured the image she painted, but added her to the mix. With her hair color, it would be stunning. They repeated their tile selection process, and he pushed his tiles onto the board. P-R-E-T-T-Y. He risked a glance her way—would she think he flirted with her? And would she like it?

She blushed. A small smile curved her lips, and he did an imaginary fist pump.

"What's your favorite thing to do?" she asked.

He rested his hands on top of each other as he thought about her question. "Ever or during a specific time?"

"Ever."

His stomach tightened. *Spend time with you.* He shoved the thought aside. "Swim in the ocean, listen to music, create things of beauty."

"Those are three things. I only asked for one."

He shrugged. "You didn't limit me."

She added her tiles to the board. C-H-E-A-T.

He chuckled, and a weight lifted inside his chest. "Your turn," he said.

"I displayed my tiles, and you haven't asked me a question," she said.

"What's your biggest regret?"

She settled into her seat. "Wow, you're deep, aren't you?"

"Is it a problem?"

She paused, then shook her head. "Not telling the truth."

"About what?"

"You only get one question at a time." Her hands were fisted on the table. He wanted to reach for them and soothe her.

"Says who?"

"I do. It's your turn." She pointed at the board, and he switched focus to his tiles. Her proximity killed him. D-E-E-P. But he wanted to know more about her answer. "Why did you lie?"

"I didn't have a choice, and you need to wait your turn."

"My house, my rules."

She stood, her body stiff, and her gaze shuttered. "I should get to bed."

He rose from his chair. "No, wait. I didn't mean to push you. Stay."

She paused, her knuckles white as she grabbed onto the chair. He could almost see her try to make a decision. The seconds stretched, and when he didn't think he could take anymore, she returned to her seat. "Fine, I'll answer your questions. But you have to answer mine."

He nodded, unwilling to think about how relieved he was. "Explain your previous answer."

She paused. He wondered if she would renege. After a few agonizing seconds, she spoke, and he leaned forward. "I lied because I thought it was the right thing to do," she said. "And it cost me. It's all I'll say right now."

He respected her wish not to continue, but her

answer filled him with more questions.

She said, "Now, you have to answer my question."

He nodded. His throat was tight. He never should have agreed to this, yet it was the only way to keep her here. The thought of her leaving was worse than the fear of her question.

"Do you have family?"

"Not anymore." His hand spasmed, and he rubbed it to loosen the muscles.

"Is your hand okay?"

He moved it onto his lap. "To quote you, 'you only get one question at a time.' " She was silent, and he raised his head. Her eyes glowed with compassion and patience. He preferred the heat from their finger-to-finger contact. He swallowed before he redirected his thoughts, because he couldn't go there. He arranged his tiles. P-R-I-V-A-T-E.

She tipped her head, as if in acknowledgement. To his surprise, she wasn't offended.

Before he could ask her a question, she spelled her own word. R-I-G-H-T.

They each knew their own boundaries. As he lay in bed that night, he realized why he was drawn to her.

She had secrets, too.

Chapter Thirteen

She burrowed deeper under the covers. Simon was private, the most private person she'd ever met. He kept away from everyone, whether he hid in his house or pushed his hair in front of his face. Yet he answered her questions, to an extent. He'd gotten a little less concerned with hiding the longer she was here. He was stern and liked to do things his way and raised his voice when he didn't agree with her. But he'd gone out of his way to apologize and reassure her.

He'd called her brave.

Did he think she was brave? *Oh please, Meg, get a grip. It was a stupid Scrabble game.* But it wasn't stupid. He'd shown more respect during the one-hour game than any of her friends ever showed her, despite all she'd done for them.

Lying in her sleigh bed, she pictured him on the roof with her, playing Scrabble with her, eating with her. She wished she could picture every detail of him, but with the dimmed lights and his hair always in his face, she couldn't fill in all the blanks. Would he ever show her his face? Her stomach fluttered. Jet black hair that was much too long, but sexy and soft. It brushed against her face when they were on the roof. She could still feel its silkiness. His broad shoulders made her feel secure and safe. His muscular arms and legs exuded strength. His deep gravelly voice was harsh at times, but never to her. And he was kind. He'd sheltered her from the storm and protected her hands from the hammer. She'd glimpsed his sense of humor during the game, and his rusty laugh? It brought her to her knees.

He was shy. He had his secrets.

And now she was falling for him.

Crap.

****

The next morning, Claire called Meg and invited herself over for coffee. "Don't tell Simon, though," she said. "I want it to be a surprise."

He entered the kitchen as she hung up. Her face heated, and it was she who looked away first. *This is ridiculous.* She looked at him. "Good morning."

He paused in the middle of pouring a cup of coffee. "Morning." Adding milk and sugar, he handed her the cup without looking at her. Their fingers touched, and rays of heat zipped along Meg's arm, like they had whenever their fingers made contact during Scrabble. After a moment, he poured another mug for himself.

"Last night was fun," she said. *Brilliant.*

He leaned a hip against the counter and looked at the ocean. "It was."

Did he love it as much as she did? "Want to go for a walk on the beach later?"

His body relaxed. "Maybe."

She didn't know if he wasn't talkative because it was morning, because he was uncomfortable about last night, or for another reason. She attempted to resume normal conversation. "What's our plan for today?"

"Our?" He folded his arms across his wide chest. Meg fought the urge to squeeze his forearms and feel the play of muscles beneath his sweater. Right before she smacked him for his stubbornness.

She ignored the urge, focused on her coffee, and sighed. "I thought we settled this yesterday."

"I'm cleaning the yards—yours and mine."

"I'll help."

He looked like he was about to argue. She placed her coffee cup on the counter and went to get her jacket. Heavy footsteps stomped behind her. There were many ways to deal with stubbornness. Ignoring it was her go-to for now.

Somewhere between the kitchen and the end of the drive, Simon must have adjusted to the idea of a helper, because he caught up to her and didn't try to dissuade her. He adjusted his long strides to her shorter ones, stuffed his hands in his pockets, and walked next to her.

He cleared his throat. "A walk on the beach later sounds nice."

This was his idea of being friendlier. Meg's lips twitched as she suppressed a laugh. "I love the sound of the waves crashing against the rocks. Although it's too cold to swim."

He nodded. When they reached the house, Simon gave her a rake, took one for himself, and they piled the debris away from the house. She spent much of her time watching him from the corner of her eye, enjoying the way his muscles bunched as he swept branches and leaves. The ease with which he moved entranced her. She wondered what it would be like to move with him in different ways. Images of dancing with him, their bodies flush against each other, flitted through her mind, and she shook her head to clear her thoughts.

Twenty minutes later, a car turned into their lane and drew Meg's attention from the corner of her eye.

"Oh, it's Claire!"

Simon stiffened. "Why is she here?"

"She asked to come over for coffee. She said she wanted to surprise you."

Claire stopped the car and climbed out. She waved and walked toward them. "Hi, Simon! I have your books!"

Simon scowled and retreated toward the shadows of the house as Claire walked toward them. He tilted his head, though his hair already covered his face, and there was no way Claire could see from that distance.

"Come on, Simon, it's me," Claire said.

Simon muttered. Meg put her hand on his arm, and he stilled. "I didn't mean to make you uncomfortable."

He looked at her hand.

"You can join us if you'd like."

He swallowed. "I've got work to do."

Meg left to meet her friend. Claire gave her a hug and nodded toward the other yard. "Guess he's not coming?"

"No, I tried."

With a sigh, Claire walked with Meg into Simon's house.

"I brought Simon's library books and also printed the plans he's made for the empty land. I wrote my comments and suggestions, as well as my boss' on the plans. Will you give them to him?"

"Sure."

"So, I asked the library director, my boss, and we're hiring if you need a job."

Meg exhaled. "Great, thank you. I was nervous."

"Nervous? You haven't been here long enough."

Meg bit her lip and wondered how much to tell her.

Claire swallowed. "I'm sorry. I shouldn't pry."

"No, it's okay. Sit. I'll make us coffee." She rummaged around in the refrigerator and withdrew the milk. "I have debts I need to repay. I used to be a publicist. Now...well, now I'm rediscovering myself, and I'm never sure what will be available. But thank you for checking. I'll fill an application right away." She needed to make money to pay off her friend's father, Mr. Adams, and convince her dad her life was now her own. The familiar frisson of fear snaked along her spine. She didn't want to be alone, but the days of her dad controlling every aspect of her life were over.

"A publicist? The town could use help with publicity for Simon's project. We are in desperate need of funds to develop the land into a garden and avoid selling it to developers. The book fair raised a little money, but not enough."

"How much do you need?"

Claire shrugged. "We need money to fight off the developer who wants to turn twenty acres of land into townhomes and a golf course. Simon created alternate plans—the ones I gave you—but turning them into reality will cost around $100,000. We have donors, but our committee still needs to raise a certain amount."

"Oh, I had no idea. Where did the land come from?"

"It's open space and has become attractive to outside developers. We'd like to keep it open, but make it useful to the town."

"Oh. I see."

"Who did you work for?"

Meg brought over two steaming mugs of coffee, along with the milk and sugar, and joined Claire at the table. "Different people."

"Anyone famous?"

You could say that. "Probably not anyone you'd know."

Claire shot her a look, and Meg's eyes widened in surprise. No one had looked her in the face in days. "Try me."

"Do you want anything to eat with your coffee? I'm sure we have something…"

"I'd love to be a fly on the wall when you and Simon have conversations. You're both good at avoiding questions," Claire said with a smile. "You're perfect for each other. And no, coffee is enough."

"I'm sorry, I don't like talking about my past." It was more than dislike. She wasn't allowed.

"I've noticed."

Meg fiddled with her mug, sliding it around on the table, until Claire reached over and grabbed the other side of it, immobilizing it. "I'm a good listener if you want to talk, and my husband is the local newspaper editor. He has a lot of contacts. If either of us can help you—listening, talking, helping you find a job—let us know. Okay?"

Conflicting thoughts overwhelmed Meg. Claire's husband was a newspaper editor. She needed to keep quiet, at least until she'd paid her debt to Mr. Adams. According to a lawyer she'd consulted, the confidentiality agreement only lasted as long as she used the money. If her debt was paid, she was free to come clean—about everything—to a few close friends. It was hard to wait. Being beholden to others was harder. She'd been burned too many times to count. But she'd been alone a long time, and a sudden desire to confess everything overwhelmed her. Would Claire understand? If she told her, who else would learn her secret?

Claire rose and gave her a hug. "I've got to get to work. Thanks for coffee, and say hi to Simon for me."

When Claire left and Meg put away the dishes, she walked to The Gatehouse. As expected, Simon wasn't in front. Meg walked around back.

"Simon?"

He faced away from her. His powerful shoulder and arm muscles bunched as he raked. His motion stopped and after a few seconds he answered. "Yeah?"

"Claire's gone." Meg walked toward him.

He stiffened. "I don't need your help, Meg. I've got it. I'm good at being alone. I like it."

****

Simon spotted her on the beach and watched her from above. She stood with the cliffs behind her, hands in her pockets. Wind from the surf blew her hair into a red halo. Once in a while, its force pushed her back a step, and she'd replant her feet in a physically defiant "screw you" kind of way. He couldn't imagine her saying it. Although, after the way he'd behaved today…

He was an ass. She'd never once done anything to make him feel like a monster. What did he do in return? Hide away and order her to leave him alone. He was a coward. Part of him wanted her to see him, to see who he was inside. To know him. But the other part of him couldn't let her in.

She probably thought of him as a cowardly ass slave driver. Perfect.

His phone buzzed, and he looked at an email from Claire.

"Nice of you to stop and say hello."

He rolled his eyes. Crap from her was the last thing he needed, especially when she was right. Jabbing the off button on his phone, he shoved it in his pocket, and scrabbled his way along the rocky path to the beach.

His steps slowed as he approached. Inhaling the briny air didn't provide him the ease he expected, because his heart stuttered at the sight of her. He cursed. The wind and light made it impossible to hide his scars. He squared his shoulders. Approaching the shoreline, his shadow loomed near, dwarfing hers. But she remained silent. Of course—waiting for him to speak. He was ashamed of his behavior.

He stole a glance. Chin tipped toward the sky, eyes closed, nostrils flared as she let the sun shine on her face. Oh how he longed to do the same thing. But not here and not now. Now he needed to speak, except he was at a complete loss for what to say.

She walked away.

"Wait!"

She stopped. "Why?"

"I thought we were supposed to walk on the beach." Yeah, great way to avoid the issue.

Meg shrugged. "You prefer being alone."

Crap. "I'm sorry. It was a lousy thing for me to say."

She breathed a deep sigh. "I rent a house from you. And as your renter, I'd like to know when I can return to my house. Because I can't live forever in yours."

The words she left unspoken hurt as much as the words she said. For a person who didn't raise her voice, she was pissed. Her anger shimmered in an aura around her.

"I thought we were friends," he said.

"Are we friends when you act like you can barely stand to be around me?"

"Whoa, time out." He turned toward her and reached for her.

She retreated a step.

"You're mad. I deserve it. Yell at me."

She blinked.

"I treated you like crap. I was an ass and a coward. You should scream at me."

Meg bit her lip and took another step away from him. "No."

"No, what?"

"No, I don't scream."

"I want you to."

She paused, as if she considered it. "I do what's best for my friends. But it doesn't mean I'm not mad."

"I'm sorry. Claire's arrival threw me. What do you mean you do what's best for your friends?"

"Never mind."

He frowned as he tried to understand her, but once again, she stumped him.

"I should have asked you first, or warned you, about Claire, although she asked me not to," she said.

"No!" His vehemence made her freeze. "You had no reason to warn me or ask me. You're free to do what you want, with whomever you want."

"But it's your house."

"Which I share with you right now. But you're right, I shouldn't force you to stay here forever." No matter how much he might want her to. He paused and turned toward the ocean. Forever? When had the idea entered his mind? "I'll rush the construction guys, offer them a bonus to come right away—"

"No." Now it was she who raised her voice. "You don't have to. I mean, I can't live at your house forever," she smiled, and his chest warmed, "but if you're not in a rush, I'm not either."

He looked in her direction for as long as he could without making eye contact, an interesting feat. But the anger he sensed evaporated. His Meg had returned.

He coughed. When had she become "his" Meg?

"Do you want to take that walk?" she asked.

Action was better than thought. He'd examine his feelings for her later. Right now, she asked to walk with him. He'd be a fool to say no.

Chapter Fourteen

Meg walked with Simon on the rocky beach, waves on her right, cliffs on her left, and seagulls overhead. This time, her lungs expanded, her respiration slowed, and she became hyper aware of him. He took longer strides than she did, but after they'd gone a few feet, he shortened his.

She appreciated the consideration. It only made her more aware of his muscular thighs. Their arms brushed as they walked, and tingles shot up her neck. It was an accident, wasn't it? He stepped away, but a few strides later the uneven ground pushed them together, and their bodies brushed against each other. She listened to his breath hitch at the contact, and he didn't move away.

Nervous laughter bubbled in her chest. They'd been close before and held hands. Granted, he'd covered hers on the ladder, but still. It wasn't the first time they touched. Why was this different? She remembered the sensations when he'd covered her hand on the roof—warmth and roughness and safety. And she wanted it. She bumped her hand against his, on purpose, to feel his skin. It wasn't smooth like hers. Its texture, unique to him, fascinated her. A moment later, he rubbed his arm against her.

Was it accidental, too? She snuck a glance at his profile. Although his hair blocked most of his face, she'd swear when the wind blew it, a ghost of a smile hovered, like they shared a private joke. Her belly warmed, and the air between their knuckles, where they almost touched, crackled with electricity.

The next time their bodies touched, she slipped her hand through his elbow. His body jolted before he pressed her arm against his side, and they walked to the curve of the shore connected.

When they stopped, they watched the waves lap over the rocks, their froth sputtering into the cracks.

"This is the only place I've ever not felt alone," he whispered.

"How long have you been alone?"

"Too long," he replied.

"This is the only place I've ever felt seen."

"I can't imagine you invisible," he said.

"When "It Girls" and camera bulbs surround you, it's easy to fade into the background."

The sky and water darkened as the light faded, and she shivered in the chill air. Her hand grew icy as he pulled away from her. As she was about to complain, a weight landed on her shoulders. His arm drew her close. He remained still, as if he waited to see if she'd object. Instead, she leaned against his side. Heat emanated from him, and tingles ran through her body. A desire to turn into him, to press her body against his, to kiss him, overwhelmed her. He positioned her in front of him and rested his chin on the top of her head. His heart beat against her back. A soft moan escaped her lips, and they both froze. All of a sudden, she was aware of how close she was. His jacket was warm from his body and smelled like him. His low chuckle brought her out of her reverie, and he took a step away.

"What's funny?" She didn't like the cold space

between them.

"You look like a poppet in my jacket."

She turned and raised an eyebrow. "A poppet. A poppet?" She fisted her hands on her hips and gave him her best glare.

His mouth twitched.

"Don't you dare laugh at me, you gargantuan man."

A noise, like a combination of a rumble of thunder and a groan emanated from him; despite her warning, he laughed.

"The only reason I look like this is because your jacket is ridiculously huge!"

His shoulders shook, and he ducked.

"Yeah, you keep it up, mister. See if I return your jacket."

He walked with her to the house, adjusting the jacket every time it slipped off her.

****

"Let's watch a horror movie." Meg flopped on the couch and wiggled into the soft cushions.

There was a beat of silence before Simon turned away from her and poked at the logs in the fireplace, sending sparks up the chimney. "I'm not a big fan of horror movies."

She liked horror movies because the monsters were obviously fake. You didn't have to dig deep, to wonder about anything. It was black and white. Meg's heart constricted. She hadn't thought about it from Simon's perspective. Did he consider himself a monster? Could this amazing man see himself in those movies? Her throat thickened. She wanted to run away and cry. But he'd think she ran from him. With a deep breath, she sorted through the list of her favorites in her mind and threw away several until she thought of the perfect one. "How about Dracula?" Her voice rasped past the emotion, but she forged ahead. "The old one. It's totally cheesy, which makes it funny. 'I vant to suck your blood!' " she said with a fake accent.

"Do you?" he asked.

Returning the poker to the rack, he walked toward her, and held out his arm, wrist up. She took it in her hand. His skin was warm beneath her fingers, his pulse steady, and the hair on the other side of his arm was wiry. She stroked her thumb along the inside of his wrist. His breath stuttered. She wondered what he'd do if she kissed him. Desire flooded through her. Never mind him, what would *she* do?

"Next time," she said. She was brave, but maybe not that brave, at least not yet.

Slowly, he lowered his arm to his side, but remained close enough his knees brushed hers. His skin was flushed, his eyes ablaze. Heat pulsed between them. After a moment, he stepped away, as if he wasn't brave enough either. "Do you want popcorn?"

She nodded, and he left the room. While he was gone, she turned on the TV, her pulse racing. While the movie room upstairs was a fun place to watch, she usually preferred the living room. With the lights off, the TV provided a white glow, along with the orange light from the fireplace. Usually, it was cozy, but this time, it was intimate. The movie began, and Simon joined her on the sofa with a bowl of buttery popcorn. The cushions dipped under his weight. Less than the width of a person between them this time. Merely a bowl.

As the movie played, she rested her hand on the edge of the bowl, and a moment later, his hand appeared on the opposite side. Its presence drew her attention, and she forgot to watch the screen. At the same time, they each reached for the popcorn, and their hands bumped in the bowl before they brought the popcorn to their mouths. Her pulse pounded in her ears. She wanted those hands on her. On screen, thunder boomed. He laughed when she startled, so she poked him, making him jump. Simon shook his head. When a spider web appeared on screen, Meg's hair brushed her neck, and with a screech, she turned. Simon's hands grabbed the ends of her hair. Wolves howled on screen, and once again, she poked him.

This time, he grabbed her hand. His fingers clasped her wrist and slid to her palm. A trail of heat snaked from her arm straight to her heart. All her desire returned. The only thing she could think of was him. His thumb circled against her palm, and she opened her hand to give him more access. Her fingers fluttered as he performed the most seductive, silent palm reading she'd ever experienced. Her breath stuttered in her chest, and her gaze was drawn to the hypnotic motion of his thumb. When she thought she could bear it no more, he stopped, but now it was worse. Because he pulled his hand away, and she was bereft.

She moved closer, but he shifted. The bowl of popcorn tipped. She grappled with the snack, lost her balance, and somehow landed sprawled across his lap. He stiffened as she leaned against his chest to right herself, their bodies close. His eyes widened. This man, this hard, lonely, kinder-than-anyone-she'd-known man, stared at her in fear. She recognized his fear as easily as she recognized his scarred face—the deep lines and grooves of scar tissue along his cheeks and forehead, the crooked formerly broken nose, the puckered burns along his jaw. The blatant evidence of his pain mixed with the waves of fear rolling off him. She blinked and shifted her gaze to his lips.

Lips that begged to be kissed. Perched on his lap, she couldn't imagine not kissing him. She braced her arms on the sofa cushions on either side of his face and lowered her head.

She got no more than an inch or two closer when he grabbed her upper arms.

"What are you doing?" His voice was raspy and sent shivers along the length of her body. His hands made warm imprints on her skin.

"I want to kiss you."

His gaze hardened, and his jaw clenched. "Don't mock me."

"Never."

He stared at her. In the background, the movie played and from the hallway, the grandfather clock chimed.

Straddling him, she shifted in his lap for better balance. He inhaled. There was no escape.

****

If he allowed his mouth to open, he would gasp like a marathoner at the end of a race. Or yell to rival her original shriek when she saw him on the beach. But he didn't want to betray his emotions. He clenched his jaw and suffocated in silence.

She, whom he'd desired from the moment she'd walked on the beach the first day, was on top of him, touching him, aware of him and his scars.

It didn't matter she'd never said anything cruel in the four days she'd been in his house. It didn't matter her actions showed her to be as kind and as funny and as genuine as he fantasized her to be.

She was too close. No matter how much she might say she cared, no one wanted a face like his. A face like his was for nightmares, horror movies, not fantasies. Any minute now, she would realize her mistake. Any second...

"Simon."

Her voice was no more than a whisper, and it took him a moment to realize she spoke.

Dammit. If only he could disappear.

"Simon, open your eyes."

No. If he opened his eyes, his emotions would pour from them, like tears. Hope, desire, need. And once they escaped, he'd never rein them in again. Better to keep them locked away forever, if necessary. He pushed farther into the sofa, as if he could fade away into nothing.

"Simon, look at me."

He had to hand it to her. She was good. Her voice didn't sound any different than usual. Her hands remained where they were against his face, drawing maddening circles over his eyebrows. She trailed lines along his cheekbones, massaged his scalp, brushed his hair away from his face. For the first time in forever, a woman touched him with desire. Her skin was soft, her touch warm. This was Meg, his Meg, touching him because she wanted him. The sensuality of it all crashed against him like the waves in his cove, endless, hypnotic.

Brutal.

As if seeing more of his face was an improvement.

"Simon. Please. I need you to look at me."

She'd said please.

His iron control slipped, and he cursed.

He opened his eyes.

The desire and heat reflected in her eyes slammed into him with the force of a linebacker. Lust raged through him. His heart banged against his chest, he hardened beneath her, and blood pounded in his ears. He wanted her right here, right now, before she had the good sense to change her mind.

In the halfway place between dreams and nightmares, not wanting to destroy the very thing he'd waited for, he swallowed and raised his hands. He let them skim her sides, giving her time to adjust to his touch, as he learned the contours of her body. He could feel her ribcage beneath her soft cotton shirt, as well as her shoulder blades as his hands rose higher. She was a contrast of delicate bones and innate strength in his arms. He continued his upward motion until he held her face between his hands. He tried to flatten his palms against her cheeks, but his scarred fingers didn't straighten. Damn his damaged hands and their never-ending stiffness, but her petal-soft cheeks, her delicate ears, her silky hair made him forget himself. He focused on her, on her textures. Slowly he drew her closer, until he was immersed in the scent of her soap and the tickle of her breath.

Her pupils dilated with desire, and her nostrils flared. Her chest rose and fell, accentuating the breasts he ached to touch.

Holy hell, she wanted him.

Him.

Before either of them could change their minds, he brushed his lips against hers. The contact sent a jolt of desire straight to his groin. He stifled a groan and opened his mouth to taste her. She was salty and buttery from the popcorn, and oh, so sweet. He'd swear this was a dream, one from which he didn't ever want to awaken.

Her hands slid around the nape of his neck and stroked him, made him burn beneath her touch. His hands splayed against her back, drawing her closer. She whimpered against his mouth. Why? Did she want him to stop? He froze for a moment, before he opened his mouth over hers. With a small amount of encouragement, she slid her tongue inside his mouth, hesitantly, as if she wasn't sure she'd be welcome.

She wasn't sure?

His tongue met hers, and they tasted each other, danced with each other. He sucked. She sighed in pleasure, gripped the hair at the base of his skull, and wound her fingers through it, sending shards of pleasure along his spine. For the first time ever, he was glad his hair was long.

He scattered kisses along her jawline, the long column of her neck and across her collarbone as she arched against him, exposing her throat. His hands supported her and entwined in her hair. He couldn't get enough of her. She placed her finger against his lips. Not wanting to stop, he drew it into his mouth and sucked.

She rose on her knees against him, left her finger in his mouth, and caressed his face with her other hand. It bumped along his scarred cheek. He frowned and pulled away.

"Let me," she whispered, "please."

There was that damned word again. He loosened his lips a little, and she removed her finger. She framed his face with her hands, and he waited for her to realize her error. Instead, she traced his scars like a blind person mapping a lover's face. He sighed. It had been ages since anyone made him feel wanted. His breath caught, and a prickle formed behind his lashes. She covered his face with kisses, and he focused all his attention on her smooth lips against his scarred skin.

With a sigh, she pulled away and curled against his chest. He wrapped his arms around her, rested his cheek on the top of her head, and listened to her breathe as he fought to get his racing pulse under control.

"Thank you," she said.

"For what?"

"For letting me do that."

"I never thought anyone would want to ever again."

"You must not hang out with the right people," she said.

He raised her hand to his lips and kissed the palm. He swallowed past the sudden lump in his throat. "Seven years ago, my home burned to the ground." He turned his face away in an attempt to forget the heat, the crackling, the burning. The house had caved in on itself, filled with smoke and flames and turned into a torture chamber. "The fire killed my parents and the staff and injured me," Simon said.

Meg gasped.

His throat was dry, as if the memory of the smoke wrung every bit of moisture from his mouth. It had formed a wall, a living, breathing barrier. "It's how I got these burns. A guest set the fire accidentally, during a party."

He shuddered at the visions in his mind—pulsing music forever mixed with dancing flames. His jaw twitched.

Meg took his hand in hers and massaged it with care. "I am so sorry." Her voice shook. The light from the fireplace illuminated her tearstained face.

She pulled him into an embrace and held him, and he let her sympathy wash over him. "You don't need to hide from me," she whispered when they separated. Maneuvering her hand in between his, she tried to entwine their fingers together, but his were stiff and uncooperative and cupped around hers instead.

"Sorry. I don't think…"

"This is perfect."

He eyed her askance. "You have an odd idea of perfection."

She shook her head. "No, I know what to look for now. You're more than the scars, Simon. And someday, you'll realize I'm right."

****

Now what?

The question flitted through her brain, never far from the surface as she sat in Simon's lap and stared blankly at the screen.

But instead of the movie, she saw the hulking shell of the destroyed mansion. She couldn't fathom the pain he'd suffered. How could he look at it without thinking of everything he'd lost? No wonder he pushed everyone away.

Everyone except her.

She'd kissed him. More than kissed him. Devoured

him. And he'd done the same.

Her attraction had built for days. The kiss was unplanned, unexpected, and unbelievable. She dissolved into a puddle at the thought of it. His scent filled her nostrils, his warmth made her drowsy. She purred in satisfaction as he lightly stroked her hip. But after hearing about his past, how could she not confess hers?

"I can feel you thinking," Simon said as he buried his nose in her hair.

"Mm."

His breath against her neck sent delicious waves of desire once more curling along her spine.

He stiffened. "In case you have any regrets…"

She gave him no time to finish his thought. Instead, she covered his mouth with hers. He went from expressionless to pleased to aroused. Only then did she pull away. "I have no regrets. I'm…scared."

Cradling her face between his hands, he tipped his forehead against hers. "Scared of me?"

"No!"

"Then what?"

She didn't know how to answer his question without telling him about her past. No matter how much she owed him the story, she wasn't able to.

"You're excellent at avoiding my questions," he said.

She decided on distraction. Starting at the notch in his collarbone, she stroked over his pectoral muscles, paid attention to each rib as she worked her way toward his waist.

About halfway there, he covered her hand and pressed it against his stomach, which rose and fell in time with his breaths. "You're also good at distraction." He brought her hand to his lips and turned toward her. "Tell me what you're afraid of."

She wanted to focus on his lips against her fingertips, or his drown-into-oblivion silvery gray eyes. But he'd allowed her to see him and touch his scars. She couldn't brush off his trust.

"I'm afraid you won't like what you hear." A careless partygoer had set a fire and destroyed his life. Would he see the similarities and blame her?

He pulled away from her. "You're kidding me, right?"

She stroked his face, the face she became fonder of the more he let her touch it. "You don't know me." How could she ever explain the difference between who she was and who people thought she was?

"I want to." He held her close.

She swallowed. "People have wanted to know me before because of what I could do for them." It took her a long time to realize this. Too long.

He pulled away. "Why? What did you do?"

She shook her head.

"I'm not one of them," he said.

"No, you're not." She stared at her lap and wondered how to explain.

Simon tipped her face to meet his gaze. "I want to get to know who you are inside. I want to know your soul. The rest of it—it doesn't matter to me."

She blinked. "I know. But the memories are still there."

"So let's make new ones. Dance with me."

Chapter Fifteen

He turned on the stereo and pulled her to her feet. Her warm palm sent streaks of pleasure straight to his chest. He drew her close and wrapped his arm around her. He swayed, and after a few beats of the music, she joined him.

Her body was soft, her bones delicate, and he inhaled her lemony scent as he rested his cheek against the top of her head. "Hallelujah" played through the speakers. Simon's chest swelled as the guitar strummed, but whether from the beautiful music or the lovely woman in his arms, he couldn't tell for sure.

Meg looked at him. She didn't shudder and run away. She looked beyond his scars, and she was happy to be in his arms. He hoped this song lasted forever, because he didn't ever want this dance to end. Behind his splayed hand, he could feel her heartbeat, feel her ribs expand as she breathed, and then feel a vibration. He listened.

She was singing.

Under her breath and wildly out of tune as usual, but she sang.

He joined in, and his baritone rounded out the stereo music.

She pulled away from him and stared in accusation. "You can sing!"

He stopped mid note and nodded.

"You never told me you could sing."

"You never asked."

"I'm a terrible singer." The song drowned out the rest of her words as she lowered her voice, and he pulled away from her once more.

"What did you say?"

"I'm a terrible singer."

"No, after that."

She looked away. "My friends told me I sounded like a drowning cat."

He might have agreed or teased her because she couldn't carry a tune. But what kind of friend says that? What kind of man would he be if he agreed? He hugged her close and whispered against her ear, "You can sing any time you'd like."

"You like my voice?"

He smiled. "I like that you use it."

And for the next five minutes, they danced to her off-key, out-of-tune, beautifully awful rendition of "Hallelujah".

When she finished, Simon stood still and held her against him. She moistened her lips with her tongue, and he watched it run from one corner of her mouth to the other. Her lips parted, and her breath reached his chin. She rubbed against him, and he hardened. He didn't want to frighten her. She shifted again. This time, her movements were slow, like she wanted a reaction from him. His chest tightened. His heartbeat increased. His hips twitched against hers, and her pupils darkened.

When she bit her lip, he stifled a groan. He wanted her lip between his teeth. He wanted her mouth on his. He ran his hands along her spine and cupped her butt. It was firm and fit perfectly in his hands. As he pressed her against him, she whimpered, but rather than pull away, she edged closer.

She smoothed her hands from his head to his cheeks, and it was all the encouragement he needed. He touched his lips to hers, tasting her. Once again, he pulled her against him. As she tilted her hips, he flared his nostrils to draw in more oxygen. He should step away, take things slow, but his pulse pounded in his ears, her scent enveloped him. He couldn't. He lifted her and let her slide the length of his body until once again her feet touched the floor. With a moan, she arched and stood on tiptoe, as if she begged him to do it again.

First, he needed to find condoms—condoms he hadn't needed in ages. Leaving her where she was with a kiss as his promise he'd return, he found the box in the back of a closet, said a silent thank you they weren't expired, and rushed to her.

This time, he lifted her so their faces were level. Her eyes were deep blue, like his beloved ocean. Holding her, he turned toward the sofa, and she wrapped her legs around his waist, as if claiming him. If he had his way, he'd never part from her. Laying her on the sofa, he kissed her, gently at first, then harder. He shuddered with pent up desire. His tongue plunged into her open mouth. She tasted sweeter than he'd imagined. He mimicked what he wanted to do with other parts of his body. In and out, in and out, until she moaned and let her head fall backward. Her neck exposed, he trailed kisses across to her ear and along the creamy line of her neck until he reached her collarbone. He inhaled her scent. Blood rushed away from his head and made him dizzy with need. His hands twined through her hair as he admired her with his lips. He kissed his way from her collarbone until he met her mouth again.

"I want you," she whispered against his lips. Desire slammed through him like a physical jolt.

He pulled away, gave her one last chance to say no.

Her eyelids were heavy with desire, her lips swollen from his kisses, and her fingers sent chills along his spine as she stroked his neck.

Sliding his hands to her waist, he lifted the hem of her shirt to reveal her body. She raised her arms, and he slid the shirt off. He froze. It had been years since he'd been with a woman, seen her body. He wanted to do this right. As if she read his mind, Meg took his shaking hands and placed them on her breasts. The silky lace of her bra teased his stiff fingers, her soft skin enticed him, and he played with her breasts until her nipples hardened against his hands. He brought his face lower and buried it against her chest.

"One of us seems to be overdressed," she whispered.

Without breaking eye contact, he rose and pulled off his shirt. She covered his hands with hers, and he dropped them to his sides, waiting for her reaction.

A flicker of a frown crossed her face, as she leaned forward and traced every scar with her tongue, until his skin was wet, covered in goose bumps. If he'd thought he was turned on before, he'd been a fool. Blood rushed to his groin, made him dizzy with need. She removed her bra. In the recesses of his mind, he'd wondered how he would manage to unclasp it, but now, all he thought about was touching her. All of her.

He hugged her against him, skin to skin. The

difference in textures—hers smooth, his scarred—created friction as they rubbed against each other. He ran his hands along her spine and felt the indentation of her backbone and the individual vertebrae beneath the pads of his fingers. Her hands stroked his back, making his muscles quiver.

When her hands slid around to the front and fiddled with the snap of his jeans, he had his answer. Her button-flies were beyond him—there were too many small buttons to grasp, and his fingers slipped off them—and he pulled her face toward him in a kiss to ease his frustration. When he pulled away, her jeans were undone, and they both shed the remainder of their clothes.

Naked and silent he worshipped her from the tips of her cotton-candy-painted toes to the birthmark on her right hip, to her bellybutton, around her breasts, and to her blue-green eyes.

"You're beautiful," he said, his voice hoarse with need.

"So are you." She kissed his chest before she slid her lips lower and lower...until he risked ending it all right there against the sofa.

"It's been a long time," he ground out as he pulled her up into his arms, "and I want you to enjoy yourself, too." He lowered them onto the floor. The carpet was plush, a lucky coincidence, and he lay with her.

Free of clothing, their hands and lips ravaged each other. She kissed him, plunged her tongue inside his mouth, ran her hands over his skin. Even the scarred areas, where he had less sensation, felt her touch, and his breath became choppy as he strained against her. With a low, sensual hum, she pulled away and reached for a condom. The air cooled. He shivered as sensations overwhelmed him. A moment later, she climbed on top of him and rubbed against his body. He bucked as he reached the end of his self-control and gripped her hips. Her hands wrapped around his length as she slid the piece of rubber over him, and blood once again rushed in his ears. She rose and lowered herself onto him, inch by exquisite inch.

It took every ounce of his strength not to rise to meet her, but he sensed she needed to do this on her own. Gritting his teeth, he met her gaze as she took him inside of her. When she was settled, he expelled a breath that came from his toes, and they rocked in tandem. She slid her hands along his chest and around his neck and arched against him.

The need, which had built in him from the first time he'd seen her, which had frustrated him since they'd kissed during the movie, which he'd suppressed for what seemed like forever, overcame him. He slid a hand off her hip and caressed her stomach, enjoying the way it contracted beneath his touch. When she squirmed, he slid his fingers lower and stroked her skin beneath the soft hair until she gasped, arched away, and screamed. He pulled her toward him, kissed her, and felt the aftershocks running through her. Cradling her so as not to hurt her when he rolled, he flipped them so he was on top.

"Yes," she whispered. He increased the speed of his pumping until with one last shout, he released himself into her, heart thudding in his chest, sweat rolling down the sides of his face.

When he was spent, he rolled once again, and they lay on their sides still joined. Breath intermingled, skin slick, they looked at each other. Simon couldn't be sure what Meg thought, but what they'd done was indescribable. With his fingers, he memorized the slope of her eyebrows, the smattering of freckles across her nose, the divot in her upper lip.

She gave a drowsy smile. "Thank you."

"Again? What for?"

"For the new memories." She curled against his chest.

She thanked him? Did she have any idea what this meant? As he inhaled her scent, her breath provided background music, her skin warmed him, and he vowed he'd tell her as soon as she awoke. Because he couldn't keep something this amazing to himself.

****

Meg looked at the man who slept beside her. Curled around her like a cocoon, he kept her safe, protected, and showed her she was desirable, all at the same time. Now she understood what everyone talked about, what movies showed, what books described. No longer did she equate making love with hooking up, because for the first time, the man she had sex with stayed. She didn't have to wonder who should leave first, how long was too long, or wonder if he felt anything other than satisfaction from a physical release. As much as he'd wanted it for himself, he'd waited. He'd let her lead. He'd made sure she'd gotten her fulfillment before him. From the first moment she'd seen him, she'd known he was different. Today was the proof.

She studied him while he slept. There were more scars than she'd realized, and they were horrific, but they didn't repulse her. Instead, they filled her with sadness for what he'd been through and what he'd lost.

With one finger, she traced his face—across his brow, around his cheekbone, over his nose and to his lips. When they stretched into a smile, she knew he'd awakened.

"Hi," she whispered.

"Hi." He opened one eye and wrapped his hand around hers, pressing it to his lips and kissing it. "You are amazing."

Meg caressed the side of his face and brushed his hair off his cheek. "You're sexy."

He raised an eyebrow, and she kissed it.

"You make me feel desirable and secure, like I'm special, rather than any interchangeable living being who can scratch your itch and be done. You have no idea how appealing it is."

He hugged her close and ran his fingers through her hair. She shivered, and he raised his head. "Are you cold?"

"A little." As he rose, she protested. "No, don't go anywhere. Hold me."

He lay with her until the sun peeked over the horizon, its rays streaking through the window, creating yellow stripes along the floor and furniture. Simon groaned.

"As much as I'd love to stay here all day with you, I need to work," he said.

"I need to shower."

His mouth opened, and he watched her walk naked toward the stairs.

"I'd join you, but I'd never leave," he said.

She winked and went upstairs to the bathroom, showered, and dressed. When she finished, Simon was in the kitchen frying eggs. "Can I help?"

"Nope." He nodded toward the stack of mail on the counter. "You're famous."

Her heart stopped. "What?"

"Look at the paper."

Beneath a stack of yesterday's mail was a newspaper. With shaking hands, Meg pulled it out. *The Gull's Point Herald,* the town's weekly paper. The front page covered the harvest festival from last week. She scanned the article, but found no mention of herself, and she breathed a sigh of relief. The article covered the library's sale, the Halloween festivities, and the yearly anonymous donation to the town's schools. She turned the paper over. Below the fold were photos from the day. Her breath knocked out of her once again. The center photo showed people perusing the books in the library. One of those people was her. She gripped the paper hard and shook.

And like a flipped switch, she returned to that awful day. The press of the crowd, the flash bulbs, the shouts to "turn this way," people grabbing her clothes.

And the awful thump.

Her hands sweated. She couldn't breathe. Too many people crushed her.

"Here are your—Meg, what's wrong?" Simon dropped the plate on the table with a clatter and knelt beside her. "Sweetheart, what is it?"

She jerked. Why was Simon there? He wasn't there the last...she looked around and noted the cheery yellow kitchen. Her palms were slick with sweat, and she rubbed them on her legs. "My photo. I'm in the paper."

"I know. It's a nice picture." His voice was low.

Images of other photos flashed through her mind. Mug shots, perp walks. No, those were not nice pictures. "No."

Simon slid the paper from under her hand and looked at it, a frown on his face. She couldn't tell him. He'd never understand. "I can't be here. They can't have used my photo. I have to go." She rose, and Simon reached for her. She struggled against him. "Let go of me!" Once again, she pushed against the crowd and tried to break free. Her breathing increased, and she gasped for air. Simon released her. She stumbled and banged into the table.

"Meg, stop. What's wrong?"

She tried to stay calm, but she couldn't.

"Meg, come here. Please."

Simon's arms were outstretched. All she wanted was the safety he offered. But she couldn't stay here, she was scared. If anyone learned who she was...

He walked toward her, each step careful, as if he waited for her to bolt. After what seemed like minutes, he drew her against him. His body was warm, his heartbeat steady.

"Easy, sweetheart, easy."

Despite her terror, his words penetrated her brain. He'd called her sweetheart. He crooned a soothing hum. His touch calmed her.

"Tell me what's wrong. Why are you scared?"

She took a shaky breath. "It doesn't matter. I have to go."

"What? Why? Meg, talk to me. Let me help you."

She laughed and teetered on the edge of hysteria. Pulling away from him, she reached for the door. "You can't. No one can."

Because all she needed was one person to recognize her photo, and everything she'd run away from would return.

****

What the hell? One moment she walked into breakfast, all rosy from sleep, sex, and a shower, and the next she raced from the house like the hounds of hell chased after her.

He walked over to the window. She stood on the cliff and stared into the ocean. Her hair blew in the wind, and she hunched over from the cold. *She should have taken a jacket.* Should he take her one? She wanted to be alone. With a sigh, he walked away from the window. Maybe the cold would give her an excuse to return. To him.

His gaze fell on the photo in the paper. She stood in line, a stack of books in her arms. Her hair was pulled beneath a white wool hat, and her black pea jacket was draped on her shoulders. She looked pretty. He brought it closer to the light but couldn't find any hidden clues. She'd never seemed the type who was concerned with her appearance anyway. Then again, he couldn't be sure. She always dressed well, even when they did yard work. Had a bad picture sent her running?

He hunched his shoulders, trying to rid his approaching anxiety. They'd had sex. He shouldn't relate it to her reaction, but a part of him couldn't help it. They'd connected in more than physical ways, at least to him, yet she'd run from him. Did it mean as much to her? Was it because of his scars?

His phone rang. It was Claire. Maybe she'd have insight.

"Hello?"

"Well, it's good to know you answer phone calls from me, despite how you hide from me when I visit."

He pinched the bridge of his nose as a wicked headache formed.

"I'm not in the mood, Claire. Did you call for a specific reason, or to bust my balls? Because if it's the latter, I'm hanging up."

"What's wrong?"

"It's Meg." He relayed what happened this morning, leaving out the sex. "I don't know why she freaked out like she did. She left before we could talk, and I don't know if I should go after her or let her be."

"Hmm, I saw the photo and thought she looked great. I'll call her later and see if I can find out what's bothering her. In the meantime, go take her a coat and use it as an excuse to see if she'll talk to you. But you, more than anyone, should be able to understand if she doesn't want to talk."

"Yeah, well it's different when you're on the other end."

"Welcome to my world, Simon."

He snorted. "Did you actually call for a reason?"

"Oh yeah, what do you think of my comments on your designs."

"I haven't had a chance to go over them, but I will."

Simon hung up, grabbed Meg's coat, and walked to the beach. She'd moved on from where he'd seen her last and for a moment, he thought she'd left the beach. But he found her and approached her with caution. He was afraid to invade her privacy.

"You left your coat inside," he said, his voice low. He held it out and waited.

She faced away from him and made no move to take it. "Thank you."

"Do you want it?"

She shook her head. His vision tunneled as her rejection of him penetrated his brain. His arm remained outstretched, the coat hanging like a curtain.

"What can I do to help you?"

"Nothing."

Chapter Sixteen

Seated on the window seat the next day with an
unread book on her lap, Meg figured she could either
isolate again—leave Gull's Point altogether or stay in
Simon's house until her own house was fixed—or she
could make the most of her time with him until the shoe
dropped.

He was the first person who had been kind to her in
a long time. When he'd followed her outside with her
jacket, all she'd wanted was to take it from him, wrap
her arms around him, and hide in his warmth and
solidity. She wanted his company—to see him smile,
listen to his voice. No matter how reasonable or rational
option one might be, she went with option two.
Chances were, once he knew who she was and what
she'd done, she'd be alone anyway. It was only a matter
of time before it happened.

Decision made, she closed her book, unfolded from
the window seat, and knocked on his office door.

"Come in." His voice was deep and modulated.

She peeked around the door and watched Simon
turn away from her. Her stomach plummeted. Whatever
walls she'd knocked down, he'd rebuilt. If he repaired
her house as fast as he did his emotional walls, she'd be
back there in no time. She blinked before she entered
the darkened room. Once her vision adjusted, she
walked over to his desk.

"Hi," she said.

"May I help you?"

Oh, what a loaded question. But she knew he meant it in the most perfunctory way. He always protected himself.

"I'm sorry," she said.

She moved closer but left a foot of space between them. Simon didn't move to lessen the distance, but he didn't lean away.

"There are things about me you don't know. But you've been kind to me. I should never have responded to your attempt to make me feel better about the photo in the way that I did."

He furrowed his brow and gripped the armrests, stretching the scarred skin on the backs of his hands. His shoulders rose. He met her gaze for the first time, pushing his hair away from his face, his jaw tight.

"I've been kind."

She nodded. He shoved his chair away from his desk, rose, and paced the small space between his desk and the wall. Meg followed his movements and noted his resemblance to a caged tiger. Any moment he would pounce.

"So you fucked me to thank me? For being kind?" A vein in his neck bulged. His voice was deceptively quiet, but he spit out each word like a bullet.

Each one hit their mark, and she jerked as if shot. Her jaw dropped, and her pulse pounded in her ears. Didn't he notice how much she cared for him? She'd given plenty of signals. In fact, she'd fought the attraction for what seemed like forever. She'd reacted to the photo, not to their intimacy. He should know that...unless it didn't mean nearly as much to him as she thought.

"I don't repay kindness with sex." The words left a bitter taste in her mouth, and she spun around and stomped toward the door.

"Wait." His voice was low, but his tone made her stop. "Why, exactly, did you have sex with me?"

She rested her hand on the doorknob, its cool metal a contrast to her overheated palm. He didn't know?

"Because you turn me on. Because when I was with you, time stood still, and I couldn't breathe when I was away from you. You made me feel valued and worthy, and you saw me for myself rather than what I could do for you. But if I'd known you thought so little of me, I never would have touched you, much less had sex with you."

His body was against her before she stopped speaking. He pulled her against him and wrapped his arms around her, cocooning her within the warmth of his body. She stiffened and pulled away, but his grasp tightened. He rested his cheek against the crown of her head, crossed his arms across her chest, and stroked her upper arms. She gritted her teeth.

"I was an ass," he whispered. "What we shared was special. It's been a long time...I can't think straight about you. Fear kicks in before sense does. I hate being scared. I got angry and lashed out. I never meant to hurt you. What I said was horrible. Please forgive me."

His solid chest and warm body melted some of her anger. She inhaled, listened to his steady heartbeat and his sincere tone. What he'd said earlier stung, but he'd asked for her forgiveness. Was she ready?

"Please, Meg."

She pulled against his hold. This time, he let her

go, tipping her chin. His pain mirrored her own and she relented.

"I'd like to stay. Here. With you."

Relief flooded his features. "Good."

It was what he said now. But what if he knew her secret?

****

Simon sat at his computer and typed an email to CAST. He'd repaired things with Meg. Now it was time to get things moving with Claire. She needed help, and if she wouldn't accept his, he'd find another way.

"You guys saw the information I sent you earlier about my friend's open-space project. Since the animal rescue project is a no-go, I'd love to address this project. What are your thoughts about it? Can we help without directly linking my name at this point? She's reluctant to accept assistance from me, but probably won't object to a third party."

He didn't want to outright lie to Claire and would let her know his involvement once she'd accepted CAST's assistance. In fact, helping her would barely put a dent in their funds. Their tax accountant would probably urge them to find additional projects for this tax year. But what was the point of all that money if they couldn't enjoy their investments?

Chapter Seventeen

Simon ushered Meg outside right after sunrise the following morning. Dressed in jeans and a hoodie sweatshirt with dark sunglasses, his tight jaw betrayed his discomfort. It had been days since she'd been out of the house, and the thought of venturing into the world filled her with a mixture nerves and anticipation. Why he chose to leave now, though, was an interesting question. Especially after his behavior yesterday.

"You have a car?" she asked, as he held open the door. She'd never expected a guy as reclusive as he was to own a vehicle. Then again, she hadn't given it much thought.

"I have a Jeep."

She arched a brow at his emphasis of "Jeep."

"Sorry, caffeine hasn't yet kicked in. Yes, I have a car. I used to have several—an Aston Martin, a Porsche, and a few others. Now I have a Jeep."

"But where do you go in it?" His groceries were delivered. Claire brought him library books. What did he need a Jeep for?

"Not too many places. But occasionally, I drive around in the middle of the night."

She wanted to say more, but remained silent. The idea of him driving around in the dark, alone, filled her with sadness.

"Where are we going?" she asked when he pulled

into the gravel drive and stopped at the mailbox.

"My favorite spots. Ready for an adventure?"

"An adventure? In public?" Her voice squeaked, and she swallowed. Usually it was he who avoided attention. This time, after the shock of her photo in the paper, she had an overwhelming desire to run to the safety of his house.

He reached over and patted her knee. "Trust me?"

After a moment, she nodded. *I can do this.* Simon pulled onto the two-lane winding coastal road. On one side, cliffs overlooked the sea. The sun peeked over the ocean, lightening the sky to a dusky gray—traces of yellow streaked throughout the horizon. The cliff face reflected in the stark beauty awed Meg. On the other side were rolling hills, dotted with houses and farms. The peacefulness soothed her. As they got closer to town, he gripped the steering wheel until his knuckles whitened. She wanted to soothe him, but at the same time, her stomach knotted. After last night, she was hesitant to initiate contact. How would he take it? Now that they approached civilization, would they see anyone? She stared at her lap; hands clutched tight.

Luck was on their side. They sped through town without encountering anyone. The road led through tall pine trees, and they drove inland, over streams and rivers. She rolled down the window and breathed in the varied scents of salt and pine. It was a beautiful drive, and once on the road, Meg relaxed. She leaned against the seat, one hand rested on her thigh, the other on the armrest on the door. The breeze blew through her hair.

Simon reached for her. She clasped her hand around his, the last of her nerves easing. Something inside of her loosened, and she realized how much she craved contact with him. They passed most of the ninety-minute drive in companionable silence, interspersed with comments about the scenery. Meg made a few attempts to learn their destination. But Simon was irritatingly closed-mouthed about it, and eventually she gave up

When they once again approached the coast, she tried again. "Where are we going?"

He smiled. "My favorite destination."

"Which is?"

"Botanical Gardens."

Of course. If she could think straight, she would have concluded a landscape architect loved botanical gardens. But she'd been too caught up in the lull of the ride and the changing scenery after days of isolation in the house.

Twenty minutes later, they pulled into the parking lot and found a space at the far end. Turning off the engine, he faced Meg and took her hand in both of his. "When I was in the hospital recovering from the fire, one of my therapists learned I was a landscape architect. She knew about this garden's therapeutic horticulture program, gardening therapy for people with all kinds of disabilities. I came here every day for months. It was the only thing that kept me sane. And it helped with my fine motor skills, although they'll never be the same." He pulled his hands away from her, wiggled his fingers, and stared at them as he turned them over.

Her throat clogged as she thought about the work required to recover from his injuries. Had he been alone? He never mentioned other people. How lonely and scared he must have been.

Meg looked at him with compassion. After another moment, she took his hands in hers, he squeezed and continued. "Anyway, I come here once in a while to say hello and walk through the gardens."

"To say hello?" She dropped his hands. "I didn't think you let anyone see you."

"Jed is different."

They exited the car, and Simon paused. Meg scanned the gardens and walkways. This early in the day, the place was empty. Birds chirped and flitted from branch to branch. Inhaling, she smelled hydrangeas and the last roses of summer. Simon pulled his hood up and took her hand in his. He led her through the raised stonewall gardens, and she admired the autumn plants, herbs, and flowers. As they walked toward the pavilion, a man appeared.

"There's Jed." Simon pulled off his hood and raised a hand as the other man approached. The older gentleman barely reached Simon's waist, with gray hair and beard and bowed legs.

"Frankenstein! It's good to see you." Meg frowned.

"You, too, Garden Gnome. Let me introduce you to Meg." Simon bent over, and the two shook hands. Meg stifled a gasp but must have betrayed her shock because Jed laughed—with his cheeks spread wide and the pitch of his voice, he sounded like a hyena. As she looked between the two men, she regained her composure and greeted Jed in a shy manner. Jed and Simon must have a special relationship if they could call each other names. She wrapped her arm around Simon's waist, and he exhaled.

"Pleasure to meet you, Meg. Simon, it's been a while."

"I thought we'd wander the gardens a little after we visit with you."

Jed nodded and walked with them to the pavilion. In the shade, they sat on benches while Jed told Simon about his latest gardening projects.

"How about you?" Jed asked.

Simon shrugged. "Nothing's working."

Meg frowned. Simon disappeared into his office for hours at a time. She'd assumed he was busy. But if nothing was working, what was he doing?

Jed looked from Simon to Meg. "Well, you might like to look at the new plantings over there." He pointed toward the north corner. "We've got special exhibits, but I assume you'd prefer to walk the paths."

Simon nodded and rose. "We'll stop to say goodbye before we leave."

Jed turned to Meg. "I'm glad to have met you. Simon's a lucky guy."

Meg blushed. "I'm pretty lucky, too. It was nice to meet you."

Simon took her arm and led her in the direction Jed pointed. The walkways were deserted, and Simon was in his element. She warmed as he talked about how much he admired the flowers and herbs, climbed on walls to get a different view of the plants, or crouched to see the stems, mulch, and rocks on the ground. His excitement was contagious, and although she didn't know what half of the plants he named were, she admired their colors and textures.

After a few moments, he pulled his phone from his pocket and dictated notes. When he put his phone away, Meg spoke. "These gardens are beautiful."

"Want to see what I planted when I was here?"

His work was here? "I'd love to." She hadn't seen any of his finished projects, just his plans. She was eager to see what he'd done. He led her once again toward the pavilion. In one area, sweeping in an arc, were leafy plants and flowers. At first glance, they looked as if they'd landed there any old way, but as she studied them, a pattern and a purpose emerged. Varying shades of greens and golds merged with reds and oranges.

She gasped. "They look like flames! They're beautiful."

He smiled. "When they're in full bloom in the summer, you can see the design more clearly."

He'd created this because of his accident. To think he'd intentionally planted to make a thing of beauty out of destruction…her chest swelled, and she blinked away unwanted moisture. She wrapped her arms around him. "Does it help you to look at it?"

He shrugged. "Now, it matters less to me. Then? I needed to remove the image from my mind and this formation helped. Instead of seeing the fire that destroyed my family, I turned those visions into something that created life—flowers that stunned and soothed at the same time. Plus, the ability to do the work myself was therapeutic as well."

"You're amazing." She looked around, turning in a slow circle. "I don't think I could ever do anything like this." The car accident and flash bulbs flickered in her mind once again. What beauty could she possibly create from her experience?

He massaged his hand. "Took way longer than it should."

"And probably involved a lot of cursing."

Simon huffed. "In the beginning, I made sure to only be here alone. Toward the end, Jed allowed a few select people to work here at the same time as me. But never children. Because, you know, language."

He draped his arm around her as they meandered along the pathways. At the sound of voices, Meg turned toward them, but Simon steered them away from the other visitors.

She wanted to protest, to convince him he had nothing to fear from strangers, but she acquiesced. She, of all people, understood his fear. Instead, she followed him and absorbed the beauty of the flowers and the gentle scents that mixed and mingled around them.

The pathway wended toward where they entered, and soon the pavilion came into view.

"I'm going to talk to Jed for a minute. Will you be okay on your own?"

"Of course," Meg said. "Take your time."

****

Simon left her admiring the hydrangeas and found Jed in one of the potting sheds. The loamy, musty smell, sharp with a tinge of fertilizer, made him take a deep breath. He'd missed this.

"Mind reaching that for me?" Jed pointed to a large planter on a high shelf.

Simon grabbed it and followed Jed outside.

"So I assume you want to talk to me," Jed said. He nodded toward Meg. "She seems nice."

"She's more than nice."

Jed's face crinkled into a lopsided smile. "So what's the problem?"

"I'm empty."

"What do you mean?"

"My designs, my inspiration. I can't find them. My clients are satisfied enough, but I'm not. I can't figure out how to infuse my designs with more than 'plants.' "

"Maybe the problem isn't with your designs."

Simon sat on a bench. "What do you mean?"

"You've been alone for a long time now."

"I don't know if I'm ready."

"Yeah, you do. Your heart knows, in any case. Your thick head might take a little longer to come around though."

"What does Meg have to do with my designs?"

"Maybe nothing. Maybe everything. Landscape architecture is your passion. And passion needs nurturing. Think about it."

He returned to Meg. Jed was right. It was time to let Meg in and do what his heart begged him to do, even if it meant kissing her senseless in public. Heat flooded through him, and he coughed.

"Everything okay?" Meg asked.

He blinked and forced himself to focus. "Come on, I have another stop in mind."

"Will you tell me or do I have to guess?"

"You'll have to be patient."

"Ugh." She poked him in the ribs.

Reaching for her, he tickled her waist. With a shriek, she ran for the car. Simon chased her. He caught her as she was about to open the Jeep's door, swung her around and brought her against his chest, claiming her mouth with his own. Their kiss deepened. Blood rushed in his ears and his body hardened, as he let her slowly slide along the length of his body.

Her eyes were deep blue with desire, and her lips were redder than normal. "You're such a tease," she whispered.

He grinned, handed her into the car, jogged around to his side, and turned the key. They pulled onto the winding road and followed the coastline. Waves crashed against the rocks.

"Look how beautiful that is," Meg cried.

Simon smiled at her excitement.

"Oh, look." Meg pointed to a shack on the other side of the road. "Crab cakes. I'm starved. Let's stop."

He took a deep breath and pulled onto the gravel lot, crowded with cars. A line of people waited their turn at the shack. Turning off the engine, he gripped the steering wheel, heart pounding. He could do this.

"Tell me what you want, and I'll order," Meg said.

"No." He put a hand on her arm.

"It's fine." She covered his.

Relief and shame washed over him. As much as he wanted to refuse, to conquer his demons and exit the car, he took advantage of her offer and watched as she placed their order.

As they ate, her cries of delight over the succulent crab covered his shame and should have made their food delicious. But it was dry and tasteless because he couldn't get past his fear of being seen.

When they finished, Meg threw away their trash, and he once again pulled onto the road. Ten minutes later, he turned off onto a rocky trail. When it became too bumpy, he stopped the car, and they walked. He took her hand in his and led her toward the rocks. The breeze and the pounding surf and her soft hand in his took away his dismay, and as mist from the waves sprayed his face, he relaxed at last and inhaled.

He pointed to her right. "There's an old abandoned

lighthouse over there. It's got great views. Come on."

He helped her over slippery rocks and led her to the gray, semi-collapsed stone lighthouse. Hardy weeds grew along its foundation and within its crumbling cracks. An exposed wall displayed spiral steps that used to lead to the top. Now it was an empty shell.

Like him.

He dropped Meg's hand and stared at the lighthouse, his gaze following its jagged lines and edges. His heart twisted at the exposed emptiness.

"What's wrong?" Meg approached, concern on her face. He wanted to smile as if it were nothing, but he couldn't.

His throat squeezed shut and pressure built in his chest. And then her arms surrounded him and rubbed his back, while her head rested against his chest. He wrapped his arms around her and held on tight. They listened to the crashing surf until Simon pulled away.

She turned. "Tell me what's wrong, Simon."

"I meant this to be for you." He watched the white froth bubble and let the ebb and flow of the tide hypnotize him. "I'm lost. I've spent all my time alone. Nothing makes me happy."

"Nothing?"

He looked at her upturned face, her expression somber. "Well, there is one thing."

She linked her fingers through his, ignoring how clumsily his hands worked. "Maybe your heart knows it's time to return to the world."

He pulled away, but she objected. "Not all at once, but a little at a time. You've survived spending time with me."

He smirked. "Yeah, it's been a real chore."

"So maybe we expand a little bit." She pointed around her. "You left your house."

"There's no one here. And when there was, you took care of it." He could feel his face heat, and he looked away.

"Because caring about a person means supporting them. If ordering a silly, but delicious meal made things easier, I'll happily do it for you."

He hugged her and pressed his lips to her hair. How was he this lucky? And how could he manage to keep her?

"So maybe the next step is to open your world a tiny bit to other people. Like Claire."

Claire. She came to the hospital and his house. She called over and over again, and ignored his grumpiness. And she emailed all the time.

"What's going on inside your head?"

He startled. He was used to solitude, thinking through things in his mind. But Meg was here with him. "Claire is the one person who has never let me retreat from her."

"Sounds like she'd be the perfect person to start with."

"I don't know if I can do it alone."

"You have me. We could invite Claire and her husband to dinner."

He swallowed. "I don't know."

"Look, even the most ill-mannered people know not to make fun of the person who feeds them. Not without a taster at least." She grinned, and the pressure in his chest eased. "And Claire's not ill-mannered. Neither is her husband, I'll bet. The first five minutes will be awkward. Anyone can handle five minutes.

Even you."

"Well, when you put it that way."

****

"Whose stupid idea was this, anyway?" Simon mumbled as he pulled the sweater over his head.

Meg smoothed it over his broad back, and taking him by his shoulders, turned him around to look at him. Denim jeans hugged his thighs and should be considered hazardous to a woman's health. A cream cashmere sweater showed off his tapered waist and his wide shoulders. A perfect specimen of maleness.

But his face. Meg stifled a gasp.

Now, his face was twisted in a scowl. His jaw was clenched. His body loomed in front of her. He'd cause anyone who didn't know him to run in the opposite direction for reasons unrelated to his scars.

Sliding her hands through his hair, she massaged his scalp and dragged her hands over his cheeks and waited until he unclenched his jaw. Cupping his face, she looked at him head on.

"It was my 'stupid' idea, and it will be okay." She worked on the clasp of her necklace.

He took her hair in his hands and raised it off her neck. With a smile of gratitude, she clasped the necklace, and he let her hair fall against her shoulders. She met his gaze in the mirror before she spoke again. "You get one free pass for calling what I do 'stupid.' The next time, it'll cost you."

"If your next idea is like this one, I may have to sign my bank account over to you," he grumbled.

"Ha! You think I'd charge you money? Money is way too easy."

He sat on the bed and rested his foot on the

opposite knee. "Really?"

She watched the tension ease from him. "I'm not someone you want to mess with."

"I'm learning." He pulled her collar away from her neck, and trailed kisses over her skin that sent shivers along her spine. "Definitely don't want to mess with you." He nibbled her ear. She tilted her head to give him better access. "You're scary. Terrifying."

When he took her blouse from her jeans, she pulled away. "Later."

"Now."

"They'll be here in five minutes."

"Cancel."

"No. You're not using sex to avoid the dinner."

With a sigh, he stepped away, and Meg fixed her clothes and hair. As they made their way downstairs, the doorbell rang. Simon froze. She gave him an encouraging smile. "They're your friends, not the firing squad."

"Says you," he grumbled.

She opened the door and gave Claire a welcoming hug. With a smile at Tom, she ushered them inside. Simon took a step toward Claire.

"Oh my God!" Claire gasped.

Simon jerked as if slapped.

"Your hair! It's so long!" Claire stepped forward and reached out a hand to touch it. The contact must have flicked a switch because Simon laughed. It was deep and rumbling, as if it came from his toes. His entire body shook, and his long hair shimmied.

After several moments, Simon pulled Claire into a hug and shook Tom's hand. "It's been too long."

"Since your last haircut?" Meg asked. Everyone

else burst into laughter.

"No, since I've seen you two." He nodded toward the other couple and put his arm around Meg.

"It's about damn time you invited us over." Tom lifted a covered dish he'd placed on the side table and handed it to Meg. He held her gaze for an extra beat, and Meg hid her discomfort.

"It's been forever since I've been here," Claire said. "Can you give us a tour?"

With a nod, Simon led them through the house, highlighting the changes he'd made. Meg's cheeks warmed as she remembered the first house tour Simon gave her. This time, he didn't hide his face, and he pushed his hair behind his ear at one point, as if he disliked its distraction.

In the living room, Meg sat next to Simon, and he brought her as close as possible without pulling her into his lap. She leaned into him and listened while Claire and Simon dominated most of the conversation.

"Do you remember that time we played hide and seek," Claire asked, "only we were at the big house—that's what we called the mansion," she said. "You decided instead of hiding in the big house, you'd hide here." She rolled her eyes. "It took me hours to find him. When I finally did, he sat at this table, eating cookies!"

Tom and Meg burst into laughter.

"Hey, I got hungry," Simon said. "You took too long."

Tom made eye contact, and she smiled. Simon was in his element. He was more animated than she'd ever seen him. And obviously, she'd imagined Tom's stare when he first walked in.

The timer in the kitchen beeped, and Meg rose. "Dinner's ready."

"I'll help you," Claire said.

Away from the men, Claire gave her a hug. "Thank you."

"For what?"

"For returning my friend to me. I've missed him."

"Thank you for showing him he could do this," Meg said. "And for showing him I was right," she added with a grin.

"We have to stick together—girl power."

They brought the steak, salad, and bread to the table where everyone quieted while they tasted their food.

"So, Meg, where are you from?" Tom asked.

His gaze pierced hers and the discomfort returned. The piece of steak she chewed lodged in her throat, and she choked. Chair legs screeched against the floor as Simon rushed to Meg's side, but she waved him away, tears streaming, and took a gulp of wine. Clearing her throat, she turned to Tom. "I moved here from Texas."

"You don't have a drawl."

Meg fidgeted. "No, I don't. I grew up on the West Coast. Beaches, shopping, movie stars."

"Venice Beach or Hollywood?"

Claire placed her hand on Tom's arm. "Tom, you're an editor, not an investigative journalist."

He nodded. "Didn't mean to pry."

"Anyone want more wine?" She gripped the bottle to still her hand.

"So, Simon, I could use your help presenting your plans for the garden to the committee," Claire said. "How about you come to a meeting and let everyone meet my great landscape architect in residence?"

He looked at her sideways. "How about you don't push your luck?"

Tom snorted. "She's good at that."

"I'd rather give you the money," said Simon.

Claire shook her head. "No, you don't. After the way people treated you, you said you wanted nothing to do with them."

Simon shifted in his chair. "Maybe I'm coming around. Let me help."

"As much as I appreciate your offer, I can't let you do it, Simon. Not with the way the town has ignored you for all these years. The committee is trying to raise enough money to buy the property from the town."

"How much money do you need?" Meg asked.

"About a hundred thousand dollars," said Claire.

"Which is why I'd like her to consider my help," Simon interrupted.

Claire colored. "Even if I did, the committee is uncomfortable with the idea of one person purchasing the land. What's to stop him or her from exerting control over how it's used?"

"You know I wouldn't."

Silence stretched for a few seconds before Meg spoke.

"Have you tried a big fundraiser?"

"What kind?" Claire asked.

"Something on a much larger scale. I handled publicity for a living. I could help you plan an event if you want."

"That's fabulous. Thank you!"

"Simon, maybe you could show me the plans you have?" Meg asked.

"I haven't finalized them yet. They're giving me trouble."

She remembered his conversation with Jed. "Well, when you get to a point you can show me."

Claire turned. "I hope you finish it soon."

He shrugged. "There's something missing. I'll figure it out."

"We'll still be able to present at the next town council meeting, though, right? My boss is counting on it."

Simon's jaw tightened. "You will."

"I'm glad the land will be put to good use," Tom said. "Less chance of kids messing around over there and getting into trouble, or screwing it up."

Simon cleared his throat. When she looked at him, she noticed his white knuckles where he gripped his fork. Meg placed her napkin on her lap, smoothing it to remove all wrinkles and straightening it to align just so. She rested her hand on Simon's knee.

"I think kids would hang out on the beach," Meg said.

Tom nodded. "They do, mostly. And there are the town-sponsored events, like fireworks over 4th of July and the bonfire during Memorial Day."

When Simon's fork dropped, she noticed his face, white around the scars.

"Sorry." Tom glanced away.

Simon rose and grabbed his plate.

"I've got it," Meg said. Claire joined her, while Simon and Tom remained at the table.

"Sorry Tom put his foot in his mouth," Claire said under her breath.

"What do you mean?"

"The bonfire. It's how Simon's house and family were destroyed, and he got all those burns. His family hosted bonfires on the mansion grounds before the accident. Now the town hosts an official one, but Simon wants nothing to do with it."

More of the mysterious pieces of Simon's past fit into Meg's puzzle. And evidently, Tom had a habit of unintentionally stirring up trouble. Although she sympathized with Simon, she was glad his stares at her and questions about her background meant nothing. In the doorway, she called to the men, "Do you all want dessert now?"

"Yes!"

After dessert, Claire and Tom got ready to leave. Claire pulled Meg into a hug. "Thank you again for returning my friend to me."

She walked over to Simon and gave him an even longer hug. Reaching for his face, she grasped his jaw and turned his face to one side and the other. "You've got a very dashing, dangerous look going on here, like a boxer who's been in the ring one fight too long."

Simon, who stiffened at her touch, huffed, but the spark in his eye told Meg he wasn't offended. *Go Claire!*

Tom shook her hand and pinned Meg with his stare. "It was nice to meet you. Thanks for the invitation."

Meg and Simon stood arm in arm at the door and watched their friends pull away. When their taillights faded into the distance, Simon pulled her close and kissed the top of her head.

"If I say you were right, do I have any chance of living it down?" he asked.

"Don't count on it. I'm liable to mention it at the most inopportune times." She clasped her fingers around his waist and rested against his chest. His heart beat strong and steady. "You amazed me tonight," she whispered.

"I couldn't have done it without you."

"And Claire."

He chuckled as he walked with her into the kitchen. "I thought it was over right there."

Simon washed while Meg dried.

"So, maybe you'll break out of here once in a while?"

"We'll see."

****

With any luck, the library would be closed. He clasped his hands in his lap as he watched Meg's car eat the road in front of him. As if she'd read his mind, she'd insisted on driving today. At least if he'd driven, he could have changed course and taken them somewhere more romantic, more interesting…and more secluded. But this morning, she'd suggested she drive and when he'd begun to argue, she'd said "*please*." What was it about the word on her lips that killed him every time?

His hopes were dashed because they drove around for ten minutes before they found a parking spot.

She turned off the engine, unbuckled her seatbelt, and opened the car door.

He remained where he was.

She leaned into the car. "You coming?"

No.

He climbed out of the car. Had he not been concerned with making sure his hair covered his face and no one was around to see him, he would have appreciated the chance to get out of the tiny box she called a car. He would have made a wiseass comment about her trying to cripple him by forcing his body to bend in ways he didn't think were possible before now to fit inside. He might have inhaled the autumn air and appreciated its crispness.

Instead, he pulled up his hood, stuffed his hands in his pockets and walked with her into the library. He kept his gaze focused on her back as he followed her through the foyer and into the adult section. He didn't stop to talk to anyone and made no eye contact.

"Any books you're interested in?"

She'd stopped, and he looked around. They were in the biography section and between two stacks, which were deserted. For the first time since they entered, he took a deep breath.

"I have no idea where the horticulture section is," he said.

"We can find it."

"No, thanks."

"But it might help you with inspiration."

He sighed. He hated when she was right. Well, not really. But right now, it annoyed him. "Fine."

"Let me pick one or two books first."

All too soon she was finished, and they left the sanctuary of the particular deserted stacks he hid in and meandered through the more populated areas of the library. After the slowest hunt in the history of mankind, she stopped. "Here it is." They were in the agriculture section, and lucky for him, there wasn't anyone else here, either. In this small library, the section encompassed three shelves. He took a half-hearted look around, until he spotted a book that piqued his interest—*Flora Illustrata.*

"I didn't know they had this one," he said. "This won the American Horticulture Society's Book Awards."

He pulled it off the shelf and flipped through it, glimmers of ideas flashing through his mind.

"While you're here, I'm going to find the romance section," Meg said. "I'll be right back."

He nodded, already absorbed in the book.

A rustling behind him made him realize he wasn't alone. Someone bumped into him. He turned. A teen gasped.

"Uh, s-sorry." The kid retreated.

Simon's face burned.

"Man, you should see the face on that guy," the teen said to his companion as they left the section. "He was a monster."

Laughter covered whatever else the kids said, but Simon heard enough. Images of his time in the hospital right after his injury flashed through his mind, along with the grief, embarrassment, and shame around people he'd known his whole life. He backed out of the stacks and bumped into another person. The man dropped his pencil. Simon scooped it into his hand and gave it to him. The man's face reddened before he took the writing implement and hastily turned away. Nothing had changed.

Coming here was a mistake. Didn't matter how much time had passed, or how old the people were, no one saw him as anything other than a monster.

A hand on his arm made him jump.

"I'm ready to go if you are," Meg said.

He swallowed. She looked happy here. He didn't want to tell her what happened. He didn't want to show her how right he was. His stomach churned. She'd done so much. The last thing he wanted was to destroy her happiness.

They made their way to the checkout counter. Simon stood off in the corner while Meg borrowed the books and chatted with the librarian. He was a coward, but it was the best he could do right now. He wasn't doing this again.

Chapter Eighteen

Meg was giddy with excitement and bounced on her bed, unable to keep still. Her plan worked. She'd made a difference. She wasn't propping up the work of someone else. She did it on her own, for the good of someone else, and it worked.

She paced to the window and looked at the crashing waves. Her mind raced over possibilities—restaurants, movies, strolls through town. It wasn't easy, and it wouldn't happen overnight, but there was a future outside these walls for Simon to grasp. She, more than anyone, knew what it was like to be imprisoned, knew how rejuvenating freedom could be. Little by little, she'd help Simon reenter the world, to relearn the benefits of a community, to expand his horizons.

And now he'd be able to work on the land development project like Claire wanted. And his gardens. Oh, he'd complete his gardens, and they'd be beautiful. He'd find himself, he wouldn't be lost anymore. He'd be happy.

She couldn't wait for their next outing.

****

Simon walked into his office. The sight of it almost made him ill. Everything he needed was here to ensure he never had to see anyone again. All the latest technology, all the gadgets, and none of them made him happy.

Opening a hidden panel within his desk, he removed a photograph of him with his parents taken before the fire. He didn't recognize himself anymore. When he'd awakened in the hospital and taken one look at his face, he'd shouted in horror. Despite what the nurses and doctors told him, and no matter how much plastic surgery he might agree to, he'd never look the same. When he'd walked the halls of the hospital and rehab and saw the horrified or pitying glances from other people, he realized he was better off keeping away from everyone. When a group of friends surprised him with a visit, their reactions seared themselves into his brain and affirmed his decision.

But then Meg came along. She'd provided companionship and friendship and...more. Maybe. He could fall in love with her if he let himself. He couldn't think of anyone he'd rather be with. Sex with her was amazing. She'd given him Claire, and her husband as well. She'd taken him to the library. His venture in public, and the walk through the botanical gardens, gave him enough inspiration to help him work. After poring over the book he'd borrowed, he had more ideas than he'd had in months, which helped him further develop his plans for Claire. Maybe his feelings for Meg helped, too. They crept in when he didn't expect them to, brightened rooms when she was in them, improved the taste of food when they shared a meal, and lightened his steps when they walked together. Jed said he needed to open up. As usual, Jed was right.

Still, his attempts to go out in public weren't without pitfalls. He avoided everyone at the botanical garden. And the crab cake shack? He couldn't exit his car. And when people did see him, they still reacted badly.

Thanks to the speedy contractor, her house was almost finished, much faster than anticipated, which meant she was leaving. Back to her house, to her life, not hidden from the world. How could he be a part of her life? Unless she moved in with him and stayed here. His chest lightened with the thought of waking every morning next to her, spending his days with her, his nights with her. Her laugh. Her smile. Her touch. Except he stayed in his house. She'd get bored, remaining sequestered with him, no matter how much she might care for him. If he loved her, as he suspected he did, he couldn't make her unhappy.

As for public excursions, he'd gone to the library, and it was a disaster. How could he bear the looks and horrified expressions of the public? Thank goodness Meg wasn't with him to hear what those kids said, but he might not be so lucky next time. He couldn't expect her to deal with it or the burden of him. He was dependent on her, and it would get exhausting. She'd been the friendly and outgoing one, talking to everyone they'd met, sparkling with enjoyment as they escaped from his solitary life. She deserved a life unfettered by his fears.

****

Their last night, she lay in bed with Simon, tucked against him. His heart beat against her ear as she drew lazy circles across his chest and toward his abdomen. His skin jumped beneath her finger, and finally he grasped her hand in his and pressed it against his lips.

"You're killing me," he whispered.

"I didn't think you could feel it."

"I can feel it enough that you're driving me mad."

"Good."

He raised an eyebrow. His pupils were dilated, and she suspected he was as affected as she was.

"Want to keep tickling me?"

She swallowed and struggled to put together a coherent thought. "N-no."

He rolled them over until he was on top of her, his arms supporting his weight, his warmth enveloping her. Restlessness and pressure built as he hardened. She rocked her hips and created a delicious friction between them. He trailed kisses across her eyelids and her cheeks until he reached her breasts. He sucked first one, then the other until her breath came in gasps. She arched against him, whimpering. She dragged her hands along his back and cupped his buttocks, and he whipped his head up, nostrils flared.

He stared at her, as if he waited for permission. "Please," she whispered and reached for the foil package. When he handed it to her, she opened it and sheathed him, his harsh intake of air signaling how much her touch affected him. Finally, finally, he entered her. They rocked together, each stroke and thrust building toward exquisite climax. Sparks exploded behind her closed lids, and her muscles gave her sweet release. Only when she'd reached her own peak did he withdraw and drive himself in again, shouting her name.

She lay with him once again, panting, floating in the blissful aftereffects of their coupling.

Moonlight streamed through the window and created luminescent white shards of light in the otherwise shadowy room. "When I leave tomorrow, you'll be able to come to my house." She gave him a wicked grin. "There are new rooms to christen."

His tone, when he spoke, was forced, and her heart thudded in her chest. "You don't have to go, you know," he said. "I could rent the house, and you could stay here."

She angled to see his face, his expression. For once, he held her gaze, his features intense. All the oxygen evaporated. He asked her to live with him. Her throat squeezed, and her mouth quivered as she imagined how hard it must have been to suggest. This lovely man valued his solitude, and now he wanted to spend it with her?

With a trembling hand, she caressed his cheek. He pulled her toward him. If she stayed with him, she would hide away. She needed to go into the world, reclaim her place, and exert her independence. As much as she loved Simon, she couldn't use him as an excuse to hide. He deserved more.

She traced the outline of his lips. "You don't know how much I wish I could say yes to your wonderful idea."

He rose on one elbow and ran his hand along her body from shoulder to hip, leaving a trail of goose bumps. "Say it."

"I can't." Her throat clogged. She pushed the words from her mouth. "I value my independence as much as you value your solitude. For too long, I've hidden from my past. I can't do it anymore. It's too tempting never to leave this place and let them win. And I can't."

She kissed his forehead. "Besides, if I don't go, I'll never drag you out of here." *Please tell me you'll join me. Tell me you won't withdraw again.*

"I'd never prevent you from having a life, Meg. I love your independence and your strength."

"We could explore life out there together. There are restaurants to eat at and towns to walk through, and…"

He grasped her hand. "I know what everyone in town thinks about my looks. Every child thinks I'm their monster under the bed. But you could do everything you need to do and still come to me at night."

"And watch while you hide yourself away? Simon, I love you too much to be your enabler."

"What do you mean?"

She sighed and pulled away from him, covering her body. "I mean, people change."

"My face hasn't."

"But you have. You've said you needed to find inspiration. Hiding in your house won't help."

"Hiding in my house?" He raised his voice, the rasp giving away his fear. "You think it's easy for me to stay here without anyone around me? I hate it, Meg, but I hate the stares and the whispers more." He sat in bed and watched her pace the room. "I'm not ready. I don't know if I ever will be."

She swallowed. "I know." She couldn't force him to be what he wasn't. But she also couldn't encourage the man she loved to do what was hurting him. "This won't work, will it?"

"You have no idea how much I wish it could."

She turned away from him and blinked away tears. Silence filled the room. She wished she could force him to be what she needed.

"I could get you a job if you'd like."

She shook her head no. "I'm not good with plants."

He huffed. "I have contacts in other industries. I'm sure one of them could connect you with something."

"I don't want anything too big." No matter how much she needed money, the idea of "contacts" scared her. If Simon was as wealthy as he indicated, his contacts might know people from her old life. She wanted small and simple. Besides, how many contacts could Simon have if he never left his house?

"So what will you do?"

Without him? She didn't want to contemplate it, so she focused on the job aspect. It was a good question. "I'll see if the library needs anyone, like Claire said. If they don't, there are plenty of shops in town that could use help, I'm sure. Or I'll waitress. And maybe you'll visit me while I work?"

He smiled, but it didn't reach his eyes, and she knew his answer before he said anything. No.

Chapter Nineteen

Simon stood on the porch and stared at Meg's house. He'd walked her over an hour ago, gotten her settled, and come home alone. And ignored every fiber in his body that screamed at him to take her with him.

He'd spoken about the quality of the workmanship, about her plans to get a job, and about his next steps for the land development project. He'd reassured her he'd bring over anything she forgot.

He didn't tell her how much he cared about her, or why he would miss her. He didn't tell her how much he needed her. He hadn't begged her to stay.

If he did, would it make a difference? Would she stay with him? Probably not. Would she change her mind about going into the world? Definitely not. It would pull her in another direction and force her to make a decision she shouldn't have to make—between her life and his. It wasn't fair.

It wasn't fair to him either. He needed time alone again to figure where to go from here. She'd given him a glimpse of normalcy, and it was better than he'd expected. Going out gave him a hint of the freedom he could have if he was brave enough to grasp it.

But to have a normal life, he needed to do a hell of a lot more than sneak around a library, avoiding people. He wasn't sure if he could do it. In the meantime, he'd let her go, if only across the road. It might kill him, but it was the only way for her to live. He'd kept his thoughts to himself.

Meg deserved freedom. He couldn't cage her. He'd put himself into a self-imposed prison, not only because of the way he looked, but in order to keep order and stability in his life. He couldn't risk recklessness. Look what happened last time. Recklessness killed his family and burned his house to ash. He had to be careful and cautious.

If he wanted to be part of her life, it was time to escape from his cell walls.

****

"Meg?"

She turned away from the library's front desk toward the sound of the voice. "Claire!" The librarian behind the desk gave her a disapproving glare, and she lowered her voice. "I wasn't sure if you were working today."

"Just finishing. What are you doing?"

"Job application. I don't know if they'll hire me because I don't have a library science degree." *And I have a criminal record.*

Claire straightened. "We always need assistance. I'd love to have you work here." She pulled Meg away from the stiff, older lady. "Don't worry about your background. Give me your application when you're finished, and I'll pass it along to Bill. He's the one who makes the final decision."

Meg finished the application and gave it to Claire.

"Actually, publicity experience is a bonus," Claire said as she took the paper from Meg.

Thinking about her previous publicity experience—patronizing trendy clubs with society girls who looked for attention—Meg swallowed the bitter taste in her mouth. "I guess it depends on the kind of publicity you need."

"So you're not one of those people who believe all publicity is good publicity?"

Meg shuddered. "No."

"Let's grab a cup of coffee," Claire suggested.

They left the library and sat in a blue booth near the window in the sandwich shop. After they ordered drinks, Claire leaned forward. "You look sad. What's wrong?"

"Simon and I broke up." It was the first time she'd said those words out loud. Her throat and chest ached. "I moved into my house this morning." She sipped her coffee, but her stomach rebelled.

"Oh no!"

"After dinner with you and Tom, and our trips out, I thought he was ready to break out of his shell. But he climbed right back in and is wedged in tighter than ever." She gripped the edge of the table.

"Simon's walls are hard to breach, Meg. The fact he's let you in as much as he has, and as fast as he has, is amazing. But I don't know how much more he can do."

"I know. I can't push him. I care for him, but I can't lock myself away. I spent too many years molding myself into what other people needed. I can't do it again."

Claire studied Meg over the rim of her coffee cup. Meg wanted to squirm. Her new friend was easy to talk to, but it didn't make Meg any less nervous.

"You keep alluding to your past," Claire said, her voice slow and deliberate. "Was your life before so different?"

What a loaded question. "The short answer is yes," she said.

"And the longer answer?"

Something about Claire told Meg she could trust her. "Out in LA, it's all about who you're seen with, what people can do for you." She ran her finger around the rim of her cup. "Who you are inside gets buried, especially if you want to protect it. You become what others need from you." She shrugged. "I was good at it for a time, and I paid a horrible price."

"Don't give up on Simon. You two can still work on your relationship from separate houses. Maybe with you no longer under his roof, he'll see how much he misses you and do something about it. I know he cares for you. It was obvious at dinner the other night."

"I can't force him, Claire. He has to want to do this on his own."

"Look, most people develop a relationship and then live together. You two have done it backward. The few days you spent in his house sped everything up. Maybe if you take things a little slower, he'll acknowledge what he already feels."

"He needs to change because he wants to, not because I want it."

****

"So have you given anymore thought to presenting your plans to the committee?" Claire's voice over the phone was a welcome distraction to Simon, after he spent most of the day in his darkened office, moping about Meg.

"Why can't you do it?"

Her laugh made Simon wince. It was higher and

lighter than Meg's. It made him miss Meg's rich, throaty one more.

"I'm not one of the premier landscape architects in the country. Besides, without Meg around, you'll have more time to finish them. Speaking of Meg, I hope you don't let her get away."

Her mention of Meg knocked the wind out of him.

"I don't need you playing matchmaker, Claire."

She remained silent. When he caught his breath again, he focused on her request. There were many reasons to say no, but they were all petty. If Simon were honest, he couldn't blame people for their initial reaction. His actions and demeanor probably contributed to their opinions of him.

"I'll finish the design for you. But I won't present the plans to the town, and don't ask me about Meg. It's not part of the deal."

There was silence on the other end of the line. "Okay. Oh, and before I forget, Tom wanted me to tell you he needs to talk to you."

"What about?"

"I have no idea. But he said it was important."

Chapter Twenty

Simon braced before he opened the front door. Swinging it wide, he forced what he hoped was a smile on his face.

"Hi, Tom. Come on in."

"You look thrilled to see me," Tom said and held out a hand.

With a snort, Simon shook it and led Tom into the living room. "Don't take it personally. I'm still adjusting." He froze as the words slipped, but Tom nodded, and Simon relaxed. Simon might not know her husband as well as he did Claire, but Tom was a friend.

"Right. Wanted to talk to you about Meg."

His heart skipped a beat before it thudded in his chest. "What about her?"

Tom leaned forward and rested his forearms on his knees. "I'm not sure. She looks familiar. What do you know about her?"

Everything and not nearly enough. "We didn't sit around quizzing each other, Tom." *We have passionate sex, and she leaves. Every. Damn. Time.*

"At dinner, she said she'd lived in Texas for a while but she had no accent. She mentioned California. Do you know where she lived in between? Why'd she move? What does she do?"

Simon held up his hands. "Whoa. Okay, hold on. I have her rental forms here somewhere, but without knowing more, I'm a little concerned about sharing private information."

Tom sighed. "You're right. Ever get a feeling, though, you know a person and you can't figure out how? Maybe I read about her."

He felt like he'd known Meg forever. "Her last name is Clancy if it helps, but I doubt Meg's done anything to give you cause to be concerned."

"She's too smart to be without a plan or a job. Any idea why she came here?"

Simon shook his head. "Have you asked Claire these questions? The two of them are friends."

Tom laughed. "She thinks I'm nosy. Says Meg is a private person and deserves to be." He rose. "I'm sure you're both right. I wish I could put my finger on what's eating me." He turned to Simon. "It's good to see you again."

As Tom got into his car, Simon couldn't help the niggle of doubt along his spine. Tom was a newspaper editor. What happened with Meg to draw his attention?

****

Simon frowned so hard his face hurt. He relaxed his facial muscles with effort and walked closer.

Claire had invited him to the movies with her and Meg. His initial response had been an automatic no. He'd refused her invitation, softened a little so as not to offend her. And she'd given in, far easier than usual.

But when he'd gotten off the phone, he'd felt like a coward. Again. He'd spent the rest of the day trying to persuade himself to go. He hadn't been successful until right before the movie began, which was why he frowned. Because when he'd arrived at the movie theater, he'd seen Meg walk inside, talking to a group of people.

She'd looked...carefree. She should socialize, attend parties, meet friends. For the first time, he understood what she'd miss if they were together. What he'd missed. His stomach clenched, and he took a deep breath. His hands cramped at his sides, and he strove to relax them. Having Meg alone those few days made him forget that side of life existed.

He'd intended to approach Meg and Claire and let them know his plans to join them after all. But the other people with them distracted him. They made him remember things, remember what he looked like and how his looks provoked reactions. Instead, he'd bought a ticket to the movie and sat in the back and watched Meg and Claire and the group instead of the movie.

Claire knew them. He didn't think they were from school, but it was a long time since Simon went about in town and things changed. He couldn't be sure. From his vantage point, he watched everyone in the group socialize. They occupied an entire row in the theater. Popcorn jostled, and the guys tossed a kernel or two at each other, reminding Simon of puppies who couldn't be contained in a cage. They weren't unruly per se...just carefree. Meg appeared to enjoy herself with them.

He watched a few of the guys, gauging their interest in Meg. She was beautiful, he couldn't deny it. He could wax poetic about her for the rest of his life, and he still wouldn't do her justice. Did the guys have a crush on her? Were they girding themselves to ask her out? Sour bile rose in his throat, and he wished he'd stopped at the concession stand to buy a soda. Meg wasn't his. She was free to be with anyone she wanted.

He inhaled. He and Meg were...nothing. If he were honest, they were barely friends. He hadn't spoken to her since she moved into her house. What right did he have over her? None. But it didn't protect him from shards of jealousy. He wanted her smile directed at him.

He walked over to them when the credits rolled, and the house lights came on. "Hi. Did you enjoy the movie?" he asked the women.

"Simon!" Meg's low exclamation warmed him, but he kept his attention on the people near them. At the sound of his voice, they turned, and as expected, froze when they made eye contact with him. His heart thudded in his chest. Perspiration formed on the back of his neck, and he tensed, the urge to flee overwhelming. Before he could turn away, everyone rose and left the theater. Claire and Meg made hasty introductions. Simon paid little attention to their names. They did their best to avoid looking him in the face. Perfect.

"I introduced Meg to friends I know," Clair said. She lowered her voice. "She attracted interest."

Simon eased the tension in his muscles. What was Claire doing? Is this why she'd invited him? Meg's hand brushed his. He grabbed it, not caring they weren't together anymore. The feel of her fingers in his made him want her more than he already did. After a moment, she slid her palm from his. The space it left filled him with longing.

He blinked and turned. "Want to come over?"

"We're going for a bite to eat." She nodded toward the rest of the group. "You can join us if you'd like."

He ignored the weight in the pit of his stomach, and the doubt in her voice as she extended the invitation. She didn't think he'd join them, and she was right.

"You go and have fun. I'll see you around."

He watched Meg catch up with them. The group left the theater together, and he resisted the urge to call to her. He was too proud to beg.

Chapter Twenty-One

"What's going on with you and Meg?"

Simon frowned when he opened his email the next day and read Claire's message.

"I told you I don't want to discuss her."

He pressed send and scrolled through his other emails, but his mind was on Claire's message. Why did Claire have to butt in? He was giving Meg space. He still needed to solve his own issues—how to rejoin society without being reckless—not to mention whether he could bear to be in public. She was making a life here. He couldn't stop her.

His email dinged. "Are you sure? Because you looked like you wanted her."

"I won't discuss this."

"You can't pull her in two different directions. You're either broken up or you're together."

"Claire, we're friends."

"Then define the boundaries. Because it's not fair."

Did Meg complain? Had his reaching for her hand bothered her? He wanted to ask Claire. His fingers hovered over the keys, but he paused. Using Claire as a go-between was how the old Simon worked. Could he talk to Meg without making her feel bad?

He grabbed a jacket and walked along the lane to her house. The ground was pocked and pitted from the tree removal and construction equipment. He'd have to fix it soon. At least get the holes filled so he could plant grass in the summer. He noticed the empty flower beds in the front of the house. Great landscape architect he was.

Striding to the porch, he rang the bell and thrust his hands in his pockets while he waited. He should have called first. What kind of carelessness made him arrive without warning? He strode down the lane to his house.

That night, after he cleaned up dinner, he dialed Meg's number. He missed her. She'd worked her way into his soul, and life wasn't the same without her here.

"Meg, it's Simon."

"I was on my way out."

"Never mind." Disappointment ran through him, and he cursed.

"I've got a little time. What's up?"

I want you. I need you. Come back to me. "Are we okay?" He rolled his eyes at his words.

"What do you mean?"

"I don't know." He was an idiot.

She sighed. "Did you like the movie?"

He took a moment to track her thoughts. Oh, the movie he didn't watch. "Yeah."

"I'm glad you came."

"Claire invited me." He paused. "I'm trying."

"I know. But don't do it for me."

"What do you mean?"

"I mean you have to want to get out there for yourself. Not for me."

Did she mean she wasn't hanging around waiting? He didn't expect her to, but on the other hand, a huge part of him hoped she would. He was used to solitude, to the orderliness and the routine of his days. Being out there meant a certain recklessness and an abandon he wasn't sure he could handle.

"It's your choice, Simon." Her voice was soft, like velvet, and he let the sound of it wash over him.

He wanted to ask her to come over but thought it pathetic. *I'm too scared of the possibilities to go out in public, so come hide away with me in my lair?* He didn't want her pity.

"Look, I've got to go," she said, her voice a whisper.

When she hung up, he stared at the black TV screen as the room darkened around him. He *was* a coward.

****

Meg resisted the urge to throw her phone across the room. Her living room had been repaired and reeked of fresh paint. She didn't want to damage it with a phone-sized dent in the wall. Not to mention if she broke her phone, she'd have little chance of contact with Simon again, even if the added difficulty of her father and Vanessa reaching her was a welcome change.

She didn't intend to make it easy for Simon. He'd come to the movies, and she'd gone out afterward with Claire's friends. Today she told him she was busy, when she had no plans. If her goal was to show him she could do without him, she did a damned fine job. He'd done what she'd asked. Every time they went out in public, it was for her. Well, other than the botanical garden. She couldn't have him do something uncomfortable because she asked. He had to want to change.

She loved him. Admitting it didn't hurt or surprise her anymore. Listening to the deep rumble of his voice on the phone made her knees tremble, and an ache bloomed low in her belly. She wanted him. She needed the cocoon of his arms around her. She missed the sound of his heartbeat against her ear, the feel of his breath against her neck, the rasp of his fingers on her skin. Nothing aroused her like his scent.

Ugh! These thoughts didn't help. She went into the kitchen and made a cup of tea before bed. Except she was too restless for a soothing drink. Turning off the kettle, she grabbed a jacket, shoes, and a flashlight and went outside.

A hint of the winter filled the biting air. Wind from the ocean blew her hair in her face. She walked with care, shining her light in front of her so as not to trip. She stopped when she reached Simon's house. She didn't mean to end up here...or maybe she did. She stood still. Outdoor spotlights illuminated the eaves. Lights from within showed he was home, and through the gauzy curtains she could see movement as Simon walked within. A shiver ran through her as she watched him, and it took every ounce of willpower not to run to his door and knock.

She squinted as light from a flashlight shone in her face. A moment later, Simon lowered it.

"What are you doing here? I thought you went out." His tone was a mixture of surprise and annoyance, and she retreated a step.

"I...I was...out for a walk."

"You shouldn't walk outside alone in the dark. Anything could happen."

She frowned and turned in a circle. "We're in the middle of nowhere. What could possibly happen?"

"You could trip without anyone knowing. You

could fall into the ocean…"

She threw her hands in the air. He stopped talking. A frown creased his already lined face. "You're kidding, right? Fall into the ocean? What do you take me for?"

Simon ran a hand through his hair and sighed. "Meg, think about the consequences."

"Consequences? Are you kidding me?" Flashes from that night played in her mind—the mass of people and flashbulbs, the accident, the decision she made— and her heart pounded in her chest. "I never stop thinking of consequences. I'm the least reckless person you'll ever meet." Without another word, she raced to her house.

****

Simon watched Meg's figure retreat until the darkness swallowed her. What the hell? He wanted her to be careful, and she jumped all over him. He followed her, his long strides eating the distance between them until she jogged onto her porch and into her house. He knocked on the door she'd left wide open and followed her into the kitchen. She was making tea, her movements sharp and angry. Yanking the cabinet door open, she grabbed a mug and slammed it on the counter.

"Meg."

She didn't look at him or utter a sound and moved away from the stove. Randomly banging things, as if the sound or the action gave her comfort, she shoved a chair and opened and slammed drawers. Arms folded against his chest, he watched her as she made her way around the kitchen. It was the one time she calmed, although tension stiffened her posture and altered her movements, removing their natural fluidity and grace. Once she put the kettle on the range, gentler this time, she bowed her head. She looked tinier than usual. His heart ached.

"Please tell me what's wrong. What did I say?" Simon approached her from behind with care. With a few inches of space between them, he caressed her shoulders. They rose as she inhaled, her breath shaky. He pulled her toward him, until she leaned against his chest. She stayed there a moment before she pulled away.

"Don't!" She spun away and refused to meet his gaze.

"Don't what, sweetheart?"

"Don't try to take care of me." Her voice wavered. "Don't call me 'sweetheart.' I'm not your girlfriend. Don't tell me I don't think about consequences. I've always been the careful one. Always. And it got me in more trouble than you can imagine."

He caught her and turned her around until she faced him. Anger shimmered, drew his attention to Meg's flared nostrils and the mutinous set of her jaw.

"What do you mean being careful got you into trouble? What kind of trouble?"

Tears spilled, and he wiped the salty trail with his thumb.

"Never mind."

"Meg, talk to me."

"I can't." She blinked away the tears.

"Why not?"

"Because it will change things."

"I thought you liked change," he said.

"Not this kind."

"And you won't tell me what 'kind' you're talking about?"

She shook her head again.

Anger flared. "So you expect me to change, to venture out of my comfort zone, but the second I ask you anything that makes you uncomfortable, you shut down." He clenched his hands at his sides. "Maybe it's not me who needs to change, maybe it's you."

He turned. If she wouldn't talk, there was no point in staying. Except...the way she carried herself hinted at a vulnerability, one he hadn't seen before. It made him think she needed him and lessened his anger.

"Will you be okay?" He wanted to stay with her, but he didn't know how to ask.

"Of course I am! I'm capable of taking care of myself."

He held up his hands and waited for her to calm. "I know. But you're the one who walked over to my house. I thought, maybe...well..." Dammit, he was a fool.

"You thought what?" She stood with a hand on her hip.

All he wanted was to beg her to let him take care of her. "I thought maybe you missed me." His voice was no more than a whisper. He looked past her, rather than see her disdain. When she moved toward him and stood toe-to-toe, he had no choice but to stare directly at her.

"I do. But it doesn't change anything."

Arousal and anger fought for control. He squashed the guilt that sliced his chest as he dampened his desire. He'd never wanted her more than he did right now, though.

She bit her lip before moistening it with her

tongue, and he stifled a groan. Her irises deepened to midnight blue with specks of silver.

"I shouldn't want you this much," she said. She placed her hands on his chest. Like a brand, they burned through his shirt.

He pulled her close. "Do you want me to stay?" he asked.

"I want to do the right thing and say no."

He walked toward the door.

"Where are you going?"

"Home," he said. "No matter how much I want to stay." The last part he whispered. He was pushing his luck, but he didn't care.

"Don't go, Simon."

Maybe if he stayed, he could fix things. "Claire said we've done things out of order, and I can't blur the lines between friends and…more."

She walked over and hooked her fingers through his belt loops. Pulling his hips against hers, she rubbed against him until he hardened once more.

"I don't care what Claire says."

Chapter Twenty-Two

Meg's body vibrated. Shock and longing pulsed through her. Had she dangled such a blatant come on to him? They'd broken up. What happened to giving him time to find himself? To waiting until he found the motivation for *himself*, not her?

He stroked the sides of her face, cupped her chin to tilt her face toward him. She couldn't bear to pull away. He brushed his lips against hers. She tasted a hint of mint on his breath. Their noses bumped. He smiled against her mouth, not breaking contact. Shivers ran along her spine and warmth pooled in her belly as she reveled in the feel of his lips against hers.

Just a kiss. That was it. She'd tell him to leave as soon as they finished their kiss.

His mouth devoured hers, his lips firm yet gentle. Their tongues met, explored, teased, made her yearn to get closer, deeper. She whimpered, the sound absorbed into their kiss. His hands trailed from her face to her neck to her breasts. His thumbs made maddening circles. She wanted more.

They were not supposed to do this. Nope. Not right now. Because she needed to find herself, he needed to come out of his shell, and they needed to determine if their lives could work together. She pulled away.

"Do you want me to stop?" His voice was hoarse and raw.

Meg swallowed. Her brain screamed yes, her heart screamed no, and her mouth remained swollen from his kiss. Her tongue still tasted of him.

With a shuddering sigh, Simon removed her hands from around his waist and retreated a step. If she didn't already love him, his actions sealed the deal. Because no matter how much he wanted her, no matter if she were the one to initiate this, he would stop.

"No, I want to."

Tomorrow they could return to individual growth.

Taking his hand in hers, she led him to her bedroom and turned on the bedside table light. The soft glow cast his face in a geometric relief of lines and planes, and accentuated his scars.

She brought him over to her bed and pushed him so he sat on the edge. She stood between his knees, took his face in her hands, and finished the kiss he'd begun earlier. He moaned—or was it her? He met her thrust for thrust. Their tongues danced together as their kiss got hotter and deeper. Her skin burned. She needed to be closer.

Pulling away with another moan, she dragged the waist of his shirt out of his waistband and drew it over his head while he rose. She ran her hands across his shoulders to his pecs, reveled in the rough texture of his hot skin and sculpted muscles beneath her palms. She trailed kisses along his scars on his abdomen to where his skin disappeared beneath his jeans. He let his head fall as she worshipped his body. Skin and scars, the different textures beneath her lips drove her mad.

"This feels good," he said, his voice ragged with desire.

He reached for her top, and she let him pull it off.

His hands held her waist while he buried his face in her breasts. She massaged the base of his skull and stroked her fingers through his hair.

"Take off your bra," he whispered, and she complied. As he sucked first one breast and then the other, she whimpered and edged closer.

When he paused, she unbuckled his belt and opened his jeans. He let her remove them, before he reached for hers. He fumbled with her fly button, but she let him work it loose on his own, and his triumphant smile reminded her of a wolf about to devour his prey.

She shimmied her hips as he pulled off her jeans and stepped out of them. Pressing against him, she marveled at how their bodies adapted to each other's shapes like pieces of a puzzle. His hands roved across her shoulder blades. She grabbed his arms, forced him to keep them at his side.

"Wait," she whispered against his lips.

Starting at his collarbone, which was as high as she could reach unless he bent over, she licked a trail from shoulder to shoulder. She splayed her hands across his chest and teased each of his nipples with her teeth, listened to him hiss and felt his bulge harden and lengthen against her stomach. Making her way lower, she licked, kissed, and blew small breaths across his skin, watched it ripple beneath her touch. When she reached the waistband of his underwear, his stomach sucked in convulsively, and she caressed his backside. As she lowered his underwear, he bucked when her hand touched his shaft. Focused there, she admired the velvety soft skin, the pulsing heat, and the size as he grew beneath her fingers.

She knelt, brushed her lips against him, and he

groaned until once again, she reached his collarbone. This time, he bent and met her lips with his own, grasped her elbows and drew her against him. His body trembled from her teasing. He wound his hands through her hair. Her hands fluttered before landing on his buttocks. His muscles clenched and unclenched, his hips rocked against hers, creating delicious friction between them.

"I want you," she whispered.

Tilting his head, he plunged his tongue into her mouth, and she whimpered at the sensations running through her body. Her knees shook and knocked against his, and he lifted her against him.

He lowered them both onto the bed and flipped her beneath him. His desire mirrored her own. She reclined against the pillows and watched as he sheathed himself with shaking fingers. When finished, he rose above her, a question in his gaze. She nodded, and he lowered into her, teasing her until she could not breathe. When he was finally inside her, she wrapped her legs around his waist and rocked her hips against him.

"Baby, when you do that…" he rasped.

She did it again, and reached for him. He threw his head back and bared his teeth as he hissed.

"Do you like this?" She wondered at her own temerity.

"Oh God, yes."

His voice rasped. The sound increased her desire. Pressure built low within her and brought her closer to the edge. Her respiration increased and joined his choppy breaths. Her skin tingled and burned where their bodies touched. She dangled on the edge of the abyss and tilted her hips, taking more of him inside her as she reached for something just out of her grasp.

As if he knew what she needed, he flicked his fingers over her folds, stroked her until the pressure built beyond anything she imagined.

"Simon," she mouthed, and he covered her lips with his own. Another stroke of his fingers and she screamed his name as pulses of desire exploded, creating rippling aftershocks in her body. She'd barely drawn another breath when his shout matched hers, and he pumped into her.

Their bodies slick with sweat, they collapsed, limbs entwined, breaths mingled. As she curled against him, his heartbeat echoed in her ear. He stroked along her spine, and she shivered as her skin cooled. He drew her toward him and flung the blanket over both of them.

They should talk—about how things hadn't changed, about the last time she was "careful," about her need to brush her teeth. But this closeness, this intimacy, was what she missed most while they spent their time apart. She remained silent, adrift in the fluttering aftershocks.

****

The light of the bedside lamp enabled him to watch her sleep. Dark lashes created shadows against the delicate skin beneath her eyes. Auburn hair fanned across the pillow, reminding him of a bird of paradise flower, except he preferred her deeper, richer hue. The faint smell of sex hung in the air along with her sweet scent, and he inhaled deeply. The sheet draped across the curves of her body, and his breath caught as her shape beneath the sheets—its hills and valleys—gave him inspiration he'd lacked.

Sliding from under the covers, he riffled through

his jacket pocket for a pen and paper. He preferred his computer—drawing was a bitch with his hands, but his idea wouldn't wait so he knelt next to the bed, sketched as fast as he could before Meg awoke. When he had enough to jog his memory, he stowed the paper and pen in his jacket pocket and crawled into bed. He contemplated what she'd let slip earlier—how being careful got her into trouble.

What kind of trouble? Did she miss out on an opportunity? Why didn't she tell him about it? She'd said she didn't want things to change between them, yet she wanted him to change his habits and get out more. Why the paradox?

He raised his arm and let it hover over her. He wanted to wake her and drag the information out of her to understand. But instead, he extinguished the light and shifted in bed to get more comfortable. He hated it when people forced him to do what he didn't want to do. What right did he have to do the same? With a sigh, he burrowed into his pillow and shifted his thoughts to the muted sounds of the ocean and rolling waves as he drifted into unconsciousness. He wanted answers, but he needed her here more.

The next morning, sun streamed through the window, and she was gone. Again. The bright glare of the white sheets highlighted his solitude. Why did she always leave after sex? Sitting in bed, he looked around the room. His clothes were folded and stacked on the chair. She took such care of him. He got out of bed, put on his jeans, and walked into the kitchen.

She made coffee.

"Morning, sleepyhead," she said. She smiled over her coffee cup, one arm wrapped around her waist.

Simon forgot to breathe.

"What's wrong?" she asked.

He shook his head. "Nothing. Sorry. Morning."

She handed him a cup of steaming coffee. "Here, first drink, then talk. I find it works better that way."

With a nod, he did as she asked, and refrained from telling her as long as he looked at her, he'd never have a coherent thought in his mind. But the caffeine helped, or maybe it was his desire not to look like a babbling idiot. Either way, he finished his coffee and put his cup on the counter, confident in his ability not to drool over her and to be able to string words together in a coherent fashion.

"This is much better," he said.

"I can tell."

Meg cracked eggs into a bowl, and with a start, Simon grabbed her arm. "Wait a minute. You prepared breakfast for me when you stayed at my house. The least I can do is prepare yours when I'm here."

"You don't have to…"

Simon led her to the table and pushed on her until she sat. "Relax."

Ten minutes later, he served them both French toast and fresh fruit. As they ate in silence, he debated whether or not to mention their conversation from last night. With a final swallow, he spoke.

"So, about last night—"

"—you're right, it shouldn't happen again."

"Wait, what?"

"It was a mistake. I shouldn't have led you on, not when we've broken up. It's confusing. We need more time apart to figure things out. It wasn't fair to you."

He straightened in his seat. His shoulder and neck

muscles tensed. "You led me on?"

Her neck grew mottled under his stare, and for once in their relationship, she was the one to avoid eye contact. He would have reacted if what she said didn't blow him away.

"Yes, anger and adrenaline and whatever overcame me, and I came onto you and made you think things had changed," she said.

"So what does it mean?"

"It means neither one of us has answers yet. And sex only complicates matters."

Of all the "reckless" scenarios he'd thought of, he never believed her to be reckless with sex…or his heart. Oh sure, it was under the guise of kindness, which made it hurt more. She thought she did him a favor by having sex with him and setting him free to find out what he wanted. Was sex so meaningless she didn't want to discuss their relationship or their feelings?

The soft and buttery French toast hardened in the pit of his stomach. With deliberation, he crossed his utensils on the plate, wiped his mouth, pushed back his chair, and rose. His height let him tower over her. He took advantage of the psychological power it gave him over her.

"I'd like to thank you," he said, "for taking such good care of me." His words were soft, barely above a whisper, and deliberate. "I appreciate your sacrifice. I won't bother you again."

****

That afternoon, Meg dragged herself to the library for work, when all she wanted was to crawl into bed. Simon was the one man, the one person, who made her feel like she belonged. She'd never belonged before, ever. And she'd taken advantage of him, used him for sex, to try to hold onto the delicious feeling for one last moment before she let him go. She'd hurt him more than she ever intended. She owed him an apology, but before she could say anything, he'd stalked away. She'd raced after him and called to him. But he ignored her and kept walking.

She'd gone into her bedroom and climbed into bed. Unfortunately, the sheets still smelled like a combination of sex and Simon. A delicious combination, but it made her stomach ache. With a shuddering sigh, she'd climbed right out, stripped the bed of everything, and run the laundry. She cleaned the kitchen, too, but her body still ached for him. In between the dishwasher and the washing machine, she called him, but he didn't pick up. She texted him, but he didn't answer. Her email remained in the ether. She walked to his house and knocked on the door, but he didn't answer. Which left nothing for her to do but resume her life, and that meant go to work.

For the next three hours, Meg shelved books and helped patrons research and borrow books. Somehow, every book she touched reminded her of Simon. Who knew there were so many various types of books—in every section—with flowers on the cover? The self-help books mocked her with their dime store advice. Communication was touted as the key to every issue. But what if he refused to talk to you? The library patrons made things worse. One older man came in looking for Scrabble strategies. That was a thing? When her shift finally ended, she wanted to throw away every book she owned and become a reality show, binge-watching junkie.

"Meg, can I see you for a minute?" Bill motioned to her as she worked. With a nod, she followed him inside his office and sat in the extra chair.

"Claire tells me you're experienced with publicity."

She nodded. "Yes." Her heart thudded in her chest, and she struggled for breath.

"We need help fundraising for our community garden, and I thought publicity might help us raise more money. Can you put together a plan for us?"

Tension leached from her. This was different from what she used to do. And then she had another thought.

"It's not the type of publicity I did in the past, but I'm sure I can think of a plan. Who else will I work with?"

She didn't want to be difficult, but she needed to know ahead of time if she'd be working with a particular tall, scarred anyone else.

"No one right now. For the moment, this will be for me. If it changes, I'll let you know."

Good, she didn't have to worry about Simon. At least not yet. Her mind whirled with possibilities, and she couldn't wait to get home to write them in her notebook. It was a relief to have her mind occupied with something other than Simon.

That evening, she opened her laptop and developed three different publicity proposals. One was event-driven, one was publicity-driven, and one was charity-driven. The charity-driven one was her favorite, and if she were honest, her time with Simon in the therapy garden inspired it. Without much direction, she wasn't sure which idea Bill would go for, but she couldn't wait to show him tomorrow.

Chapter Twenty-Three

Simon slowed his Jeep as he drove along Main Street that evening. There were lots of people around. For once, he was curious about what they did and where they went.

He'd gone to the grocery store, a task that should have filled him with pride. Usually, he ordered his food to be delivered. But he'd only needed more eggs, and his weekly delivery wasn't for another three days. His time with Meg inspired more than his creative side. It made him want to break out of his shell. He'd braved the anticipated stares. And it wasn't bad. Fran rang at the register, and her husband, Seth, stocked shelves. They'd said hello, he'd said hello, there was small talk about the weather, and he'd left unscathed. Sure, his palms were sweaty, but it was nothing a quick swipe against his jeans couldn't handle. He didn't even drop the eggs. He flexed his fingers, gripped the steering wheel, and expelled a deep breath. He'd done it. It wasn't as bad as he expected. In truth, it satisfied him to choose what he wanted, rather than rely on others to do it for him or take care of him.

Like Meg.

He slowed to avoid two people crossing the street. Why wasn't he happier about his accomplishment? After all, she'd been the catalyst.

Call her.

He should share this with her. His eye twitched as she appropriated his thoughts, and he blinked to relieve the sharp pain. She'd be happy for him, but in a patronizing way, like the reason she had sex with him. Pain sliced through him.

She wasn't as awful as he painted her to be. He had her to thank for getting him out of the house. Because if he were honest, his hermetic ways forced others to adapt to his needs and forced Meg to take care of him. If he had any chance of building a life with her, he needed to show her he could go into the world on his own terms. Still, her betrayal hurt, and while the nice-guy side of him didn't want to be too harsh, the rest of him wasn't ready to forgive. Not yet. If it meant his pride in going out in public was a little muted, so be it.

He pulled into his driveway and slammed his hand on the steering wheel, cringing at the ache as it radiated along his arm. She drove him mad, and he shouldn't think about her. They were finished. She wanted space, and he would give it to her. Now to explain it to his heart.

****

Simon awoke groggy before the sun rose the next morning. His eyes burned, and his head ached. This was ridiculous. Thinking about Meg got him nowhere. He didn't care if Claire made fun of him. He didn't care if he played right into her hand. He needed to talk to Claire. Waiting for the morning to develop enough to talk on the phone, however, was as difficult as failing to sleep last night.

He wandered from room to room, getting nothing done. In the kitchen, he made breakfast, only to stare out the window, distracted, and burned his toast. He made coffee in the hopes a jolt of caffeine would wake him enough to function but left it on the counter and wandered into the living room. His gaze drifted to the window seat, Meg's favorite reading spot. He frowned. Stuffed in the corner was one of her books. He picked it up—it was from the library. With a sigh, he entered his office to get work done, but the print on the pages blurred in front of him, and he couldn't concentrate on any project—even for CAST—for more than five minutes. Deciding he should go to sleep until it was time to call Claire, he climbed the stairs and crawled into bed. But his head hitting the pillow was a more effective wake-up than caffeine because his mind spun in a million different directions, and his eyelids flew open wider than they'd been since yesterday. With a groan, he turned and punched his pillow. He lay on his side and stared at the window.

The ringing phone jolted him, and he sat upright in confusion. Bright sun shone through the window, puddled on the floor. He must have fallen asleep after all.

"Hello, Claire."

"Simon," said Claire, "we need to talk. It's important."

He'd seen her at his house, he'd ventured into town. He could go to her house. "How about I come over this morning?"

"Really?" Her voice was pitched high in surprise, but she recovered quickly. "That's great. I have something to show you."

"What is it?"

"An article about Meg."

Chapter Twenty-Four

It had been a long time since Simon drove his Jeep as fast as he did to Claire's house. As a teenager, he'd done his fair share of speeding. As a young man, he'd driven fast. Not any longer. When he needed to escape, he'd wind his way with care along the back roads at night, when no one was around. When he reached the highway, he'd press the gas a little harder, open the windows and drive as fast as he dared without going more than five miles over the speed limit. Speeding was reckless, and he was no longer. But this morning, he didn't care what the speed limit was. He didn't care about his safety or anyone else's.

Claire hadn't sounded her usual teasing self. Her worried tone scared the hell out of him. He'd barely gotten his clothes on—the only reason he'd dressed was because he didn't think Tom wanted him to arrive in pajamas.

Ten excruciating minutes later, he pulled into her driveway. The small white clapboard house was decorated with bales of hay, scarecrows, and mums. He stopped the car and ran along the path and front steps, to bang on the door. Stuffing his hands in his pockets, he paced the front porch until the door opened, and Claire let him in.

Without a word, she led him along the hallway to the kitchen. The table was littered with newspapers, and she pulled out a chair.

"You'll want to sit for this," she said.

Fear lodged in the pit of his stomach. It was unreasonable, but he couldn't make it go away. Nerves urged him to stand and pace and shout at Claire to get to it, but her expression stopped him. Whatever Claire said would change everything. He could feel it in his bones and cold sweat ran along his spine. He dropped into the chair at the head of the table.

Claire slid the papers toward him.

"Read these," she said.

"Why?"

"Because you need to."

Perhaps if he'd gotten more sleep the night before—any sleep—he wouldn't have accepted it as a legitimate answer. He stared at her turned-down mouth, until he could no longer postpone the inevitable. With a swallow, he looked at the pages.

The first was a photo of a bunch of pseudo-celebrities—barely clothed party girls dancing, holding bottles of alcohol—inside a club. The second were photos of the same types of girls getting into limos, posing for selfies, rubbing against well-muscled, tatted guys. Not recognizing anyone, he skimmed through them.

"What are these?"

"Look closer at them."

"I am."

With a groan, she pulled the photos away and pushed forward a bunch of news articles. "News" was used lightly, as they were from grocery store gossip rags. He didn't have time for games.

"Why can't you tell me?"

"Because you need to see it for yourself."

Pressure built behind his eyeballs. He rubbed his brow. "See what?"

Claire tapped a blue-painted fingernail on the top article. Did she always wear blue nail polish? He shifted his focus to the news article and pulled it toward him. The first one's headline blared, Billionaire Beauties Busted. "I don't understand."

"Keep reading."

He started the article again. Clubbing. Drinking. Paparazzi. Car crash. A car plowed into a crowd of bystanders, injuring fifteen. The car and driver fled the scene but were found fifteen minutes later. The passengers in the car were billionaire socialites, a Vanessa Adams and a Mackenzie Trundle. An accompanying photo showed tear-streaked mascara and mussed blonde hair. He didn't recognize either of the women. But the third one? He stared harder at the photo. Police held a brunette woman with expressionless blue eyes that reminded him of the ocean, and creamy pale skin. The hair color was wrong, but it was Meg. In handcuffs.

"What the hell?"

"Tom thought Meg looked familiar when we were over for dinner. He researched." Claire shrugged. "It was one of the last stories he covered in LA before he moved here. He showed these to me last night. I want to hate my husband for this, but I can't."

"But the girl in this photo has brown hair. Meg's is red."

"Hair dye."

He wanted to argue, but it was Meg. He'd recognize those eyes anywhere. And her name, Megan

Thurgood.

"On her lease, hell, around town, she used the last name of Clancy," Simon said. "Maybe it's a case of mistaken identity?"

"I wasn't able to get a lot of background," said Tom, "but I do remember her mother's maiden name was Clancy. Maybe she uses it."

It made sense. But… "Meg's a billionaire heiress?" Simon asked. "I'm familiar with her father, he's been after my investments for years. I knew he was loaded, but a billionaire?"

"No, but she was their publicist—society, I guess."

His face went hot and cold and hot again. Claire's voice retreated into a vacuum of white noise. What. The. Hell? She'd lied.

His mind drifted back to their Scrabble game. She'd told him she lied. Was this what she meant? How could he possibly believe her when the evidence was right in front of him?

With shaking fingers, he slid the next article over. The papers grew damp in his grip, the ink blurred as he read more details. This headline was worse. Scamming the System. The photo was of Meg outside a courtroom, climbing steps away from hordes of flashbulbs. Again, she showed no emotion. This time, she wore a modest suit. Only legs that once wound around his waist were visible.

In all the time she'd been here, she'd kept this secret from him. Betrayal burned his throat. She'd asked—no, begged—him to change his entire life, but she didn't have the courage to tell him about her past? Fury built in him, and made his hands shake.

The accompanying article said she'd been given

two years in jail and community service and hinted money accomplished this.

How the hell did she get off so easily? According to the article, she'd plowed into a group of people after a night of partying and ruined lives, and she was out so soon?

"Apparently one of the girl's father was a lawyer and got the judge to give her a lenient sentence," Claire said.

Fury shook his body. He pushed up. The chair scraped along the floor, and he paced. What happened to the victims? She'd caused the pain and suffering they had to deal with, while she lived in comfort in the house he rented. She was no different than the irresponsible people who started the fire in his family home.

"I have to find her," he growled.

"Simon, wait!"

He spun around. "What? Did you think you could show me this without a reaction?" His stomach churned.

Claire grabbed his arm. "No, I showed you the article because you, of all people, needed to know what she'd done. But don't rush to conclusions. Think first before you do anything."

"Me, of all people? I've seen first-hand what happens with reckless behavior, Claire. Someone has to judge her. Otherwise, what she did has no consequence. If you were her victim, would you be okay with this?" His pulse pounded in his ears and he squeezed the chair.

Claire twisted a strand of hair around her finger. "No, of course not. But...I don't know. When Tom showed this to me, I couldn't believe it. I still can't."

"Which article did he write?"

She pointed to the court coverage in one of the more respectable papers before handing it to Simon.

The papers creased, and he loosened his grip. "I can't believe a person who did such damage got off so easily."

She touched his arm.

He flinched.

"I know this is awful. Maybe she has an explanation."

"What can she possibly say?" He covered his face with his hands. "I can't believe I fell for her."

Claire reached for him to give him a hug, but he pulled away. "I thought you should know the truth, but I hate how it hurts you."

"I have to talk to her." He paced the room, unable to bear the thoughts spiraling in his mind. He'd trusted her. He loved her. And he was a fool. "I feel like I don't know her at all."

****

The waves pounded against the rocks, and Simon wished he could go into the ocean. To disappear under the water, hear nothing but the amplified echoes of the current beneath the surface. But it was too cold, even for him. The wind whipped his hair across his face, the salt stung his skin, and the sand was icy beneath his feet. Goose bumps rose on his arms. He shivered, but the thought of going inside stifled him.

He turned and walked along the beach. His feet kicked seaweed and sand as he scuffed along. His gaze flitted from shells to scraps of driftwood. What the hell was he supposed to do?

The last time he'd faced such sheer recklessness,

he'd been one of the victims. And his response was to shut almost everyone out of his life. He'd built a solitary existence. Granted, it wasn't much of one, but it was one he could handle. He'd been content if not happy.

Then he met Meg, and his dissatisfaction with his life rushed to the surface. He pushed himself because she was right. He needed to live again. Except everything he'd built with Meg was a lie. She wasn't the woman she'd appeared. What was the point of going into the world if his reasons were no longer valid?

He returned the way he'd come and stopped short. His reasons were valid. He'd been stuck in a rut forever. Nothing inspired him anymore. However, going out, visiting the botanical gardens, driving to the lighthouse in the daylight, visiting the library, hell, going to the grocery store, rejuvenated him and allowed him to find his creative inspiration again. Re-entering the world helped him. He didn't do this for Meg. And he'd continue without her.

But he still needed to confront Meg, to find out how he'd been wrong about her.

****

Meg pulled into the library the next day for work. She couldn't wait to show Bill her ideas, but first, she wanted to share them with Claire. She signed in and stored her laptop in the break room. Her phone rang. For the second time since she'd arrived in Gull's Point, Vanessa's ID scrolled across the screen. Ignoring it, she put it in her purse and left the break room.

She didn't see Claire. She went in search of the cart of books to reshelve. The work was mindless, and her thoughts shifted to Simon, the things he'd said, the look on his face when he thought she'd slept with him out of pity. Swallowing tears, she waited for Claire to arrive, and when she didn't, she asked one of the other librarians.

"She called in sick today. Sorry."

Meg made a note to call her later and drop off soup, then found Bill at the reference desk. If Claire couldn't help her keep her mind off Simon, maybe Bill could.

"I have three publicity proposals for you. When do you want me to show them to you?"

"Let's meet at the end of your shift."

Four hours and five million, seven hundred and eighty-four thousand thoughts of Simon later, she knocked on Bill's office door and opened her laptop. "I hope you like them."

Bill walked around to the other side of his desk and paged through each proposal. He nodded a few times. "Meg, I love them all, but the charity one resonates with me the most. Can I take a look at all three, though, and let you know in a few days?"

"Of course."

"You did a great job with these, thank you."

Meg's spirit lifted at the praise. She stopped at the grocery store, chatted with Fran, and bought soup for Claire, as well as other things she needed. As she pulled onto the street, she couldn't help but smile. She'd found somewhere to fit in.

Chapter Twenty-Five

"M…Meg, what are you doing here?" Claire asked.

Claire looked surprised, not ill. "They said you called in sick. I thought I'd bring you soup and see how you were feeling."

"Oh…um…thanks."

The longer Meg looked at her, the more flushed she got. "You poor thing, you don't look well at all."

"I'll be okay."

Obviously, she wasn't used to a friend taking care of her. Or maybe she didn't want to infect her. Meg held out the soup. "I'll call you later to check on you. In the meantime, take it easy."

Claire closed the door, and Meg made a mental note to call her that evening. When she did, Tom answered.

"Hi, Tom, it's Meg. How are you?"

"Claire can't talk to you now."

"Okay. How is she?"

"She'll call you another time."

Meg frowned as Tom disconnected the call. He'd been much friendlier at dinner two weeks ago. Maybe he was worried about his wife? Except Claire hadn't looked sick. Was there something she missed? Stewing about it wouldn't help. She grabbed her cell and texted Claire.

—Hey, I know Tom said you couldn't talk, but I'm

checking in to see how you're feeling?—

She waited. There was no response. Maybe she was asleep or in the shower. She grabbed one of her books and opened it, but reading reminded her of Simon's window seat. And Simon. The words wavered and disappeared. Blinking, she checked her phone. After twenty minutes of this on repeat, moving dots showed Claire was typing. They disappeared. She waited again, but nothing. With a sigh, she returned to reading. When her phone dinged, she jumped.

—Fine—

That took her twenty minutes to answer?

The next day, Meg returned to Claire's house once again, exhausted from lack of sleep. This time, Claire's odd behavior added to her insomnia. As she pulled into their driveway, Claire descended her front steps.

"Claire!"

Claire paused and looked behind her. Straightening her spine, she walked along the path.

"I'm on my way out."

"Is everything okay? How are you feeling?"

"Fine. Busy."

Meg watched her friend brush past her and unlock her car. "Claire, what's going on? Are you mad at me?"

Claire remained motionless before she swung around. "Mad at you? How can I be mad at you? I don't know who you are."

Her stomach dropped. She'd seen the contemptuous look before.

"Claire, talk to me." *Please tell me it's something else.*

"You don't want to do this now, Meg, not with me. You should talk to Simon."

No, she didn't want to discuss it with anyone. But it looked like she didn't have a choice "I don't want you avoiding me."

"Before Tom came here, he worked for a few gossip rags in LA."

Oh God. The earth tilted. Meg tightened her grip on Claire's arm.

"He thought you looked familiar when we had dinner with you and Simon."

"It's not what you think."

"Meg, he showed me the articles!"

Everything around her stopped, as if flash frozen. Her muscles contracted, and she clutched her stomach. Her pulse was the only thing she could hear. It pounded in her ears, drowned out Claire's voice. Her gaze focused on the glint of the sun against Claire's car keys. The bouncing light made her stomach tumble. After a moment, she gasped. The scents of hay and decaying leaves wafted around her. She swallowed and tried not to gag.

Meg whispered, "You don't know the whole story."

"Tell me. It sounds like you were some Hollywood wannabe who rammed her fancy car into a crowd of people and got off with two years in jail, while they were injured. You ruined innocent lives. Tell me what I don't know. Please. Because I want to believe you're not that person, but…" Claire's voice petered away.

Meg's hand dropped from Claire's arm She should have let things be.

"I can't believe you did what they say you did, Meg. Tell me what I'm missing."

There was no point in saying anything. She

couldn't, actually. Not if she wanted to return to a normal life. A few more repayments of the money she'd been given to keep quiet, and she'd be free of Mr. Adams and her dad's hold over her. She could finally live her own life. But until then, no matter how unfair it was, she had to let Claire and Tom believe whatever they wanted. She'd been judged before—she knew how this ended. Her vision blurred, but she refused to cry. Not in front of the woman she'd thought of as her friend. Instead, she drove home.

They'd never understand.

****

Simon watched Meg's car pull up to her house and clenched his jaw. She needed to leave. He didn't care about a signed rental contract. She'd lied about who she was. He didn't want that kind of person living on his property. Even if "that kind of person" was his Meg.

He paused at his doorway. Did he need to go over in person? He'd left her original written instructions before. Why not do it again? *Because it took me half an hour of pain to write it, and I don't need any more pain from her.* Maybe, if he confronted her, she'd explain what happened. What *really* happened. Like ripping off a Band-Aid, do it fast and get it over with. He strode to her house and pounded on her door before he could think twice about it.

She didn't answer at first. When she did, he barely recognized her. Her face was red and blotchy and there were streaks of moisture on her cheeks. A trace of sympathy snuck in, but he squashed it. He stood on her porch as desire thrummed through his veins. How could he still want this woman who hurt him?

"Simon." Her voice was scratchy, barely above a

whisper.

"I don't suppose you'll tell me what happened." He had to give her a chance.

She shook her head. "I can't."

He had no other choice. "You have a week to vacate. Leave the key on my porch when you do."

She stilled. He'd expected a reaction from her. When he didn't get any, he frowned. With a shake of his head at his own foolishness, he walked away, her gaze like a physical pull on his nape as he returned home.

Inside his house, he paced. As a child, he'd gone to the zoo with his father and watched the tigers pace in their pens. He'd wondered aloud what they thought as they paced. Now, he knew. They wanted to be anywhere but where they were.

Everywhere he looked he was reminded of her. The kitchen, where she'd cooked and eaten with him. The dining room, where they'd shared a meal with Claire and Tom. The living room, where they'd played Scrabble together. The window seat, where she'd read her books. Hell, she'd left remnants of herself in every room.

What would he do when she was truly gone?

Gripping his mug of now-cold coffee, he stared through the rear window at the rolling surf. Under normal circumstances, he'd go outside and walk the beach. But the sun glinting off the water reminded him of her eyes. All he could think of was how he'd stood here when she first arrived and watched her frolic in the water. Now she was leaving. He needed her to go, but he couldn't imagine life without her.

He shrugged into his coat and walked to the ruined

manor house. Maybe a stroll through his garden would clear his mind. It was the one thing she hadn't touched. Yet.

****

Meg glanced a final time into her rearview mirror. No amount of cold compresses could get rid of the redness and puffiness of her face. She'd done her best to cover it with makeup, but she wasn't fooling anyone. With a sigh, she walked into the library to start her shift.

She didn't search for Claire. She was here to do her job and go home—well, her home for the next six days. She'd have to look for a new place to live. And she needed to make a clean break and repay Mr. Adams. Until she'd repaid his debt, she could never be free.

"Do you have any Clifford books?" A little boy tapped her arm. Meg leaned over with a smile.

"Sure we do. They're right over—"

"Lucas, don't talk to her. We'll find them on our own." His mother pulled him away, and Meg stifled a gasp. At the checkout counter, Linda avoided her gaze and Joan shook her head.

So everyone knew.

Meg swallowed. She refused to dissolve into tears in front of all these people. It would give them more fodder for the gossip mill, which worked faster here than it did in LA, to her surprise. So be it.

Straightening, she grabbed the book cart and walked toward the adult section. She had a job to do, and she would do it. However, today moved with miniscule progress. Each person she made eye contact with turned away. One older man asked her if she was still allowed to work here. Her co-workers didn't speak and spent more time in Bill's office than she'd ever seen. Her list of jobs to do was left in writing.

The only good thing was Claire wasn't there. Meg didn't know if she wasn't scheduled to work today, or if she'd changed shifts on purpose, but she was thankful, regardless of the reason. They'd have to learn to work with each other at some point, but the pain was too raw today for her to handle it.

Right before her shift ended, Bill called her into his office. Her stomach clenched. She needed a job in order to rent a place to stay and continue to pay her debt to Mr. Adams. She had the money all set aside and ready to send, but if she lost her job, she'd have to dip into savings. She couldn't live any longer with the debt hanging over her. This job was necessary, and based on everyone's reactions today, she doubted anyone else in this town would hire her. Her palms sweat as she walked toward his door. If he fired her, she'd have to leave. Wiping her hands on her thighs, she entered Bill's office and perched on the edge of the chair across from his desk, her spine so straight it ached.

"You wanted to see me?" It was hard to get words past her choppy breaths.

"Yes, let's talk about the publicity plans. As I thought, we're going with the charity one. I like it the best. I think we can make the most of…what's wrong?"

Meg raised her hands to her face and wiped the tears off her cheeks. "Nothing," she whispered. "I'm sorry. Go on."

"Tears are not nothing, Meg." He handed her a tissue.

She blew her nose. "I thought you were firing me."

He leaned in his chair and rested his hands on his

rounded stomach. "For what reason?"

Her mouth dried, and she couldn't speak. She swallowed. "Information about my past has come to light. I'd kept it hidden as much as possible, although I did answer your application honestly when it asked about criminal records. But people have learned I was convicted of causing a car accident that injured people, and...well..."

He held up a hand to stop her. "As far as I'm concerned, there's no reason to fire you. You arrive on time, you do your job well, and you've created three of the best publicity proposals I've ever seen. Did I miss something?"

Meg blinked her tears away. Speech was beyond her right now.

"Good." He reached across his desk and handed her a brochure. "I'd like you to go to the Botanical Gardens tomorrow and talk to their horticulture therapist. See what he suggests as part of the plan you've created."

Jed. He wanted her to speak to Simon's therapist?

"I...I don't think I can."

Bill frowned. "Why not?"

Because... "Never mind. I'll do it as soon as my shift is over tomorrow. I'm working in the morning. I can get there around two."

Bill rose and patted her shoulder. "Don't give up."

Chapter Twenty-Six

As Meg drove to the Botanical Gardens, she tried not to dwell on the last time she'd been there. Her hands trembled on the steering wheel. She gripped it tighter. The hard plastic pressed against her palms. It didn't do any good to think about Simon. The meeting with Jed promised to be awkward. With luck, he wouldn't recognize her.

"You're Simon's friend, aren't you?" the garden therapis said. He didn't bother with hello, and Meg's stomach plunged.

"I was."

The frown the man gave her did nothing to dissuade her he wasn't a garden gnome. If anything, it enhanced his image, giving his craggy face grooves and causing his eyes to disappear beneath formidable brows. If Simon were here, he might have made a joke about it.

If Simon were here, Jed wouldn't have frowned in the first place.

"I had high hopes for you."

Meg resisted the urge to sass him. Bad idea to tick him off before she'd asked for his help. "Sorry to disappoint you. I hoped you could give me advice."

He hopped onto a stool and moved pots around, his back toward her. "Do you think it's wise?"

"You're the best horticultural therapist around, and

my committee is fundraising for its own community garden. We want to install a therapy area. My boss suggested I speak to you."

He faced her. "You didn't tell him you knew me through Simon?"

"No, although the town I live in is small. I'm pretty sure everyone knows everything at this point."

"Or thinks they do."

She nodded. "So." She cleared her throat. "Will you help me?"

"What do you want to do?"

For the next half hour, they discussed the library's plans. Jed made suggestions, and Meg took copious notes. He gave her a list of names of horticultural therapists to contact for assistance. By the time they were finished, Meg's head hurt with all the advice and next steps Jed gave her.

"I appreciate your help." She was halfway out of the pavilion when his words stopped her.

"I didn't expect you to return here."

She turned and met his shrewd gaze. "I wouldn't for personal reasons. It's not fair to either of you. But you're an expert in your field."

"Don't mix business with pleasure, eh?"

"Loyalty is everything."

A flicker of...something...crossed his face and without another word, he hopped off the stool and shook her hand. "Good luck to you."

The rest of the week passed far too quickly as Meg quelled her panic. Word of her past spread throughout the town, because no one returned her apartment inquiries, and the people she did speak to gave a myriad of excuses why their property was no longer available.

She had to look farther afield, which would make commuting a hassle, but if she didn't want to resign from her job, she had no other choice.

She'd spent the week depleting her food supplies. There was no point in leaving food around an empty house. But by Friday, she had nothing left to cook. Despite not wanting to face the hostile gazes of the townspeople, she braved the grocery store one last time to find food to microwave.

Despite the harsh gaze of Fran, the grocery owner, she nodded and scanned the aisles. They were empty of people, except for the frozen food section. Of course. She made her way over and waited for the woman in front of her to finish.

"Oh, excuse me," she said. "I didn't realize you were there."

Meg smiled. "It's okay. I don't mind waiting."

"You look familiar. Have we met?"

"I don't think so." She took a deep breath. "I'm Meg."

Recognition flashed across the woman's face before she banked it. "Oh, hi. I'm Steph. My dad, Bill, works at the library with you."

This was new. Meg smiled. "Nice to meet you."

"Is that all you're getting?" She nodded at Meg's empty cart, and the single box of frozen lasagna Meg held.

"I'm moving tomorrow, so, yeah."

"My dad mentioned you were looking for a new place to stay. Have you found anything yet?"

"No, I haven't." Meg forced the tremor from her voice.

"You know, we have an empty apartment above

the hardware store. We often rent it. It's available now, and if you'd like, you're welcome to stay there."

Excitement bubbled beneath the surface, but Meg paused. She didn't know who Meg was, and Meg wasn't in the mood to have to move twice in one week. "I don't think it will work, but thanks." She walked toward the counter and the disapproving Fran.

"But you don't have a place yet, right?"

Meg spun around. "No one else in this town wants to rent to me. Why do you?"

"Because I'm big on second chances. The place is yours if you want it."

Fran's shocked mutterings echoed Meg's silent ones. With a deep breath, she spoke, "Yes, I'd love it."

Steph gave her directions and the amount of rent, and they exchanged cell numbers, arranging for Meg to move in the next day. As she paid for her lonely lasagna and said goodbye to the ashamed Fran and the pleasant Steph, for the first time in more than a week, a lightness filled Meg.

****

On her way to Steph's, Meg stopped at the bank, got a cashier's check, and mailed it to Mr. Adams, with the letter she'd agonized over for three days. The wording needed to be right—appreciative but not obsequious; firm but not rude. After years of saving, she'd gotten the money together. No longer indebted to Mr. Adams, she could be free. Once she was free, she could explain what actually happened. It was only a matter of time.

Meg unpacked her clothes and her hand brushed a piece of wood. She examined the shell embedded in the scarred piece of driftwood. Its weight reassured her.

"Knock, knock!"

Startled, she looked up. Steph stood in the doorway. "Just wanted to give you fresh flowers and make sure you're okay." She walked inside and eyed Meg. "You are okay, aren't you?"

"Sure." Meg placed the piece of wood on top of the dresser and took the flowers from Steph. She buried her face in the lilacs. "Thanks."

"You know, if you want to talk, I'm a good listener."

"Thanks, but it's not right."

Steph perched against the dining table across from the living area. "Why not?"

"I'm the outsider here. It's not fair to make people take sides."

"I never said I'd take sides. I said I'd listen."

"I appreciate it."

She picked up and held the driftwood once again after Steph left. Simon hated her and made it crystal clear he wanted nothing to do with her. Turning the wood over in her hands, she traced the scars in the wood and the ridges of the shell. She missed him.

With a start, she rose and paced the room. What kind of an idiot missed the man who dropped her without bothering to learn her side of the story? She couldn't tell him all of it. She collapsed onto the sofa. She couldn't tell him much more than he already knew. How in the world could she hope for him to ever understand? There was no point in wishing things were different. She needed to remove him from her mind.

No problem.

Chapter Twenty-Seven

"How are you?"

Simon debated whether or not to answer Claire's email. Since Meg moved two weeks ago, he hadn't spoken to Claire. She'd called, but each time, he let it go to voicemail. She'd knocked on his door one day—when did she become his keeper? He'd remained near the window and watched her leave. After, she'd resorted to their former means of communication, and he still wasn't sure he wanted to talk to her.

Somehow, in the three weeks since he'd learned about Meg, he'd transferred his anger to Claire. Oh, he was still angry with Meg, but his anger was wrapped in memories of love and sadness and desire and betrayal and a host of other emotions he couldn't bear to analyze for too long. It was easier to blame Claire. She was the one who'd knocked his world off its axis, encouraging him to take a chance on Meg. He hadn't discovered a way to return it to orbit.

"Why are you avoiding me?"

The second email came on the heels of the first. Apparently, she wasn't dropping this. He growled before pounding an answer on the keyboard.

"Because."

"Because why?"

He ran a hand through his hair, his fingers tangling in the knots as he read her next message. "Would you have preferred I didn't tell you about Meg?"

Yes. "No."

"Don't be mad at me."

Like it was that easy. "Okay."

"Good. Want to come over tonight?"

He pushed away from his desk. He hadn't socialized with them since their dinner with Meg. But it didn't mean he couldn't.

"Okay."

"Pizza and a movie. Come at seven."

He signed off his email and put the finishing touches on the library plans.

That night, he arrived at Claire's with a scowl and a bag of donuts. The scowl lessened when she hugged him, and the donuts disappeared into the kitchen, leaving him free to follow her toward the yeast and garlic smell of fresh-baked pizza. Tom pulled plates from the cabinet.

"I'm glad you're here," Claire said as they sat around the table and ate.

"Well, you *are* providing food," Simon said.

Claire kicked him under the table. He thawed a bit and allowed a slow smile to creep across his face.

"I know it's easier to be angry at me than her," Claire said.

Simon held up his hand. "Don't. I don't want to talk about her." He looked between Claire and Tom and waited for both of them to nod. "I want one evening where I can relax."

And he tried. It was a house where memories of Meg didn't lurk in every corner. The three of them didn't have a long history of time spent with Meg, of shared conversations, or experiences. And yet...

226

There was an empty chair at the table. It should have been a foursome, but it was only three. Claire and Tom had a rapport between them built on their marriage. He and Meg had begun to have one. Now, it was like balancing on one leg or sitting on a three-legged chair. Something was off with their conversation.

And the movie?

Claire paused it midway through. "Are you restless?"

"No, why?"

"Because you keep moving. We can turn it off if you want."

He wasn't restless. He kept leaning over to talk to Meg, point out a funny feature, or grab her hand. And she wasn't there. By the time the movie ended, Simon was spent. Tense from trying not to move, jumpy from thoughts of Meg, and disgusted with himself for ties to Meg he couldn't break.

When Tom turned on the lights, Simon rose. "Thanks for the opportunity to get out."

"Stop being mad at me so we can do this again," Claire said.

He nodded. "I know." He gave her a hug, shook Tom's hand, and walked to the door. Tom followed him.

"I know you don't want to discuss her, but there's one thing you should know."

Simon clenched his jaw.

"I always thought there was something missing to Meg's story."

"What do you mean?"

"There was something she didn't tell us."

"Did you ask her?"

"Yes, and she always refused to talk. But it didn't add up, and I could never figure it out. Every time I dug deeper, contacted her friends, I was stonewalled."

Simon rubbed his face. "Why are you telling me this?"

"It never seemed fair to me her side of the story wasn't told, and I feel guilty for bringing it up to you. Maybe she'll talk to you."

"You assume I want to talk to her."

Chapter Twenty-Eight

Simon felt like shit. His eyeballs were hot, his throat was scratchy, and to quote an old sitcom kid, it felt like he'd swallowed a sweater. Every joint ached, and all he wanted was to climb into bed. But he had a meeting with Claire to present his finalized plans for the open space. If she liked them, she could present it to the group of townspeople who didn't want the developer to build condos.

Considering how feverish he was, he nearly requested a remote meeting. Claire would think he was a coward. He wasn't. The world didn't end when he went in public. Sure, he wasn't a fan of it, and he avoided large groups, but meeting with Claire was not a big deal. It was no different than dinner at her house. He'd go to the library, meet with her, and go home to bed. Maybe stop at the store for medicine.

As he entered the library, his face and neck heated while his hands and feet turned icy cold. He gritted his teeth and refrained from covering his face with his hair, although his hands trembled with desire. Who knew a library housed this many people in the middle of the day? Two or three adults stood in line to borrow books. Outside the children's room, young kids swarmed around several moms. And older men and women sat in the main room. At least he didn't see Meg. He reached for the hood he didn't have—he didn't think a hoodie sweatshirt was appropriate for a meeting, even if it was only Claire, but the thought of his visible scars filled him with dread. Now he regretted his choice of a Fisherman's sweater and slacks. Steeling himself for the anticipated stares, he walked to the desk.

"May I help you?"

He had to give the woman behind the counter credit. She didn't stare or look horrified. "I have a meeting with Claire Kingston."

"Oh, yes, they're in the conference room." She pointed to a door marked "Staff Only."

They're? She had to have it wrong. Thanking her, he walked over and opened the door. His hand, slick with sweat, slipped off the knob and smacked into the metal knob as he reached for it again. Dizziness overwhelmed him. The room spun. The focus was on him as he stood there, and he swallowed. *Shit*.

One of the 'they' was Meg.

"Simon, I'm Bill Thompson, library director and head of this committee. Come on in." He held out a hand, and Simon shook it. "You know Claire, and this is Meg Clancy. She's handling publicity for the project, so I asked her to join us. Sit."

He motioned to a chair, and Simon sank into it, legs shaking. "I didn't realize anyone other than Claire would be here. I don't have enough copies of the plans."

"It's all right, we can share," Claire said. She mouthed an apology to Simon.

He ignored her. The only way he could get through this meeting was to pretend Meg wasn't there. Luckily, his stuffy nose prevented him from smelling her lemony scent. Now all he had to do was not look at her, and he should be okay. He was a grown man. He could do this.

He unrolled the plans on the table and watched as they crowded around, Meg on his left. Pointing to the library, he explained where he planned the location of the garden, and his vision for it—a place for people to congregate and enjoy the peace.

"Do you have photos of the plantings?" Bill adjusted his spectacles on his nose.

"Not yet. I'm still finalizing the best ones. But I have suggestions—"

"But I thought Claire said these plans were finalized."

Before he could invent a plausible answer, a female voice interrupted. "It's my fault," Meg said.

Everyone turned, which was good because no one noticed Simon's mouth drop.

"I rented a house from him and the storm damaged it and Simon helped me and didn't get as much work done as he'd wanted. He's behind because of me. There shouldn't be a problem going forward."

Simon looked at Claire and Bill. He snuck a glance at Meg, wondering what the hell was going on. Claire looked shocked. Bill looked pensive. And Meg? She looked empty.

Simon cleared his throat and ignored the sharp pain. "I'll email photos to you next week."

"Moving on to publicity," Bill said, "Meg has created a proposal linking the garden to a charity that works with handicapped people. A therapy garden of sorts, modeled after the Botanical Garden, but on a smaller scale. Meg?"

Simon heard little of what Meg said. A therapy garden? Why hadn't he thought of it? Suddenly, the missing piece of his plan fell into place. But why did Meg suggest it? He focused on her words.

"...said we should keep it small. We'll have tables arranged with pots, and people can do what they're able. I have calls in to a couple of therapists, and I should hear within a week. Once this is a go, we can publicize our garden on a much wider scale and use it to make an appeal to potential donors, which will satisfy the fundraising issue."

"And speaking of fundraising," Claire said, "so far we've raised…"

He couldn't focus on her words, either. Tension vibrated between the two women, like electrical wires running from one to the other. Or maybe it was a symptom of his illness. He thought he had a fever.

"Simon, are you okay?" Claire's voice sounded far away. He turned toward her and blinked. "You look pale," she added. "Are you sick?"

He exhaled. "I think I'm coming down with something. But I'm fine."

"Let's wrap this up," Bill said. "Next week, you'll have photos of the plantings, right, Simon? We need everything finalized so we can present the plans to the town council and get funding from the bank."

Simon nodded and winced as rocks crashed from one side of his head to the other.

"Good. Meg, you'll line up a garden therapist and begin work on publicity. Claire, you'll put together a list of fundraising opportunities." He shuffled his papers and squared them on the table. "All right, let's get to work."

They rose. Simon swayed on his feet. "Simon!" Claire was at his side in an instant, her hand on his head. "You're burning with fever. You can't drive home like this."

"I'll be fine."

"No, you won't," Claire said. "Let me drive you."

A knock sounded on the door, and an employee peeked in. "Claire, we need you here. There's a problem with the audio books program, and no one knows how to fix it."

"It's okay, Claire," Simon said. "I can drive."

"No you can't," Meg said. "Claire, go. I'll drive him home."

No effing way. Simon opened his mouth to say no, but his knees buckled, and he sank into the chair with a groan.

"Claire, go," Bill said. "Meg, you need help getting him home?"

Oh God, they'd make a scene. From the voices in the lobby, there were more people there. Simon's face burned.

"No, I'll be okay on my own. I'm stronger than I look," Meg said.

If anyone but Meg said it, he'd thank the person and be filled with gratitude. But he didn't know what to think. His fevered brain—because he was ready to admit he had a fever—couldn't focus. He should be suspicious of…something. The information was beyond his grasp, and he was so tired, he couldn't focus on it long enough to understand. He closed his eyes. Noise faded, and Simon spiraled. His body burned. Was he on fire? He couldn't smell smoke, but flames licked his skin. Behind his eyelids, his home burned, and his parents screamed. Oh God, no!

Coolness on his neck made him shiver, and he

raised his head. The room spun, and his stomach lurched. Reaching behind him, his fingers stumbled over a hand and sank into something soft and cold.

"Relax, it's me," Meg said. "I put a cool cloth on your neck. I'll be right back."

A cool breeze and hands on his shoulders made him open his eyes again. He wasn't on fire, just sick.

"There's a door from this room that leads outside, and I pulled my car around. Can you stand?"

He rose, staggered, and leaned on the table. She ducked beneath his arm and propped him against her. His heartbeat calmed. He'd missed this. Together, they wobbled their way from the meeting room to her car. When he was seated, he leaned against the seat, panting, as she belted him in. His chest was damp with sweat from exertion. She drove in silence. He braced against the door, trying to prevent himself from swaying. When the car stopped, he looked around in confusion. He was home. His door opened, and Meg reached for him. He frowned.

"Come on, let's get you inside," she said.

His hands fumbled with the seatbelt, and he lurched out of the car.

"Whoa, big guy, I can't get you up if you land on the ground." She supported him beneath his arm, and they stumbled into the house. Inside, she half carried, half pulled him into the living room and pushed him onto the sofa. He fell with a groan and pulled at the neck of his sweater. He was hot, and he hated the burning sensation.

"You can leave now." His teeth chattered. His body shook.

"Sure." Meg covered him with a blanket and

stuffed a pillow behind his head.

It did little to stop the tremors, though, and the movement nauseated him. The silence and lack of touch told him she'd left. Images of her face—blue eyes wide with concern, darkening with compassion—played behind his eyelids.

Rattling in the kitchen startled him. He rose to see what it was, but his body was heavy. A whistling a short time later made his head throb, but something cool touched his skin. He relaxed.

"Here's another cold compress. I made you tea. If you tell me where you keep pain relievers, I can give you medicine for your headache."

How did she know he had a headache? "It's, um…" He couldn't focus. Her hands stroked him, brushed his hair away from his face, and traced his scars. He clamped his mouth shut to keep from sighing in relief. "…upstairs in my bathroom cabinet." Her hand stilled against his temple, before it disappeared. One moment more and he would have leaned into it. He drifted again, until a cold and smooth object touched his lips. Meg. He rested his head against her arm.

"Here, drink this." He opened his mouth and swallowed the pill with water. He grimaced at the pain in his throat.

"Take tea. It will make you feel better." He sipped the warm liquid and relaxed.

"You can go now. I'm fine."

"Mm-hmm."

A chair creaked. Meg settled into the upholstered chair across from him.

"I told you, you could go."

"I know."

"Why are you still here?"

"Because you need me."

"No, I don't."

She didn't rise like he'd hoped, but he couldn't move. Unable to do anything, he closed his eyes again. When he opened them, the room was dark and sweat rolled off him. He hadn't been this hot since—

Smoke filled his lungs. Heat seared his skin. Fire, the house was on fire again. Not again? He had to be certain. His parents were in the house. He couldn't leave them there. He searched, cried out, listening. Nothing. He choked and coughed. He had to get out, but refused to leave his parents. Thrashing he called, "Mom, Dad!"

Black smoke surrounded him. He couldn't see. "Please don't let me burn," he gasped. He tried to clear the fog from his brain. Flames crackled around him. His heart pounded in his chest, and he gulped air into his lungs. His nostrils flared, and he swallowed to calm the gut-wrenching fear.

His breathing increased, he swatted the covers, and he struggled to get out of here.

"Shh, easy. It's okay. Your fever's breaking," Meg whispered. She wiped his face with a cool cloth.

Her voice penetrated his panic. He exhaled and fell against the pillow. His clothes stuck to him, and the moisture was uncomfortable. Meg was too close. She could see his thoughts and fears and strip him naked. He needed to protect himself from her. Especially her.

"I got you fresh clothes to change into." She handed him a stack of folded items.

The pile was heavy, and he dropped them on his lap. His hands were clumsy, and he fumbled with the fabric.

"May I help?"

She didn't move toward him, and he wanted to say no. He wanted to tell her to leave him alone. "Yeah." The word grated in his ears.

She removed his sweater. Her skin was dry and cool to the touch, and his flesh rose in goose bumps at the contact, whether it was from unwanted desire or the change in temperature, he couldn't tell. The damp cloth she'd wiped his face with cleansed his skin of sweat, and in a flash, she put the new shirt over his head.

"Better?" she asked him as she took away his sweater.

He nodded. *No.* But he wondered if she'd return or leave like he'd told her. He couldn't decide what he wanted. Before he could make a decision, she returned.

"Since you seem a little better, why don't I help you upstairs?"

He didn't want her in his bedroom. Before he could voice his opinion, she'd moved and helped him stand. Leaning on her, they walked upstairs. He stopped in the doorway. Of all the people to enter, did it have to be her? Now?

Meg made sure he was steady, let go of him, and walked to his bed, turning down the sheets and fluffing the pillows.

"Why are you doing this?"

She bent, offering him a view of her backside. His groin tightened.

"I already told you. You need me," she said as she led him to the bed.

He didn't want to admit how glad he was of the support. "I never said I did."

"You didn't have to." She covered him with the blanket, moved his tea within reach, and perched on the side of the bed.

At one time, he would have pulled her down beside him, studied every inch of her body. But not now. Her proximity was torture. He was about to tell her, once and for all, to leave, when she stroked his cheek again. Her fingers brushed his hair away from his face in a caress that might be sweet if he admitted it.

"Rest. You'll feel better tomorrow."

He doubted that.

****

She was gone when he woke the next morning. He knew before he opened his eyes—it was the stillness of his house, the empty echo that ricocheted off the walls, and straight into his soul. Cracking one eye open, he looked at the sun peeking behind the window shade as he mentally explored his body, determining his condition. He no longer ached all over. He wasn't hot or cold. Once again, he was grounded.

He swung his feet to the floor and waited. The room didn't spin. He was exhausted, but it was to be expected. He'd be fine, once he took a shower to get rid of the sick smell. Downstairs, he felt more like himself. While he ate, he could no longer ignore thoughts of Meg.

What the hell happened yesterday? Meg took care of him, despite their lack of a relationship. He didn't remember a whole lot, but her voice saying he needed her rang loud and clear.

His phone buzzed. Multiple messages flashed on the screen. Three from Claire, one from Bill, and one from Meg. He called Claire first, since she'd called so frequently.

"Oh, good," she said. "You're alive. How do you feel?"

"Better."

"Is Meg still there?"

"She left after I fell asleep yesterday."

"Hmm."

"What does that mean, Claire?"

"It means I'm confused about her."

"You and me both."

"Her actions with you yesterday, and quite frankly, since we've met her, don't fit her newspaper profile."

But they were in line with how she'd behaved from the moment he met her. "Maybe the profile is wrong?"

Claire sighed. "I don't know what to think. Maybe we should talk to her."

"I've already talked to her."

"Me, too, but if I'm honest with myself, I didn't give her a chance to defend herself. I was too furious about her treatment of you."

Simon hadn't either. He'd been angry and hurt. He'd lashed out and didn't think about anything other than the articles. But if there were more to the story, wouldn't she have said it right away?

"I have to go, Claire."

"What do we do about Meg?"

"I don't know."

He hung up and pulled the envelope Claire had given him from his drawer. Seated at his desk, he read each article. There were ten of them, and they covered every aspect of the incident, from the morning after the accident through the trial and sentencing. There were lots of facts—what happened to the victim, who was behind the wheel and what the verdict was—but he wanted more.

Was this what Tom thought was missing?

Simon ran his hands through his hair and pulled in frustration. The only solution he could see was to talk to Meg, and it was precisely what he didn't want to do. Having her around yesterday was torture. Seeing her, hearing her…he needed a clean break from her.

Yet he still dreamed about her every night. Her presence still inhabited his house. He still missed her.

Simon paced the confines of his office and looked with desire through the window to the beach. But the beach was where he thought of her most often. He couldn't go there.

How the hell would he manage to speak to her?

Would it make things any worse?

His phone buzzed again, reminding him he had other messages he still hadn't answered. But the newest one was Claire. Again.

—*She defended you at the meeting*—

—*What?*—

—*When Bill complained about your lack of progress, Meg accepted the blame*—

He'd forgotten about that, which only confused him more. His delay wasn't her fault. It had nothing to do with her, in fact. He listened to Bill's voicemail, checking on his health and reminding him about the deadline. After marking his calendar, he moved onto Meg's. There was nothing. She'd called and stayed on the line long enough for it to register, but didn't leave a message. Why not? More unanswered questions. If he hoped for any clarity, he had to talk to her.

****

Meg stared at the text on her phone. Her hands shook.

—We need to talk—

No, Simon, we don't, she thought. She tossed her phone on the table and straightened her living space. Her phone buzzed again.

—Can we meet somewhere?—

What's the point? she thought.

—You owe me—

Owe him? She squeezed her phone so tight her hand hurt.

—I owe you nothing—

—You owe me an explanation—

—My explanation is not a payment. It's what I choose to give or not give. And I choose not to give one to someone who won't believe me anyway—

Her phone rang and when she identified the caller, she debated not answering. But that was childish.

"Simon."

"Meg, we need to meet."

"You can say whatever you want on the phone." *Where I can choose to hang up if I don't like what you say.*

"Stop being stubborn."

She remained silent. Talking with Simon wouldn't solve anything. It would only make her hurt more. Taking care of him yesterday almost killed her. She needed space and distance.

"I want to understand a few things, Meg."

"And you can't over the phone?"

"No."

She sighed. Maybe if she met with him, gave him a chance to get out whatever was in his system, they could move on. "Fine."

"Tomorrow morning at my house."

The last thing she wanted was to go to his house. But at least if things got rough, she could leave.

"Fine." She hung up as dread built.

Chapter Twenty-Nine

Driving through the gate along the dirt road toward Simon's house made her heart hurt and her throat thicken. After two years in jail and another two years looking for a place to call home, she'd found one where she thought she could be happy. But as with everywhere else, it wasn't meant to be.

Salty air greeted her when she exited the car, and she inhaled. Her hair whipped around her face in the wind. She'd missed this. Steph's apartment was fine, but it wasn't on the ocean. She stiffened her spine. It was time to get this over with.

She marched to the door and rapped on it. Simon must have been waiting because he opened it right away. The change in him was remarkable. No longer pasty white, his skin held a healthy glow. He stood straight and tall, and his scent—the one she loved—enveloped her. But he didn't trust her. And he wanted nothing to do with her. She waited for him to leave the doorway.

Instead, he joined her on the porch. He didn't want her in his house?

"Why did you take care of me when I was sick?" he asked without preamble.

"Because you needed me." She didn't understand the question.

"But why do you care?" He folded his arms across

his wide chest. She clenched her fists to keep from touching his forearms, those same arms that had wrapped around her and held her close.

"Because you were sick."

"You didn't have to take care of me. I could have managed on my own."

She couldn't contain her disbelief. He'd been incoherent with fever, barely able to stand, and he thought he could take care of himself? "Ha!"

He flushed. "You could have had Claire do it."

"You were my friend. I don't abandon my friends." She swallowed over the lump in her throat. He stood stiff and unyielding. Any secret hope she'd had of his forgiveness disappeared.

She'd gotten over the last of her anger while she'd watched him sleep. He didn't know her entire story. He had no other choice but to keep his distance. She got it. But it made her sad because she loved him. He might be able to throw away a person he loved, but she couldn't.

"It makes no sense," he said.

She put her hands on her hips. "If Claire was ill, would you have left her alone? Or would you help her? You needed someone, and I was able to help you. I don't expect you to understand, and I don't expect you to change your mind about me. But I'm glad you feel better."

She couldn't watch his blank face anymore. It was one thing to understand his motivation. It was a different thing altogether to put herself through torture. Turning away from him, she walked to her car.

"Wait," he called, and for a moment, her spirits lifted. "I'm not finished."

She refused to face him. "I am," she said and got in

her car and drove away.

He didn't understand why she'd want to help him when he'd broken things off with her. And maybe most people wouldn't. But a part of her still cared for him, no matter how he treated her, no matter how angry she was with him. You didn't stop just like that. At least, she didn't. Did it make her weak? Possibly. Did it make her a fool? Definitely.

Tears made it hard to see. She pulled into the parking lot of the bar to wipe them. It was lunchtime, but she wasn't hungry. She'd be better off working on the library proposals. About to put her car into reverse, she paused when another car pulled next to hers.

Claire. *Goody.*

Claire's window rolled down, and Meg followed suit.

"A little early to be at the bar, don't you think?" Claire asked, scorn in her voice.

"Why are *you* here?" She tempered her voice. Claire was angry at losing a friend, and they had to work together.

"I wanted to talk to you."

Meg waited, letting Claire lead the conversation. Apparently it was "Talk to Meg" day. Better to get it all finished at once.

Claire looked around before she refocused on Meg. "Let's go inside where we can sit. It's stupid to yell across our cars."

Meg followed Claire inside the bar. They sat at a booth in the corner, the last empty one. The waitress approached, glared at Meg, and addressed Claire.

"What can I get you?"

"Water, please."

She walked away before Meg could order.

"Why did you defend Simon yesterday?"

Meg frowned. "Why do you think?"

Before Claire could answer, the waitress reappeared with Claire's water and a beer for Meg.

"I didn't order this."

The waitress shrugged. "I assumed you'd want one."

Meg's face burned. She took a deep breath, avoided Claire, and looked at the waitress. "I'd prefer water, please, no lemon." She wanted to scream and rant. The people in this town already formed an opinion of her. Anger reinforced their bad opinions. It'd happened too many times before. She took a deep breath. Claire was flustered.

"What did you mean?" Meg repeated her question.

"When Bill chided Simon for not having his materials on time, you said it was your fault. Why?"

"I protect my friends."

Claire frowned. "But he's not your friend."

"He was."

"I don't understand you."

Meg sipped the water the waitress handed her. "I don't see why not. I haven't changed. The only difference is what you think you know."

"I wish you'd explain yourself to me."

Meg studied her former friend's face and searched for answers. For a moment, genuine regret shone there, before it disappeared and annoyance appeared. Meg sighed. Mr. Adams gave her money to keep quiet. After four years, she'd saved enough to repay him, and she'd mailed it to him a few days ago. With any luck, she'd be off the hook in a few more days, and maybe she'd be able to talk to her friends and tell them her side of the story. Until then, she had to remain quiet.

"Not all journalists look for the truth, Claire. Some want a juicy story. I'm sorry I can't help you." With a sigh, Meg rose. Before Claire could stop her, she left the bar and returned to her car. This judgmental crap got to her, but it would be over soon. She'd be able to confide in her friends, and it would all disappear.

****

Simon banged his hand against the doorframe. He'd spoken to Meg and still didn't have answers. She'd nursed him out of friendship? They weren't friends. Sure, they were at one time, but now? He didn't know what they were.

His heart pounded when he was near her. It was a wonder she didn't hear it. And the sight of her hair whipping in the wind before she'd come to his porch nearly did him in.

He wanted to rush to her, shelter her from the elements, and run his hands through her hair, against her skin, and feel her along his body. His traitorous body remembered his attraction to her despite how she'd hurt him.

And now she claimed she was loyal?

His phone buzzed, and a text from Claire appeared.

—*I saw Meg today. I think we might have misjudged her*—

—*Not possible*—

—*Possible. You should have seen her in the bar today*—

—*Why was she in a bar?*—

His phone rang and because Claire's ID popped on screen, he answered.

"It's much easier to talk than text," Claire said. "I saw her driving, and I followed her. But, Si, you should have seen what happened in the bar. The waitress was rude, and Meg…took it. Like she deserved it. She didn't even respond when the waitress practically forced her to drink alcohol and called her a drunk."

Simon's face burned. There was rude and there was what happened to Meg. No matter how angry with her he might be, he couldn't condone what the waitress did.

"Why didn't she get angry?" He gripped the phone.

"I have no idea. I could see she was embarrassed. I wish I'd told off the waitress. Well, I did as I left. And I didn't tip her. Whatever Meg did in her past, she didn't deserve this treatment."

Simon got a horrible feeling in the pit of his stomach. He hadn't treated her well either.

"I don't understand how she could deliberately get blind drunk and get into a car without a thought about who she might hurt with her recklessness," he said. "It doesn't make sense. On the one hand, we're told she drove into a crowd and ran people over. On the other, she's kind and compassionate and puts everyone else first. It's like she's two different people."

Claire squeaked over the phone. "What if she is?"

"Come on, Claire, she's not suffering from multiple personality disorder."

"No, you idiot, I don't mean that. What if she didn't actually drive the car?"

Simon ran a hand through his hair. "Claire, I read the same articles you did, articles your husband wrote. She was found guilty and got two years in jail. Of course she drove the car."

"Did you ask her?"

"No."

"Me neither," she said. "I assumed everything in the article was accurate. Even after Tom said he always thought there was something fishy. But after watching her take care of you, and her lack of defense against the waitress, maybe we're missing something."

He covered his face. What the hell? Had he rushed to judgment without the facts? He accused her of being reckless, but what about him?

"I have to find her," he said.

He raced upstairs and grabbed a hooded sweatshirt. He didn't know where she lived now, but she worked at the library. He'd stop there first, despite how many people were there. He jumped into his car and drove faster than he should. Parking was scarce, and as he pulled haphazardly into a made-up spot, he swallowed as he realized how many people he'd have to see. Shit. Adjusting his hood, head lowered, he strode into the library, and stopped at the front desk.

"Where's Meg?" He didn't bother with niceties. He didn't have the time. The faster he left, the fewer people he'd encounter.

"She's not working today," the woman said.

"Do you know where I can find her?"

The woman straightened, a look of disdain on her face. "I can't reveal her personal information."

Simon took a deep breath. His face was scary enough, he didn't need his behavior to add to it. From the looks of the woman, he doubted if even his scary face would convince her to break the rules. "Is Bill around?"

With a look of relief, the woman pointed toward an office, and Simon strode in with barely a knock. "Do you know where Meg is?"

Bill leaned forward in his chair. "Why?"

"I need to talk to her."

"I don't give out personal information about my employees. Shouldn't you have it? I thought you two were…friends."

He could practically see the air quotes around the word "friends." "I think I may have made a mistake. It's personal, and I want to discuss it with her." He paused. "Please?"

Simon remained still as Bill stared over his steepled fingers. As Simon was about to give up and leave, Bill relented and wrote an address.

"Don't make me regret this."

Simon nodded. "She's everything to me. Thank you."

With address in hand, he raced to Meg's new apartment. He was about to knock when a sound from inside stopped him.

Meg was crying.

****

"Please, Dad, don't make me do this," Meg whispered.

"You have to keep silent, Meg. It was part of the agreement."

"But I repaid him. And I served my time. I won't announce it to the world. I want my close friends here to know the truth about me. Why can't I tell them?"

"Because you promised Vanessa. She was your best friend. Don't you owe her your loyalty?"

Years of pressure and misplaced loyalty, combined with disappointment in her dad, finally exploded.

"Owe her? Loyalty? Don't you think a jail sentence

is loyalty enough? What do you care about my loyalty? You're more concerned with losing Gershwin Adams, as a valuable client. You don't care about me at all."

The silence echoed on the other end of the phone. *Please, Dad, tell me you love me. Tell me you'll do anything for me to help me get my life back.* She waited.

"I need you to do this for me."

She hung up. Tears streamed down her face, and she fell onto her bed. Her dad would never be the man she wanted, she needed. This would never be over. She'd never escape her dad's control. The weight of the stress, disappointment, and shame overwhelmed her, and she gripped the bed sheets in her hands and curled into her pillow as she sobbed.

Pounding on the door made her jump, and her shriek gave her the hiccups. She looked through the peephole.

Simon.

"Meg?" His voice was loud. He knew she was there. There was no point in pretending not to be. Unlocking the door, she returned to her bed. She wiped her face and turned away from him, hoping to hide the fact she'd been crying. "What are you doing here?"

"Can I help?"

Heavy footsteps approached, and she cringed. She wanted him with every fiber of her being, needed him to feel whole again. He was the one person she couldn't have.

"I'm fine," she whispered. "Please go."

The bed dipped. His scent overwhelmed her, and the tears she'd held inside when he first spoke escaped.

Simon took her in his arms and held her as she cried. She let her emotions pour from her, she gripped his shirt instead of the bed sheets, and he held her against his chest, his voice a soothing whisper in her ear.

"Talk to me, Meg. Tell me what's wrong."

"I c-can't," she said with a hiccup. She brushed at his wet shirt, trying in vain to dry it, until he grabbed her hand and pressed it against his chest. Beneath her palm, she could feel his heartbeat, strong and sure.

"Why not?"

"Because I promised. I thought there was a way around my promise, but it turns out there isn't." She cried again, and he rubbed her back.

When she calmed, he pulled her away from him and stared at her. There was no anger or hatred, this time, only compassion.

"I showed you my face."

She wrung her hands. "Nobody can know about this. No one."

"Did you tell anyone what I told you? About what I look like, about my fears, about how hurt I was?"

She'd never tell anyone what Simon told her, though she suspected people already knew at least some of it.

"Why don't you believe I can keep your secret?" he asked.

Why would he? Although he didn't look at her with hatred right this moment, she knew how he felt about her. "What do you get from keeping my secret?"

So many emotions flickered in his eyes, Meg couldn't identify all of them, and before she could contemplate them, he banked them and pulled her close.

"Isn't making you feel better enough?"

Was he for real? No one ever had the sole purpose

of making her feel better. There was always an agenda.

Climbing off his lap, she paced her living area. This wasn't something she could rush into, to allow her desire for him to blind her.

"Why aren't you angry with me?"

"I still am."

Aha, see. "And you expect me to trust you?"

He blew a breath through his mouth, quick and sharp. "I'm still angry, but there are things that don't make sense to me. How can I accuse you of recklessness if I'm doing the same thing in my judgment of you?"

She stopped. Her stomach ached as if she'd been punched. "I've told you what you wanted."

"But not everything."

"I can't tell anyone everything."

"Even when your secrets hurt you?"

"How do you know it hurts me?"

He pointed to his soaking wet shirt, one brow raised.

There were many answers she wanted to give. But she couldn't. It wasn't that she'd never lied—she'd told a huge one—but in this life, in this place, to this man, she told the truth.

"Why were you crying?"

Her shoulders slumped. "Because of a conversation with my dad."

"About?"

"What I can't tell you."

"If you won't tell me what happened, will you answer me if I guess?"

Like he'd ever guess in a million years. "Sure."

"You weren't the one behind the wheel when your

car ran over those people, were you?"

Her knees gave way, and she gasped. Strong arms grasped her and held her close against his warm, hard body.

"Answer me, Meg."

She needed to stall him. "How…why…what makes you think it wasn't me?"

He took her hand, and she let him.

"Because once I got over my initial fury, I thought about what I knew. Things didn't make sense. Knowing you the way I do, I don't think the side you've shown me is an act. Tom said there were things that didn't add up. You defended me to Bill and took care of me when I was sick. Those aren't the actions of a person who doesn't care about others. Even Claire agrees with me."

She grabbed his arm. "You can't tell her. You can't tell anyone. You have no idea what will happen. I was behind the wheel. I paid for my mistake, and it's over. We can't talk about this again."

"Hey, easy." He caressed her cheek and neck. "Take it easy, sweetheart."

She couldn't think when he called her sweetheart. She doubly couldn't think when he ran his fingers over her skin and through her hair.

"I'll keep your secret, I promise," he whispered. "But I want to know the truth."

"How do I know I can trust you?"

He stiffened before slumping as if a pin pricked him. "Look, when I first learned about your past, I said and did things because I no longer trusted you. How did it make you feel?"

"Awful."

"I don't ever want to feel like I can't trust you. I

254

can't love a woman I don't trust. And I don't want you to think you can't trust me. If I need to keep your secret, I will. But I'd like you to tell me, because maybe there's a solution you haven't thought of yet."

Mr. Adams and her dad, two of the richest men in the country, had told her what was best, but he thought he knew better? She'd call him arrogant, except he wasn't. On the slim possibility he could think of a solution, she opened her mouth, and the words tumbled forth. She couldn't stop them.

"Vanessa Adams, Mackenzie Trundle, and I were best friends, well, as best friends as people who were in it for the scene could be. It was a typical Friday night, and there was a new club that opened and paid us to attend for it to get attention. Actually, they paid Vanessa. She invited Mackenzie and me afterward. We went, and it was an ordinary club, like all the others we'd been to. But Vanessa was contracted to stay for a certain length of time, and we couldn't leave."

"Were you drinking?" Simon asked.

Meg shook her head. "No, I was the designated driver."

Her hands shook, and Simon grasped them. "Go on."

"Somehow, while I helped Mackenzie, Vanessa grabbed the keys, and climbed into the driver's seat. I swear, I tried to get her to move. You have to believe me."

"I do. Keep going."

His calm voice soothed her. "I told her to move and let me drive home, but she refused, and she made a scene and threatened to leave without me. I was afraid she'd hurt Mack, and I thought I'd be able to convince her to pull over and switch with me before we went too far."

She clenched her hands in her lap.

"She was supposed to put the car in reverse, but she put it in drive." Meg could still hear the screams reverberate in her brain. She swallowed. "When she stopped, about a half mile away, she begged me to switch with her. She already had two DUIs. She promised me she'd go to rehab and told me they'd go easy on me because I didn't have a record."

"That's why her dad defended you," Simon said.

Meg nodded. "The judge wasn't happy, and although the sentence was lighter than it could have been, it was longer than any of us expected. Her dad put money in my account to help me get on my feet after I was released from jail. All I had to do was keep quiet and never say Vanessa was the one behind the wheel."

"They should never have made you do it."

Meg stared off into space. "At the time, I thought I was being loyal to my friend and ensuring she got the help she needed."

"And now?" Simon asked.

"It doesn't matter if I wish I'd never gone along with the plan. My dad's their investment banker. They've made him millions. He depends on them for the life he's accustomed to. He told my dad if I said anything to anyone, they'd withdraw their business and make sure my dad never got another client in town. He's all I have. As much as I hate him for putting me in this position, I can't abandon my dad."

"What about you?"

She shrugged. "What about me? My friends depended on me to keep them safe. It's my fault all those people were injured. Had I done a better job as the designated driver, none of this would have happened. I failed."

Simon turned her around to face him. "You failed? You rescued your friends! They let you go to jail."

"I know, and it's why I left. And I used as little of the money her father gave me as possible and saved what I made at various jobs. Last week, I sent Vanessa's dad a check for the full amount and told him I was free now."

"What did he say?"

Her voice flattened. "He called my dad. My dad told me I still have to keep quiet."

"Your dad's business isn't your responsibility. He can't do that to you."

"I told you. He's the only family I have. I have no one. No one else believes me, no one will let me forget what happened. Two of the families of the people she hit with her car, they send me hate mail every year on the anniversary of the accident—my dad receives it. If I don't listen to my dad, he'll never talk to me again. I'll have no one."

He pulled her against him, and she went limp. His sweater was soft against her cheek, and his heart beat against her ear. The rhythmic stroke of his hands on her head soothed her and eased her breathing. Cocooned within his arms, she could almost believe everything would be okay. But it wouldn't.

"As soon as I finish the project for Bill, I'll leave," she said.

He pulled her away from him. Pain and disbelief darkened his gaze.

"I have to, Simon. I can't stay in a place where

257

everyone hates me. I thought I could, but I can't keep doing this to myself."

"Not everyone hates you."

She looked at him. "This is a small town. I need someplace bigger, where I can be anonymous."

His jaw twitched. "Don't leave."

"Why not?"

"I don't want to live without you."

God, what she would have given to hear those words from him weeks ago. "I don't have a choice."

"If I can show you that you do, will you stay?"

He wasn't a magician. There was no way he could fix this, but his voice made her want to give him a chance. "Only until Bill's project is done."

"Will you come to my house?"

"No. I think we both need the space. And it will make it easier when I leave."

"If."

She humored him.

"I'm sorry," he said.

"Why?"

"Because I didn't trust you. Because I rushed to judgment, and I hurt you. What I did requires much more than a verbal apology, but it's all I have right now. While I try to figure out what I can do to help you, will you consider forgiving me?"

A part of her wanted to scream, "I already have," but the other part of her, the mature, independent part of her, made her refrain. She'd served prison time because she'd been eager to please those she cared about. She needed to stop doing that. Because she learned no one else would. She nodded instead.

Chapter Thirty

Simon's head pounded, and the thought of what he needed to do next made bile rise in his throat. Popping two painkillers, he stretched his hands and paced his office.

As of today, the CAST Ltd fund was worth more than $200 million. And he'd convinced his partners to invest all of the money with Meg's father.

He was a weasel. What kind of father sacrificed his daughter for money? He hated the idea of climbing into bed with the man, but it was the best way to help Meg.

Simon had heard of Thurgood, had tracked his business for years, and personal distaste aside, was impressed with his list of clients and business acumen. The list was exclusive, and Meg's father had approached Alexander, another of the CAST partners, a few years ago, asking for their business. At the time, Alex, Simon, and the rest refused, preferring to handle their investments themselves. But if investing with him could help Meg? After a thirty-minute conference call with all of them, they'd agreed to let Simon approach Meg's father.

He said a small prayer and dialed the phone. A secretary answered.

"I'm calling for Clark Thurgood. Please ask him to call Simon McAlter of CAST Ltd."

Simon left his number, disconnected the phone,

and looked out the window at the rolling waves.

Thirty seconds later, his phone rang.

"Simon McAlter."

"Simon! Clark Thurgood here. Glad you called. I don't suppose you've reconsidered investing with me."

Simon imagined strangling the man. "My associates and I have given your previous proposal some thought."

"Very good. I'll have to research…"

Simon interrupted. "We'd like to arrange a conference call to discuss what we need and what you can do to help."

"Excellent. I'll have my secretary call you…"

"How is Friday?" Politeness dictated Simon phrase it as a question.

He cleared his throat. "Ah…yes, right. Friday is fine. Does one o'clock work for you?"

Simon preferred the morning, to get it over with, but he'd exerted enough testosterone for one phone call. It was time to be reasonable. "We'll email you a link for the call. Look forward to speaking with you."

He rubbed his hands together, feeling like the overly dramatic villain in one of the old movies Meg liked. But he wasn't villainous. He was the hero. He could fix this. As long as everyone followed his plan.

****

Friday morning, Simon took a long walk on the beach to settle his nerves. He'd spent the remainder of the week on the land development plans and his research on Meg's father. Whatever information he couldn't find, Caleb, Ted, and Alex provided him. They were set for the call and hoped they had enough ammunition to get what they wanted.

The wind whipped around Simon, blowing his hair across his face. He pulled his jacket closer. He hated long hair. It was messy and required work and...he wondered about cutting it. Not if he went in public. He could only handle one thing at a time, and he couldn't deal with fully exposing his face right now.

When one o'clock rolled around, all four men signed onto the conference call and waited for Clark. Simon adjusted his seat and made sure the window was behind him. Only his silhouette was visible. It was better than turning off the video.

When Clark signed on, Simon led the discussion.

"Well, Clark, we'd like to discuss what you can do for us. As you're aware, we've developed an investment conglomerate among the four of us, worth at this moment around $200 million. Until now, we've handled it ourselves. We're ready to hand it over to someone else to manage to give us more time to focus on our charity work."

Simon watched Clark's face during his speech. His chin and nose were the same as Meg's. He could read Clark's desire before he banked it and smoothed his features.

"I'd be more than happy to take it on," Clark said. "Tell me where you've been investing."

At this point, the other three men took over and explained their areas of interest and their goals. Simon remained silent. Clark's expression was hungry and focused, the way Simon wanted.

"I'm eager to take over your portfolio management. I know I could continue and expand upon the success you've seen. Are there any other questions you have for me?"

"Just one," Simon said. "It's not a question, but a requirement."

Clark leaned forward.

"We'd require you to drop Gershwin Adams from your client roster."

Clark reddened. The man could benefit from backlighting as well. "I beg your pardon?"

"We won't invest with you while you have Adams as a client."

"My client list is private. I'm not sure…"

Ted grinned, and Clark's face paled as he realized what happened.

"How did you? Why? That can't be legal!"

Ted leaned forward. "If you take us on as your client, I'm happy to give you a computer security evaluation, including all the weaknesses I found in your systems, for free."

"And if I don't?"

This time, Caleb, who ran the second largest media conglomerate, spoke. "It's your choice. But what a shame if word of your piss-poor computer security got out to the public? Not to mention your personal indiscretions call your judgment into serious question, which might make your existing clients nervous."

Clark's face took on a greenish tinge. "How long do I have to decide?"

"How long do you need?" Simon gave a half grin. Seriously, they had the man against the wall by his balls.

"I'll have an answer for you by Monday. Give me time to discuss it with Gershwin."

The four men expelled a breath after they disconnected Clark's call. "I do not envy him," Alex said with a laugh.

"Remind me never to get on your bad side, Si," Caleb added.

Simon nodded. "Thanks, guys, I appreciate this."

They hung up, leaving Ted alone on the call with Simon. "It's not like you to want revenge," Ted said.

Simon shifted in his chair and moved away from the window. He watched Ted's face, which registered nothing, but his gaze moved from the closed captions on the bottom of his screen to Simon's face. Ted was almost completely deaf, but with Simon's face lit, he could read his lips.

"I don't want revenge," Simon said. "But I do want Meg. And I want her to be free."

Chapter Thirty-One

Simon spent the next week in a flurry of activity. On Monday, Clark called him, confirmed he'd take CAST's account, and followed the call with a notarized letter and proof Gershwin Adams was dropped from his client list. Tuesday, CAST transferred their account to Clark and on Wednesday, Simon called Meg.

"Will you come over this evening after work?"

"Why?"

"I have a surprise for you."

The silence on the other end of the phone made Simon try to cross his fingers. His inability to do it was a symbol of all he'd done wrong with this relationship. He had a lot to explain, and he hoped he wasn't too late.

"I don't like surprises," she said.

"I promise this isn't a bad one."

"Isn't it better for us to make a clean break?"

A line of cold sweat dripped down his spine. *No.* "Please hear me out one last time."

The pause before she answered was endless. "Okay."

Relieved, he spent the next few hours on the phone with Caleb, Alex, and Ted. They were ready for their roles. Now all he needed was Meg.

She arrived at exactly seven.

"Come in," he said.

With a last look around, as if she searched for

someone to rescue her, she stepped over the threshold. "What am I doing here?"

"Come with me."

Knowing the uncertainty killed her, and not wanting to make her suffer any longer than necessary, he led her toward his office. He ushered her in and pointed to a chair. She perched on the edge, like a bird about to take flight.

He turned his oversized computer monitor around so she could see it. "I want to introduce you to a few people. Meg, meet Caleb, Alex, and Ted."

Because they all lived in different parts of the country, each man appeared in a segment of Simon's computer screen. One by one, they waved. The confused look on her face as she gave a hesitant wave made Simon's heart ache.

"These men are old college friends and current business partners."

"Business partners?"

"We have an investment group, where we use the extra money we make—quite a lot of it—to invest in philanthropic causes." He gave her a brief overview of the work they did through CAST, interspersed with comments from the other men.

"Okay." The word dragged from her lips.

He sat on the edge of his desk, one leg crossed at the knee, to try to explain things. "We will purchase the undeveloped land next to the library and cover all costs related to turning it into a community garden as Claire's group has proposed. We'll pay the town double what the developer offered."

"Why?"

"We often invest in projects like this, and this is

one we'd like to fund."

"It's…very generous of you. But why tell me? Shouldn't you tell Claire or Bill?"

"I will. But I wanted to tell you first because it depends on a few things from you."

Simon turned to the computer screen. "Guys, I need to mute you all for a bit. Ted, I'm also turning off my video."

Meg frowned, and Simon explained. "He's hard of hearing and reads lips. This is private. First, you agree to stay in Gull's Point."

She leaned away from him. "Simon, I can't. You know I can't. I'm not sure why it matters, anyway. I'm leaving as soon as I complete the publicity proposal and turn it into Bill. And why do you want me to? You hate me as much as everyone else does."

He clenched his jaw, his chest tight. "I don't hate you. I could never hate you. I was angry. I said things and acted in awful ways, but I promise I never hated you. In fact, quite the opposite."

She looked at her lap and twisted her fingers. Simon leaned over and took her icy hands in his and held them. "Please, give me a chance. You need people on your side. I want to be one of those people. I owe you this."

When she didn't argue, he fiddled with the computer and turned the sound and video on. "I want you to reconsider. The four of us need you to reconsider. If we finance the garden, we want you to be involved, to not only create the publicity plan, but implement it, too."

"The four of you. Did you…did you tell them about me?"

Simon winced. "Kind of."

She stilled. "What does 'kind of' mean?"

Oh boy. "It means I told them what I knew about you in order to fully develop a plan that can work."

He'd never seen a volcano erupt, but watching Meg gave him a pretty good idea of what to expect. She froze. The silence surrounded them. Her face turned red, and the color spread across her neck. She took a deep breath. And for the first time, she yelled. "You're out of your freaking mind!"

He'd thought she'd yelled at him before, but it was nothing compared to now. Her glare made him want to duck. His friends on the monitor turned their faces away. She spit every word like it burned her tongue. "I will not be blackmailed into your scheme, number one. Number two, I will *not* put myself out in public. Three, you have no idea what will happen if I do. And D, who the *hell* gave you permission to tell them private information about me?"

She jerked her thumb toward the screen. The three men had the grace to look uncomfortable. Simon rubbed a hand across his face. The men on screen coughed, and Meg jumped from her seat. He wished he could disappear. He also envied his friends their distance because he wasn't convinced Meg wouldn't smack him. Instead, she turned and stalked toward the door.

"Wait," he said as he reached once again for the computer monitor.

"Don't you dare turn it off," she said.

"I'm sorry," he said. The three men made a miserable attempt at not smiling. They were used to him taking charge. Witnessing him apologize to Meg was different. He'd get them for this later. "I wasn't trying to embarrass you or violate your privacy. They're my business partners and friends, and in order for them to go along with my plan, they need to know everything. They've sworn not to tell anyone."

She turned to the screen and looked at the nodding faces of the men. None of them condemned her. All of them looked confident. "I sure hope their word is more trustworthy than yours."

Simon swallowed and remained silent.

"It's still not okay what you did," she said. Her voice shook, but her skin returned to its normal color. She turned toward the monitor. "You all agree with my involvement?"

They nodded, and Caleb spoke. "Yes. You're an essential part of our plan, as Simon will explain."

"You're not going along with it because he's your friend?"

All three men shook their heads. "Meg, we don't invest our money because we like a person, even if he is our partner and friend," Alex said. "Hear him out."

They liked him, but did she? She'd said she didn't yell at her friends, but she yelled at him. Did she hate him…or was it possible she cared more for him?

Meg turned to Simon. "You know, telling them"— she pointed to the computer screen—"put my freedom at risk!"

Simon walked over and grasped her arm. "I didn't risk anything. I promise."

"You don't understand."

"I do."

She pulled away. "Let me go!"

He dropped her arm. "I did once. I didn't like it.

Please stay."

Meg's breath caught in her throat. "But…"

"Sit, so I can explain?"

She sat. More than anything, Simon wanted to pull her onto his lap and hold her against him while he talked. He wanted to ask if she cared for him. But this was business, his partners were onscreen, and if he wanted her to go along with the plan, he needed to be rational. And businesslike. He sat across from her. Their knees touched until she shifted and pulled away.

"Your father has been after our business for years."

"You know my father?"

"Yes, but I didn't make the connection until I learned your real name. Anyway, the four of us have always handled our investments on our own, and done a pretty decent job of it."

The other men snorted. Meg turned toward them. "Is that not true?"

"Simon's the master of understatement," Ted said.

She frowned at Simon. "Why does he say that?"

He rubbed the nape of his neck. "Because all total, we've accumulated about two hundred million."

Her eyes widened. "Dollars?" Her voice squeaked.

All four men smiled this time, and he nodded. "Anyway, we're all too busy to devote the time needed to manage our portfolio. We've discussed hiring a money manager. I contacted your dad and made him a deal."

"What was the deal?"

"He'd get our portfolio if he dropped Gershwin Adams. At the same time, Adams received a package of photos." He handed her an envelope. "Caleb is a media mogul. He employs photographers all over the world, and well, his photographers snapped these."

"When Simon told me your story, I asked my people to dig through the archives of all the papers I own that covered this story," Caleb said. "We couldn't find anything from your accident, I'm sorry. If they existed, they're long gone."

She pulled the photos from the envelope, flipped through them, and blanched. "Vanessa's behind the wheel. But if these aren't from my accident, when are they from? And why do these matter?"

Caleb spoke. "One of my company's photographers snapped these last month, when she was stopped for another DUI. Her third."

"Last month? But she was supposed to go to rehab. It was part of our deal. I'd take the blame, and she'd go to rehab so she'd never hurt anyone again. It was the only reason I took the fall."

"As far as we can tell," Simon said, "your deal is off. We sent these photos and a copy of the one from your accident to Adams and told him if he doesn't withdraw his business from your father, we will make sure they are published in every media outlet in the country. His daughter will go to jail. We also said the pictures are safe if he and his family stays out of your life and allows you your freedom. Your dad dropped Adams and gained us. Technically, our business is worth more than Adams'. Your dad is gaining in the bargain."

"If you want to go to the judge with the photos, I can help you," Caleb said.

She stared at the photos. Her voice was quiet when she spoke. "He'd put me away for perjury."

"We checked with our lawyer," Caleb said. "It's

time served."

Meg paused before she spoke. "It's over. I can't retrieve those years. I have no desire to have anything to do with those people again."

Simon leaned forward and stroked her cheek. "You're free now. You can tell people the truth about what happened if you want."

She buried her face in Simon's neck. His heart settled into its normal rhythm. Her voice was muffled, and he pulled her away. "What was that?"

"I wish your friends were here so I could hug them." She touched each of the three boxes on the screen, and they did the same. "Thank you. How did you know Vanessa's dad was my dad's client?"

Ted waved. "Computer security guy. There's a lot I can find out."

Meg blinked. "I'll remember." She turned to Simon. "I'm grateful for all you have done—all of you—but I'm still uncomfortable about continuing to be a part of this project. I think it has a better chance if I'm not involved in the publicity."

"You know publicity better than anyone. For the project to succeed, it needs you."

"The council meeting is next week. Will they be there?" She pointed to the screen, and the three men looked at each other.

"Yes," said Simon. "They'll present the financial proposal to the council."

Since the majority of their discussion was over, Simon said goodbye to his friends and disconnected the call.

"Will you be at the meeting?" Meg asked.

"No. There are too many people. I don't think I'm

ready for it yet. I have a lot of work to do before I'm comfortable in the world. But because of you, I see a future for myself if I go out there. I see a reason for living again."

He tilted his head toward her. "What can I do to fix things between us?" He clenched his hands as much as he was able and waited for her reply. His chest ached.

"You've made a good start."

"I don't know how to fix the hurt I put you through."

She shook her head. "You call what you did easy?" Her phone buzzed in her purse, but she ignored it.

He shrugged. "We arranged a few business deals, found a couple of photos, that's all."

"But you did it for me."

"Yeah."

"I've told you before, Simon. I'm loyal to those I care about. And I care about you."

"You yelled at me," he said.

"I was angry. I still might be."

He stroked her hair. "I thought you didn't yell at your friends."

She looked up, and he held his breath. "You're more than my friend."

Thank God. Everything shifted into its proper place. For the first time, Simon felt whole. It was time to tell her everything. "Every time I look at you, you fill me with joy and purpose. Joy, because I love you, and purpose because you don't look at me like I'm a monster or freak. You look at me like I'm human, like I'm worthy. You give me hope I can live a normal life. You've convinced me to break out of my shell."

He brushed a hand through his hair and stalked

around the room as her breathing slowed. "I vowed I wouldn't beg you to stay, I'd leave the decision to you to make, so you could do what's best for you. But if you're thinking of leaving, I can't let you go without a fight. I need you, more than I've ever needed anyone. I love you."

Returning to his chair, he touched her hand. She didn't flinch. Her hand was warm. Like her.

He'd said the words he should have said—twice—but those words weren't enough. His chest ached.

"You dropped me the second you thought I did something reckless."

He swallowed. "I can't guarantee something won't trigger an automatic response from me. What happened scarred me, and I don't mean just physically."

She patted the seat next to her, and he sat. The electricity between them was killing him. Every nerve was on fire. All he wanted was to hold her. Instead, he took her hand in his, and she gripped it, hard.

"But I'm learning. I'm trying. Did I react to your past? Yes. Was it a mistake? Huge. Will I learn from it? Absolutely. Please, Meg. I know it's a lot to ask, but I need you to trust me."

She buried her face in his neck, and he wrapped his arms around her. She smelled good, like citrus, like her.

Could she love him?

"I can't go through life thinking I'm forcing you to live outside of your comfort zone because of me."

He wrapped his arms around her. "You're the only one who doesn't. Please." His voice was hoarse. It cracked on the last word. She pulled away.

She lifted her gaze to his face and stroked his cheeks, loving the rough texture of his scars. His gaze

273

was bright and intense. His skin beneath her hands was home. No matter what happened, she loved him. Slowly, she brushed her lips against his. He froze before returning the kiss. She nibbled on his bottom lip, and he groaned, cupping her face in his hands. He tasted like mint and coffee, and their noses touched as their kiss deepened. Desire built in her belly. It had been too long since they'd last done this. Her fingers tangled in his hair, and he pulled her closer, as if he couldn't get enough of her. With a sigh, she pulled away and traced kisses along his cheekbone, across his eyelids, over the bridge of his nose, and across his forehead before returning to his lips.

His tongue pressed against her mouth and with a whimper, she opened for him, letting him plunge inside. Now their kiss became more intense, more desperate, and her breathing increased along with his. Their chests pushed against each other, their arms entwined their bodies, and their hands explored beneath each other's shirts. At his grunts of frustration, she maneuvered so her clothes loosened, and he had an easier time accessing her skin. Her hands roved across his chest and back, feeling the play of muscles beneath his scars. She shivered as his hands caressed her breasts.

"Wait," he rasped, pulling away. "I need to know."

"Know what?"

"If you trust me. If you believe in me. If you'll stay. I can't bear us making love and you leaving again."

When his grasp loosened, she said, "I yelled at you. I'll probably do it again. And I trust you, as long as you trust me."

"More than I've ever trusted anyone." He pulled

her to her feet, and they removed each other's shirts. "You can yell at me any time you want." Skin to skin, he devoured her mouth in a soul-baring, toe-tingling kiss.

She exhaled. "I love you, Simon." Warmth flowed through her, and her heart pounded. He pulled her toward him and hugged her tight. This is where she needed to be. Always.

"Please," she whispered, and with a groan, he dipped his finger beneath her. Moments later, their clothes strewn on the floor, he lifted her in his arms and slid her achingly slowly along the length of his body. His hardness tormented her. She shook, and her knees wobbled as her feet touched the floor.

Their mouths never separating, he lifted her once again. This time, she clasped her legs around his waist.

"Upstairs," he whispered against her mouth, and she squeezed his neck.

"I can't wait."

Moving her backward, he leaned her against the wall next to the window seat, held her in place, and thrust against her. She rocked against him, twining her fingers through his hair, massaging his scalp and trailing her hands along his body. She gripped his buttocks, and he hissed.

"Please, Simon."

With another groan, he entered her, and she gyrated against him.

"Oh God," he said. "Meg…"

As if desire neither one of them could control took over, their hips rocked together, his thrusting, hers accepting. Desire and pressure built inside her, overtaking her in waves, until with a last scream, her muscles tightened and finally released in one gigantic climax. He followed less than a second after her, chanting her name over and over in her ear. He tipped his forehead against hers, their breaths mingling as their heartbeats slowed. Cradled in his arms, they sank to the floor, and he drew her onto his lap.

"It's not how I wanted to make love to you the first time after we've made up," he said.

She stroked his chest, trailed her fingers across his pectoral muscles and over his collarbone to his shoulders. His scars tickled the pads of her fingers. She met his worried gaze with a smile. "I liked it."

"When we have sex, it should be someplace I've put thought and effort into. It shouldn't be reck—"

Meg covered his lips. "Don't say that word. Ever. Especially if you're talking about me.

****

As Meg left Simon's house, she pulled her cellphone from her purse. There was a text, from Vanessa. Her friend—ex-friend—lied, but she was persistent.

—*You've avoided my calls*—

—*What do you want?*—

—*I'm going to rehab next week*—

—*So you say. You were supposed to have gone years ago*—

—*We can't all be as perfect as you, Meg*—

—*Why do I need to know this?*—

—*My dad fixed your legal troubles. You'll get a package in the mail releasing you from all ties to him and us. When I get out of rehab, he's forcing me to go to jail. Your record will be wiped clean. You're welcome*—

Meg wanted to feel relieved, but she'd learned not to believe Vanessa. Maybe if Vanessa showed any remorse, but as usual, she didn't. *—Is that why you called me?—*

—No, I called because I missed you—

—I can't be your friend anymore, Vanessa—

—I'm sorry—

She'd waited forever to hear those words from Vanessa. Now, she didn't care.

Chapter Thirty-Two

Meg stood in the lobby of the Town Hall committee room and smoothed sweaty palms down the front of her skirt. Bill had already presented the counterproposal to the town council. The council took a break and now it was her turn to present her publicity proposal for the garden. She faced the entire town council, the library sub council which developed this project, and if the crowd was any indication, a lot of members of the community.

A community who still thought she was guilty.

This was a mistake. She couldn't do this. With a start, she recognized three of the men from the videoconference as they entered the building. Alex caught her gaze, smiled, and led the two other men toward her.

"Meg, it's nice to see you in person," he said and shook her hand.

"It's good to see all of you here," she answered. "I don't suppose you brought Simon with you?"

Ted laughed. His voice was a little flat; she supposed because he was hard of hearing. "No such luck, sorry. You've got us, though."

She faced him. "Thank you."

Caleb turned toward the open door. "Are you coming?"

"No, I think I'll wait here a little longer." Maybe

make a run for it. She gave a brief, nervous laugh.

As they left, she studied the crowd, who stretched their legs during the break. Steph and Wade were there and came over and hugged her. Claire and Tom also joined her, and Meg stiffened.

"Meg, I owe you a huge apology," Claire said. "I'm sorry about the way I treated you. I...there's no excuse for it, other than I tried to look out for Simon. But I was wrong. I hope you can forgive me."

"Thank you," Meg said. "You're a good friend to Simon. I hope someday we can be as good friends, too."

As Claire and Tom walked away, and she was about to enter the room, Bill approached her.

"Are you ready, Meg?"

"I shouldn't be the one to do this."

"Yes. You should. I'll introduce you, turn it over to you for publicity, and from there we'll move on to funding. And we'll see where they lead us."

With a deep breath, she followed him into the meeting room and stood on the side. A long table ran along the front, behind which sat the Town Council. The rest of the room was filled with chairs, all of which were taken, and many, like Meg, stood against the walls. Alex, Caleb, and Ted faced the council. A moment later, the mayor called the second half of the meeting to order. As planned, Bill rose.

"Now, I'd like to introduce Meg Thurgood to discuss the publicity plans for the garden."

A murmur went through the crowd. Meg's face heated as she made her way toward the front. *Why the hell did I let him talk me into this? I should have left when I had the chance.* She scanned the room, her insides fluttering, noting many of the doubtful faces. But she focused on Alex and Ted and Caleb. Wade and Steph. Claire and Tom.

With a deep breath, she began.

"Our goal for publicity is to make people want to be a part of our garden, of the library, and our community. To recognize this community as one that cares about its citizens. To that end, we've devoted a portion of the garden to therapy." As she explained the purpose of the therapy garden, she thought about how Simon benefited from the therapy. She watched people nod, including the ones who'd opposed her when she first came here. Maybe things would be okay after all.

"The therapy garden gives the media a reason to cover us, with more than a blurb in the events section of the local newspaper or website. We can attract speakers and hold events to pull in out-of-town folks. The more people who come to the garden, the better our town will do."

She distributed the publicity proposal to the members of the library sub council and town council. "Enclosed you'll find our full proposal. I'm happy to explain it in more detail at any time, but if anyone has questions now, I'll answer a few."

Members of the council bent over the proposal, but a man in the audience raised his hand. She nodded, and he rose. "What you say sounds great, but do we want to trust something this important to an ex-convict? Isn't it safer to go with the developer, who has a proven record and can pay our town, rather than the bad publicity you'll generate?"

Her stomach plummeted, and she swallowed.

"Whether or not I'm involved, the garden can still

happen. It's a question of when and how people are made aware of it. The more people who know about it, the more money it generates, as people pay for the therapy. My part has centered around developing the publicity plan."

"But you drove your car into all those people! How can we trust you?"

"What I've done or haven't done, in this case, is irrelevant. This project is good for the town."

"Of course it's relevant," a council member said. "The knowledge of what you did is out there. If your name is linked with this project, it'll be dead in the water before it starts. Your reputation will infect the opinion of this town. As a voting member of the town council, I can't approve this if you're involved."

The other members of the council nodded in agreement.

The scraping of a chair drew her attention to the audience, and Caleb walked to the front of the room. "My conglomerate plans to purchase the land and give it to you for free."

"And who is this conglomerate?" The council, as one, leaned forward.

"CAST Ltd. We're a consortium from a variety of industries who invest in philanthropic projects such as this one."

"Sounds sketchy to me," one of the council members said. "How can we know you're legit?"

Caleb approached, winked at Meg, and handed his prospectus to the Mayor, along with copies to the rest of the council.

The Mayor sputtered. "I…We…we'll have to have time to look at this."

"I understand. Let me highlight a few things for you. Page two tells you who each of us is. Page four gives you an estimate of our consortium's net worth. Pages six through eight lists other projects we've been involved in, and page twelve provides references. If you need more, I can get them for you."

One of the councilwomen leaned forward. "Why do you want to fund this project?"

"It appeals to one of our business partners."

"And who is that?"

"Simon McAlter. He'll donate his time to design the garden, as well as the rest of the open space, and we will also pay for materials and labor beyond what you all fundraise. We want the town to invest in the success of this project."

Conversation broke out among the council members, and the noise, which, although whispered, built to a crescendo as more people participated, realizing Simon was one of the consortia.

"And why isn't he here?" another council member asked.

Her heart thudded in her chest. He didn't do crowds.

Except...Simon stepped forward from behind a pillar at the back of the room and locked eyes with her as he cut through the crowd and approached the podium. Her heart rate increased. He'd put his fears aside and come for her.

Simon stiffened as every person stared. She couldn't blame them. Despite his scars, he was breathtaking. Tall and broad with jet black hair and probably a scowl. She couldn't fully see it from her position next to him, but it was his fallback whenever he was uncomfortable around people. Except for her, of course.

Whispers filled the room. No one moved toward him. After all he'd done for her, it was time to help him.

"Simon," she said, as she walked toward him.

He didn't answer.

"Simon."

He turned. His chest rose and fell, as if he had a hard time catching his breath. His arms were stiff at his sides. Cords stood out on his neck.

"Look at me," she whispered. She ran a hand along his arm, feeling the muscles bunch beneath her palm. "Tell them about why the therapy garden is important. Talk about what you love." She watched his expression soften, his breathing calm, and his Adam's apple bob as he swallowed.

He pulled her against him before facing the crowd. His body was stiff with nerves, but his voice was loud and strong.

"Seven years ago, my family home burned to the ground, killing my parents and injuring me, as you can see."

He allowed them to look. Meg was speechless at his bravery. Everyone stared and shifted uncomfortably, but he stood firm. She waited for him to continue.

"What helped me through it was the therapy garden at the Botanical Garden. Being there enabled me to heal. But the garden is three hours away. Although Gull's Point is not a metropolis, it is reachable for a lot of people at this end of the state. And the library garden can provide a much needed resource to more than our own residents."

People in the audience nodded in agreement.

"But it's not why I'm offering to fund this project."

She frowned. His case was made. What other reason could there be?

He stepped away from her and turned his focus to her. "I'm doing this to thank this beautiful woman standing at my side. She came forward and pulled me from my solitary existence. She didn't know what I'd lost, but she knew what I needed. She didn't listen to tales told about me." He faced the audience. "I know they exist." He paused. The silence boomed. "She took me as I was. She pushed me to start living again, when I didn't want to, because it was best for me. She supported me every step of the way, when I was too stupid to deserve it."

Meg could no longer see him. Her vision blurred with unshed tears. There was no way she was going to cry in public. Not happening.

He brushed a stray tear off her cheek with his thumb. "Meg, you told me a few minutes ago to talk about what I love. Well, I love you, and I want everyone here to know about it."

He turned to the group. "I know for a fact she's innocent. But if you all refuse to believe it, consider this: she has paid the price for what she was accused of and deserves a fresh start. I could hold a grudge against this town for what happened after I was hurt, but I choose to follow her lead and give this town a fresh start."

He turned to the council. "If you chase her away, you'll never see a penny of CAST money. And you'll do a great disservice to this town. Because the condo group doesn't care about this town the way we do."

Claire and Tom rose, walked over to Simon and Meg, and gave them a hug. "I'm sorry, Meg."

Meg nodded and squeezed her friend's hand. Steph and Wade came over next. Others joined them, until a line formed, like one at a wedding reception. The mayor banged his gavel to bring the meeting to order, but it took another five minutes before he was able to get everyone's attention.

"Do I have a motion to approve this project, subject to funding by…" He paused and examined the prospectus again. "Subject to funding by CAST Ltd.?" The councilwoman who had asked why CAST wanted to fund the project made the motion. The councilman who had thought the proposal sounded sketchy seconded it.

"All in favor?" the mayor asked and waited for the council to respond. Every person raised their hand and the mayor smiled for the first time. "Motion passes."

Caleb and Alex clapped Simon on the back, and Ted hugged Meg. Simon cleared his throat before he tapped Ted on the shoulder. Meg looked between the two men and laughed.

"Easy there," she said to Simon, while facing Ted so he was sure to understand her. "Ted and I are friends."

"Since when?"

Ted squeezed her arm. "Since you, Si. Never knew we had a such a great spokesperson in you before, though."

"One and done, my friend." He refocused on Meg. "One and done."

****

Simon left his bathroom that evening, running a

towel over his newly shorn head. Meg lay in bed, waiting. She'd told him through the closed bathroom door about the different friends she'd made on the publicity committee. Through the closed door, he'd heard the excitement in her voice about the next committee meeting. She was in her element.

He stared at her naked body. She was beautiful, and the perfect inspiration for his gardens that had begun to bloom in the ruins of his old house. God, he owed her.

He cleared his throat. "What do you think?" He gripped the edges of the towel around his neck as though it were a lifeline. There was no longer anything to hide behind. He was there for all to see. What seemed like a good idea a couple of hours ago caused him serious stress. He wasn't sure if the dampness on his neck was left over from his shower or nervous sweat.

She climbed out of bed and walked over. "Gorgeous."

He pulled her against him, skin against skin, smooth against rough. "I will never understand you. But I will spend forever trying to."

She kissed him and caressed his face. "And I'll never stop loving you."

"Perfect."

And it was.

A word about the author…

Jennifer started telling herself stories as a little girl when she couldn't fall asleep at night. Pretty soon, her head was filled with these stories and the characters that populated them. Even as an adult, she thinks about the characters and stories at night before she falls asleep, or in the car on her way to or from her daughters' numerous activities. (Anything that will drown out their music is a good thing.) Eventually, she started writing things down. Her favorite stories to write are those with smart, sassy, independent heroines; handsome, strong and slightly vulnerable heroes; and her stories always end with happily ever after.

In the real world, she's the mother of two amazing daughters and wife of one of the smartest men she knows. When she's not writing, she loves to laugh with her family and friends. She believes humor is the only way to get through the day, mornings are evil, and she does not believe in sharing her chocolate.

She writes contemporary romance, some of which are mainstream and some of which involve Jewish characters. All are available through Amazon and Barnes & Noble.

She can be reached at:
https://www.jenniferwilck.com
or
http://www.facebook.com/pages/Jennifer-Wilck/201342863240160.
She tweets at:
@JWilck.
Her blog (Fried Oreos) is:
www.jenniferwilck.blogspot.com.

Thank you for purchasing
this publication of The Wild Rose Press, Inc.

For questions or more information
contact us at
info@thewildrosepress.com.

The Wild Rose Press, Inc.
www.thewildrosepress.com

www.ingramcontent.com/pod-product-compliance
Lightning Source LLC
Chambersburg PA
CBHW051527260626
47170CB00003B/815